ALMOST
PERFECT

MARILYN
TRACY

Silhouette®
INTIMATE™MOMENTS®

Published by Silhouette Books
America's Publisher of Contemporary Romance

SILHOUETTE BOOKS

ISBN 0-373-07766-1

ALMOST PERFECT

Books by Marilyn Tracy

Silhouette Intimate Moments

Magic in the Air #311
Blue Ice #362
Echoes of the Garden #387
Too Good To Forget #399
No Place To Run #427
The Fundamental Things Apply #479
Extreme Justice #532
Code Name: Daddy #736
Almost Perfect #766

Silhouette Shadows

Sharing the Darkness #34
Memory's Lamp #41
Something Beautiful #51

*Almost, Texas

MARILYN TRACY,

author of twelve Silhouette novels and the widely praised Santa Fe Tarot Deck, written and designed in collaboration with her artist sister, Holly Huber, continues to live in Portales, New Mexico, in one of the oldest homes in town. She wiles away the hours of the day and night behind her computer, locked in the novel zone; chatting with friends while seated on the back of her forty-foot cement dragon; picking out a melody at her out-of-tune piano; or hugging her guitar, writing a new theme song to go with her books.

Marilyn speaks Russian, a smattering of Hebrew, a bit of Spanish, and claims fluency in Texan. She likes writing about real people with real problems and loves exploring that moment when two people find a connection that can bring them happiness. She also loves hearing from her readers, enjoying the glimpses she receives of their lives, interests and loves.

For John, who really wanted to know how Pete felt.
For Dad, who filled me in on drug deals and state troopers.
For Charles, who buoys me through deadlines.
For Melissa, who believes in Almost, Texas.
And for Chris, who makes fantasies come true.

An Almost, Texas Historical Perspective

Home to some six-hundred sunbaked people, the little town of Almost huddles the New Mexico-Texas border, roughly at the midpoint of what's known as the Panhandle. After nearly a hundred years of hot dispute, the small community can rightfully take its place in the Texas—and New Mexico—history books. Not because its townspeople fought at the Alamo, rousted Geronimo from their land or drove Pancho Villa from their streets, but because a government surveyor finally decided Almost should delete one state and add a comma. At that point, Almost found its current identity: Almost, Texas.

The Almost, Texas terrain is flat as the proverbial pancake, except where former rivers have carved great gullies; arid as the moon, unless a tornado and flash-flood watch is in progress; and such plant life as can survive the high summer temperatures and the extreme cold of winter appears spindly, spiky and utterly alien to the human species, except the lush green fields of maize, peanuts, potatoes or

cotton that farmers lucky enough to have irrigation rights maintain. In other words, Almost could be called a land of contrasts.

And yet, people live and thrive there.

Almost has a combination minimart grocery store and gas station and a joint Almost Volunteer Fire Department and Post Office and no stop lights. The small town also boasts of the quality to be found in the Almost Public School, covering grades kindergarten through twelfth under one roof, though the junior class consists of only one student.

The town also offers an active Almost Over-Sixty Club, and the friendliness found in the Almost Antique Store cum junk shop and the Almost Café—which serves all-you-can-eat chicken-fried steak on Saturdays and is always closed on Sundays—can't be surpassed anywhere in the Texas Panhandle.

The town's three churches—the Almost Methodist, Almost Baptist, and Almost Catholic—thrive in the small community and serve as the predominant social life in the area.

The town also maintains an Almost Historical Society which keeps exhausting records of all goings-on in the community. Alva Lu Titwater serves as current president of the society and takes pride in her assiduous accounting of all events transpiring in Almost today.

According to Alva Lu Titwater, "Dry-land farming—a method whereby farmers rely on the annual rainfall for whatever water is needed for crop irrigation and one most farmers will say destines a rich man to be poor—and graze-land ranching provide the base of Almost's economy."

As recently as the 1960s the town could boast seventeen active oil-and-gas wells. The community of Almost literally boomed. Unfortunately, the oil crunch in the eighties brought a swift closure to those wells due to the high costs of pumping and transporting oil and gas, resulting in Al-

most's annual revenue plummeting by more than two-thirds.

As Homer Chalmers, one of the seniors playing checkers in the shade of the Almost Public School's wide veranda says, "A feller asked me the other day what I'd do if I won the lottery. I thought about it awhile, then I says to him, why I reckon I'd go back to farming, 'til I used all that money up, too."

On different days, depending perhaps on his success with checkers, Homer might substitute rancher or oilman for the profession needed in his punch line.

Newcomers should understand that the town of Almost took root in the desert soil before the turn of the century—the *last* century, the old boys at the school's checkerboard games would say—and like other desert flowers, it managed to cling to life despite droughts, grasshopper plagues, hoof-and-mouth disease, vesicular stomatitis, oil crunches, violent storms, and young people wanting to move away for the lure of city lights.

People in Almost cling to the belief that crime has no hold in their town, though just last year a student shipped to an alternative school boasted his father was the biggest pornography dispenser in Almost. Since even the newest teacher at the 'fix-it' school down in Pep, Texas, knew that Harlan Waniack had served his time for distributing questionable material nearly twenty years before and, as he now serves as a bus driver for the more remote areas around Almost and has the cleanest driving record in the county and never once misses Sunday morning or Wednesday night services at the Almost Baptist Church, this assertion was taken with a huge grain of salt.

Since the small community squats a mere hour's drive from any nearby city, Almost doesn't have a regular physician, no surgeon, no tax accountant, and no real estate agency. A town of six hundred people doesn't need such accoutrements. Almost only needs townsfolk.

Notable people in Almost include Sammie Jo Spring, co-

owner with her husband Cactus Jack, of the Almost Minimart and Gas station. Sammie Jo serves as the town gossip
and is the beloved aunt of many of Almost's children. She's
an avid movie buff and television watcher and stocks the
store with any movie she considers interesting. Cactus—
nobody knows where he came by the nickname and because of his garrulousness, everyone seems loath to ask—
runs the gasoline end of the operation while Sammie Jo
handles the store inside. Cactus is as heavy as Sammie Jo
is slim. It's rumored in Almost that the couple were sweet-
hearts in the Almost Public School some fifty years before
and no one doubts this as the two of them are obviously
still enamored with each other. No one refers to the fact
that Sammie Jo has breast cancer and is undergoing che-
motherapy, but on chemo days, extra casseroles always appear on her kitchen counter.

Dr. Charles Jamison, a veterinarian of both small and
large animals, moved to Almost some twenty years ago and
townspeople still consider him a newcomer. In his time in
Almost, and to his continual amazement, Doc Jamison has
delivered twenty babies, of the human variety, and treated
nearly every soul in town for one ailment or another. His
wife, Thelma, regularly won prizes for her rhubarb-
strawberry pie every year at the county fair in Levelland,
and women in her church group were dismayed when she
passed away without passing along her prized recipe. Because Almost lies in a 'dry' county, Doc Jamison doesn't
have the heart to tell her Almost Baptist friends that the
secret ingredient was a generous fourth of a cup of rum.

Carolyn Leary, the widow of Sammie Jo's nephew,
Craig, who left Almost to go to college and became the
town's first real celebrity by becoming Almost's first citizen
to obtain a law degree and practice his craft in Dallas,
moved to Almost only a month ago, settling into the run-
down ranch house on her husband's deceased parents'
place. Since most of the ranch land was sold for taxes years
earlier, she inherited only some eighty acres of land plus

the house, bunkhouse and barn. In prime country, eighty acres might count for something, but in Almost, during drought years, she was lucky to find her house with a roof and a barn that could stall a horse. The full value of the land appraised at less than the cost of the U-Haul that moved her and her two girls out to Almost. And she arrived to graffiti on her door warning her to leave town or else.

Another Leary of note is Taylor Smithton, Carolyn's sister-in-law, a Leary by birth and another widow forced to pick up the threads of her life when her peacekeeping husband was killed in the line of duty. She's done a fine job of raising her triplet eleven-year-old sons, and considers her life full and rich, if a little lonely at night. Her boys, on the other hand, want a new dad and have just the right man in mind. Through exhaustive research, the boys have discovered that all their prospective new dad needs to do is see their Mom once and he'll fall instantly in love. But a little mayhem might expedite matters.

Craig and Taylor's sister, Allison Leary, is yet another of the legendary beautiful—and reportedly unlucky—Leary women. Everyone in town knows Allison left home abruptly and hasn't been back to Almost since the day her parents were buried fifteen years before. Typically, however, the afternoon Allison pulled back into town after her long absence, old Homer Chalmers looked up from his checker game and asked, "Been to Lubbock, have you, girl?" No one knows where Allison's been all these years or why she's come back. But there's something very different about her.

There are plenty of other folk living in Almost, Texas, but Alva Lu Titwater, Jackson Bean, Dallan and Mickey Peterson, and the nearly six hundred other Almost souls, are Almost born and bred and adhere to the principle that governs the small town in West Texas: what you don't know can't hurt you; what you know can bring you grief; and what you learn is probably best left untold.

And that would be true except for three stories of three Almost Leary women—Carolyn, Taylor and Allison—because the telling of their stories put Almost, Texas on the map.

Chapter 1

Carolyn Leary drove the Ranger with one shaking hand and wielded the huge, attached flood lamp with the other. The lamp strafed a good two acres at a time, highlighting half-a-dozen pairs of red, startled eyes, rabbits caught unaware, mice, owls, nighthawks, even a coyote or two.

Her heart thundered in her chest and her eyes felt strained beyond endurance. She didn't have to glance for the eight-hundredth time at the clock on the dashboard; the ink black sky with its millions of indifferent stars painted an all-too-accurate picture of the late hour.

Where were they?

Bratwurst, the old dun gelding named both for color and temperament, had lathered into the corral shortly before dark, reins trailing, eyes still rolling white from his obviously furious run. He hadn't been bleeding anywhere and the burrs he'd collected in his tail suggested he'd run through the tall careless weeds on the MacLaine place.

She'd *told* the girls not to venture too far from the main house. They *knew* what dangers lurked out there these days.

But they'd gone out anyway, deliberately disobeying her, riding off while she'd been closeted with the biggest stack of bills this side of the Pecos.

When she got her hands on the pair of them...*if* she got her hands on them...

Carolyn choked back a sob. She wouldn't cry. She didn't have time; she had to find Shawna and Jenny. She rounded a small rise and slammed her fist against the horn in three long blasts, their long-ingrained search signal—a desperate message she'd never had to employ before. If it had been daylight, the girls would know, at that sound, to head directly—and as fast as possible—to the main house. At night, they were to sit tight, make as much noise as they could and start a fire. They always had matches in their pockets for just such an emergency.

It didn't comfort her any to know she wasn't the only one out searching for her children. After her second frantic pass by the house and finding them still missing, she'd called Doc Jamison, the veterinarian and town brother figure in the nearby village of Almost, Texas, and asked him to rally the other ranchers for help. The only official authority in the vicinity, a deputy marshal, had left the area some six months before without replacement, so it was up to the local populace to form search-and-rescue parties. She'd also called her sisters-in-law, and they were calling all possible friends and relatives to see if the girls might be somewhere accessible. The trouble was there were far too few actual people and too many real miles to cover.

And the girls were so terribly young.

And the Wannamacher brothers so terribly vicious.

Deep into the MacLaine's property, she began driving more cautiously than she had before, since the MacLaine place was riddled with deep gorges carved by a river long since run dry. It was worthless as farmland because of the ravines that scored the property and less than worthless as ranchland because cattle could easily fall prey to the dangerously loose ledges along the old riverbed.

But Shawna and Jenny found endless enjoyment in exploring the riverbeds, the strange rock formations, and in speculating on the seemingly multitudinous number of Indian encampments they claimed to have discovered.

What if a rattler had spooked Bratwurst and he threw them right into the deadly desert creature's fangs? No, that was impossible; this was February and rattlers weren't a problem in winter. What if the horse had stumbled on the precipice of a ravine and her daughters lay broken and hurt at the base of a shallow cliff? What if...?

She couldn't think about what could have happened. She'd go crazy that way. All she could do was continue her search, pausing every few agonizingly long minutes to blast her message on the horn and light the countryside with her blinding flood.

The bright, daylightlike flood lamp revealed a sharp, conical hill directly in front of her, a rise her Ranger couldn't begin to ascend and Carolyn threw the vehicle into a rocking Park and clambered from it. The rise was the single highest spot for miles around and if the girls had lit a fire out there somewhere, this hill would let her see it.

She reached the apex of the rise, gasping for breath, not because she was out of shape, but because she was so desperate to see some indication her daughters were all right. Were *alive*. She could see the glow of Almost's few lights off to the right, and those of the larger and aptly named Levelland far off to the left. And directly in front of her, south and a bit east, she saw the telltale flicker of a campfire. She nearly sagged to her knees in relief. It had to be them—*Oh, God, let it be them*. Her daughters *had* to be alive.

She couldn't begin to guess how far away the campfire was. The rarefied early spring air in the desert high plains, some four thousand feet above sea level and unimpaired by pollution or moisture, played tricks with the eyes. What seemed within a short walking distance might be as much as five long miles away.

But surely the fire was theirs, which had to mean they were well enough to light it. Please let it be them, she prayed. Let them be warm and safe.

And if they were, the moment they crossed the threshold of the ranch house she would take both of them apart, piece by beloved piece.

She carefully pushed the Ranger across the flat plains, mindful of the dangerous ravines and sudden pockets of sand that would bog down even her four-wheel drive. She kept veering south and a bit east, slowing only every two minutes or so now to blast the horn.

And then she saw the campfire plainly. And saw her children weren't alone. Her heart jolted once, then again, and her hand gripped the steering wheel with near breaking intensity.

Was it the Wannamacher brothers? Had they done the unforgivable and stolen her children in their determination to wrest her from her land? Had her refusal to back down to them resulted in the worst of unthinkable fates?

She could only see one man, a great hulking silhouette standing before her two children. Neither Shawna nor Jenny—both fairly tall for their respective ages of eight and ten—came up to his waist. He couldn't be one of the Wannamachers. Broad shouldered like they were, yes, but surely he was much, much taller.

Even taller than Craig had been.

She shoved the memory of her husband from her mind. He wasn't there to help her. Couldn't be there. This, and the host of other problems, was hers alone to deal with.

She shouldn't be worrying about this stranger. She should be thinking how to go about thanking him for rescuing her daughters. She wasn't a suspicious person by nature, no matter how much fate had thrown at her in the past year. This trouble with the Wannamachers had her conjuring all sorts of bogeymen out of shadows.

She told herself all that, but she pulled to a halt a cautious thirty yards from the camp, keeping the flood lamp

on the three figures in front of her. She stepped down from the cab, but not before taking the .38 revolver from the glove compartment and firmly gripping it in her shaking hand.

The Wannamachers had forced her to this unprecedented distrust, this fear-induced display of weaponry. The hell of it was, she didn't even know if her gun was loaded or not.

The man before the fire was a dark shadow, his hands slightly out from his body, his knees bent a little as if ready to run...or fight. Without speaking, he shoved Carolyn's daughters behind him.

Carolyn's heart felt as if it were about to explode within her chest. She held the .38 up in a double-fisted grip and held her breath to stop her hands' violent shaking. She expelled it swiftly.

"What are you doing with my kids?" she demanded, fear making her voice harsh and uncompromising. "You let them go this second or I swear to God I'll kill you where you stand."

"For God's sake, lady, take them! I've been trying to get rid of them for hours!"

"What?"

"Mom!" her daughters cried in unison, jumping out from behind the stranger and pelting across the desert floor, into the pool of bright light and straight at her.

"You found us!"

"Pete shot a skunk! It didn't stink or anything."

"Bratwurst ran away!"

"He wouldn't let us look at the skunk. I've never seen one up close."

"Pete fed us dinner and complained the whole time!"

"Tell him we are *not* hooligans on the loose!"

"Were you worried, Mom?"

"Did Bratwurst come home?"

"Did you think we were dead?"

Carolyn, holding the gun skyward and above her daughters' heads, hugged her girls tightly to her with her free

arm, half lifting both of them off the ground. She fought tears of gratitude, the release of adrenaline-laden terror, and clung to the sweet, smoky warmth of her children. She felt an entirely new wave of love sweep over her, a tidal flow of relief and an aching need to hold them close.

She looked up and across at the man she'd threatened with death if he didn't release her children. He'd apparently kept her children safe, rescued them from a skunk and fed them dinner. And she'd pointed a gun at his chest. She straightened slowly.

He'd walked forward into the light of the flood lamp. He was as tall as she'd thought, somewhere in the six-foot-four-inch range of huge. His short hair stuck up in spikes, as if he'd run his hands through it several times—after an evening with her precocious children, she could sympathize—and glowed in the combination of fire and flood lamp with auburn and gold highlights. She couldn't see the color of his eyes nor a glint from his teeth, which could only mean he wasn't smiling.

She released her daughters and let them grasp her free hand and drag her forward "to meet Pete." The unfamiliar weapon hung heavily at her right side.

"I'm sorry," she said, shaking loose of her daughters' hands and transferring the gun to her left before holding out her palm to the tall stranger.

He looked down at her outstretched palm for several seconds as if debating whether or not to touch her, before engulfing her hand in his. His grip was firm and her hand felt lost in the sheer size of his. Since she was a tall woman, five-eleven herself, she wasn't used to feeling small around many men. But she did now. She couldn't help looking down at their clasped hands.

He gave it one short pump and released her as if her hand burned him. "Pete Jackson."

Carolyn resisted the urge to wipe her palm against her trousers. His touch seemed to linger on her fingers.

"I can't thank you enough," she said as he stepped back, closer to the fire. She followed him. "I was worried sick."

He flicked a glance from her daughters to the gun at her side. "I can see that." He didn't say it with amusement.

She didn't have to explain herself; she had problems he couldn't begin to guess, and her daughters had gone roaming against her permission and scared her to death. But for some reason, perhaps the lack of humor in the man standing before the fire, she felt she had to exonerate her behavior. "We've been having some trouble with a couple of people and I was afraid—"

He waved a hand to cut her explanation short. "It doesn't matter," he said.

"Mom—?"

"Wait a minute, Jenny," Carolyn said. "I'm really sorry about the threat."

"Forget it," he answered gruffly, and turned his back on her. He reached across a narrow camp bed and collected the girls' parkas and handed them across without looking at their mother. "This is everything, I think. It's been real," he added rudely as he backed away slightly, out of the glare of the flood lamp and into the shadows at the skirt of his camp.

Another trick of the High Plains, she thought, knowing he stood within mere feet of them but was totally invisible to her due to the sharp contrast between light and dark. But if he'd really left, she'd have heard his boots crunching the dry grasses and crusty soil. And she could feel his eyes upon her still.

Pete shoved his hands into his jeans pockets, curling his fingers around his palms. How long had he stood there holding her hand? He couldn't begin to guess. But for a moment the clear February night had seemed colder, the stars strangely brighter. He watched her now and was oddly sorry he'd been so gruff with her.

The girls, in their endless prattle, had gone on to some

extent about their mother's prettiness. He'd ascribed ninety percent of their evaluation to daughter loyalty and love. He realized now, watching her, the girls had already mastered the fine art of understatement.

She wasn't pretty, or even good-looking. Shawna and Jenny's mother was drop-dead, staggeringly gorgeous. Model tall, she didn't have the anorexic build of most models; instead, her generous curves pushed at her blouse, nipped at her waist and perfectly filled her snug-fitting jeans. Her hair, longer and darker blond than her daughters', danced on the slight breeze like a cloud of silk. Her face, oval and peach colored, seemed to invite a caress if only just to see if her skin was as soft as it looked.

And Pete, who hadn't felt a moment's twinge of nerves in almost ten years, found himself suddenly tongue-tied and thinking of the girls' offer to help their mother with her Wannamacher brother troubles.

"We found him digging in the riverbed," Jenny said. "He collects arrowheads, Mom!"

He'd shown the girls the points he'd found and had discovered an oddly satisfying feeling of pride when they'd asked so many pertinent questions and admired the arrowheads with such wonder and awe.

He hadn't wanted the girls with him, God knows, but when their horse had run away when he shot the skunk, he couldn't very well send them into the desert alone. He hadn't fed them or chatted with them out of any desire for reward or altruism, but simply as a grim matter of necessity.

For the first time since he'd glimpsed their shadows in the dry riverbed, he was glad their horse had shied, glad they'd stayed.

And when their mother searched the darkness for him, smiling, some hard piece of the ten-year-old granite that had become his soul seemed to shift a little, chip somewhat in the face of her open, frank relief. He felt as if just by touching her, just by staring into her beautiful face, he

could be like one of the arrowheads he dug from the ground; a treasure waiting to be found by a caring soul.

He literally shook his head at the fanciful notion. Whatever part of him had softness or could have been tender had died years ago, was buried so deeply no amount of digging could ever drag it to light.

"What are you shaking your head at?" Shawna demanded, joining him at the edge of the camp.

"I—nothing," he said, far more curtly than he would have wished.

She grabbed his hand and pulled him into the light. "Mom, this is Pete. Pete, this is our Mom. Her name is Carolyn," Shawna said, her upbringing evident in her swift recital of names. She even waved her hand between them.

"We had steak for dinner, Mom!" Jenny said, grabbing her mother's hand and pulling her toward Pete. He forced himself to stay put. "Pete barely cooks the steak at all, I mean like he eats it almost *raw!*"

"It's called *rare,*" Shawna corrected primly. "Lots of people eat it that way."

"Well, not me. Eeyucko!" Jenny stated flatly. "Come see the arrowhead Pete gave me. It's too cool!"

"It's not just yours," Shawna said, her elder-sister dignity forgotten in the fear of losing her share of the precious trophy.

"We'd better head for home," Carolyn said, and Pete sympathized with her daughters' cries of dismay. A part of him didn't want her to leave, either. Another part would have paid her good money to do so.

"But we can't leave without our arrowhead," Jenny said.

"Please, Mom? Can't we stay awhile?"

Carolyn looked from the girls to Pete and he felt something catch in his throat. He knew, from reading, from television, from a thousand impressions, that some lucky men out in the world had the good fortune to spend time with women like Carolyn Leary. Decent men with impeccable

pasts. Men like doctors, lawyers, CEOs of major corporations...men who had never used might as right or threats as promises. Men, in other words, utterly unlike him.

Blithely—and luckily—unaware of his thoughts, she shrugged a little and looked over at her still-running Ranger. "Let me call Doc and tell him I've found you two."

Shawna grasped the significance of the remark before Jenny. "Oh, no! Is everybody out searching for us?"

"Really?" Jenny demanded. "Cool!"

Carolyn's smile disappeared and her glorious eyes narrowed. "It is anything but cool, Jennifer Leary. You weren't supposed to be even close to this deep into MacLaine's place. You were supposed to stay near the main house. You really, really, scared me."

Both Shawna and Jenny ducked their heads. Mumbled sorries came from two mouths Pete had sworn couldn't turn down. He looked at Carolyn with new respect.

"But maybe we're keeping Mr....?"

"Jackson," Jenny filled in. "But call him Pete. We do."

Pete's lips twitched. "Stay for a cup of coffee," he said, and immediately wondered what on earth possessed him to offer such a thing.

She hesitated then smiled. "All right. Just give me a minute."

If he were a different man, one of the lucky ones, he'd give her far more than that, he thought.

He could hear her clear, resonant voice rise to overcome the static on her cellular phone as she told Doc she'd found the girls safe and sound on the MacLaine place. It was too bad the girls hadn't had a cell phone when they left their mother's care; her worry could have been averted and he would have been rid of them a lot sooner.

Jenny and Shawna both seemed awed that an honest-to-goodness search for them had been in progress, and were eager to explain to him who Doc Jamison was, how the man had lost his wife only a year ago, and what he'd done to fix up their animals when they'd gotten sick.

"And last week? Bratwurst ate something that didn't agree with him, you know? And Doc said..."

But Pete was only half listening to Jenny's story; like salmon seemingly inexplicably drawn upstream, he found himself unconsciously memorizing Carolyn's slow, Texan drawl, her laughter, her lilting farewell.

She hung up the phone, turned off the car and the flood lamp, plunging them into the intimate desert darkness the campfire did little to dispel.

"All's well," she said, coming to join him.

It was anything but well, he thought. Anything. But he noticed she'd left the .38 behind. He wanted to tell her she was a fool to trust a complete stranger. At the same time, something about her made him want her to trust him, to accept him at face value, to recognize him as the man he used to be, long ago.

He forced a smile to his lips and said, "Coffee's hot." He grimaced as he noted that his hands were shaking a little as he poured the coffee.

"The best way," she replied, accepting a mug. She took a cautious sip and said she found it delicious. "What are you doing way out here?" she asked.

He shrugged a non-answer.

Shawna piped up, "He's collecting arrowheads. We were right, Mom. Indians were here!"

"He's got lots of them. Like millions."

"Yeah. You should see them!"

Carolyn appreciated the fact that Pete didn't correct their exaggeration, and felt warmed by an almost tender smile that crossed his full lips as he listened to her daughters.

After having spent all her life in the desert southwest, she was accustomed to reticent men. Her husband had been a man of few words, not shy by any means, but careful with his verbal expenditure. Therefore, Pete Jackson's solemn quiet didn't jar her as it might have another woman.

But as she followed him into the campfire glow, she found a few things about him that triggered more than one

alarm bell. The first was his presence on private property without any visible vehicle. The second was his accent: he wasn't from around these parts. The third was the newness of his clothing. Dusty as they were, his fairly expensive hiking boots had obviously been purchased in the past few weeks. His turquoise shirt probably hadn't felt the inside of a washing machine more than once and he wore it over a still-snow-white T-shirt. The hard water in this part of the desert precluded hospital white without copious amounts of bleach and he didn't seem the bleach-in-the-wash type. His jeans, though stone-washed, still had the broad leather label fully intact on his back pocket, a dead giveaway as to their recent purchase. No one she knew could afford new clothes meant to be used for digging in the sandy desert and those that could wouldn't be caught dead in them.

Another thing that set off the alarms in Carolyn's mind was the meticulous arrangement of his camp. Military in its precision, the camp looked like a movie set, a mock site. Somehow he'd even confined Shawna and Jenny's clutter to one small pile.

In her previous life, before low wages and bank foreclosures forced her to move them to Almost, Carolyn had worked as a social psychologist, specializing in helping newly released parolees readjust to mainstream life. Recently released prisoners seemed to fall into two categories: wildly disorganized and incapable of dealing with the smallest detail of outside life, or meticulously tidy, in furious control of each single aspect of their new lives. Both types of men, if they remained out of prison, would eventually moderate their personal habits to less extreme ends of the order spectrum.

But Pete Jackson's campsite painted the picture of a man recently, very recently, either ejected from prison or from years in the military. Either of those two backgrounds might account for the tidiness and the newness of his

clothes, but both of them established him as a man outside of the normal rules of society.

"Cream?" he asked. "I've got some half-and-half."

A man in the middle of the desert with all new things, no vehicle in sight, no horse grazing nearby, and a container of half-and-half? Curiouser and curiouser, she thought, thanking him while rejecting the offer.

He opened another tidily arranged container of cold food items, pulled out a thermos and added a generous dollop of cream to his own mug. Most men would have carelessly pushed the cooler lid shut, but Pete Jackson swiftly, precisely, moved his large hands over the seams to ensure its airtight sealing.

Maybe he was just a rigid control freak, she thought, but when he turned, and his gray—his eyes were definitely *gray,* she realized with a sense of shock, though she couldn't have said why she felt surprise—eyes met hers, she had the dizzying sensation that while control might be a distinct issue in this man's life, he was anything but rigid.

Which led her to the biggest thing about Pete Jackson that set her inner alarm bells to cacophony. She felt a strong attraction to him. A total stranger in the middle of the West Texas desert, and she was standing inches from him in the glow of a campfire, noticing the precise color of his eyes, listening to her racing heartbeat and feeling her mouth go painfully dry.

"I'm afraid I only have the cot to sit on," he said, never once taking his eyes from hers. She had the oddest sensation that they were alone in the star-studded night and that the air had been withdrawn from this small camp.

"Th-that's fine," she said, turning with relief to the bed. His bed. She took a gulp of the hot coffee and welcomed its scalding reality.

He knelt cowboy-fashion, resting on his upraised heels, and stared into the fire. And yet, she knew he wasn't from the West. He was no more a cowboy than she was a dance-hall girl.

"Will you show Mom your arrowheads, Pete?" Jenny asked. "She'd be interested, honest."

Carolyn was curious to know how much experience he'd had with children, for he turned his shadowed gaze on Jenny and studied her for a long moment, as if trying to understand child speech. For a moment she thought he would deny Jenny this treat, that he was unaware it wasn't the arrowheads that were important, interesting as they might be, but the connection between his treasures and him.

After a long appraisal, he nodded and flicked a glance at a large tackle box. "Why don't you?" he suggested, conferring singular trust on Jenny by allowing her to touch his things.

Carolyn's breath caught, watching him, and she wondered if he had any idea how his face softened when he talked to her daughters. Though she knew nothing about him, she had the intuitive impression that he wasn't a man who had encountered much tenderness in his life. Or gave it easily.

Though it was cool where she sat on the bed, his proximity to the fire must have gotten to him, for he set his mug aside to roll up his sleeves. He stopped in the act of reaching for his right sleeve, rolled the first one back down and moved away from the fire. Carolyn had to wonder if it was her open contemplation of his muscled forearm that had stopped him.

He didn't say a word while Jenny and Shawna carefully—far more carefully than they would have treated anything at home—set the box beside her on his bed and opened the treasure chest. Without touching the items inside, they reverently described each find, every point. They stammered over some of the names, looking to him for confirmation now and then—he would nod without smiling—and proceeded through the entire collection as if they'd been memorizing it for weeks instead of a single afternoon.

Carolyn felt a pang of pride in her daughters' bright, alert

minds, but overriding it she felt a sharp stab of appreciation for Pete Jackson's obvious gift of an archeology lesson for her girls. He'd taken the time to explain each and every artifact to them, and in such a way that they'd been totally captivated by it.

"What's the littlest one called?" Shawna asked him.

"Which one?"

"You know," Jenny interjected, "the baby point."

He frowned a little and pushed upward to come join the circle at his bed. He knelt again slightly to the side so the light from the fire could illumine their question. His shoulder just brushed Carolyn's thigh, making her hands tremble a little. She had the oddest desire to rest her hand on his back, a companionable, easy gesture of affection. But there was no intimacy between them. They were total, complete strangers.

When he reached with his left hand for the arrowhead the girls were pointing at, his forearm lightly rested on her knee. A breathlessness nearly alien to her after all these years left her feeling remarkably weak—and stupid. She wasn't any adolescent, snared by rampant hormones; she was a woman in her mid-thirties, a widow, a person fully accustomed to loneliness.

But nonetheless, she was somewhat gratified to note that when he apparently realized he was resting on her leg, his hands shook a little, too. She forced herself to look away from his sculpted profile to see what he held in his hand. He didn't jerk his arm away, merely transferred it to his own upraised knee. But she knew he was as overconscious of the contact as she.

"...don't you think, Mom? Mom?" Jenny jiggled her shoulder to gain her attention. She blinked at her daughter, trying to focus on the question, trying *not* to think of how his weight had felt against her leg.

After an appropriate ooh and ahh, she gathered what little rational thought she had left and stammered, "I—I think it's time we went home." As she told the girls to gather

their things, she found she could still manage to sound perfectly normal when everything in her was screaming for them to run away as fast as they could.

Pete didn't say anything as he pushed to his feet and closed the tackle box. Carolyn didn't know whether she was relieved or disappointed.

"It's getting late," Carolyn added, wishing she didn't feel so inept.

"Aw, Mom!" Jenny complained. "You just got here!"

"Don't you think Pete could help us with the Wannamacher brothers?" Shawna asked suddenly, just as Carolyn was about to stand.

"No!" she said sharply. Though she wasn't looking at him now, she was aware of his absolute stillness.

"He shoots real good," Jenny offered, blithely ignoring grammar in her eagerness.

"Really well," Carolyn corrected automatically.

"Yeah, really!" her daughter corroborated, misunderstanding.

"We've already troubled Mr. Jackson enough," Carolyn said, blindly handing him her coffee mug, not daring to look at his face, hoping he wasn't able to read her chaotic thoughts. His fingers brushed hers as he took the cup from her hand. She jerked back as if he'd tried branding her.

"We tried to hire him, Mom," Shawna said.

Carolyn was appalled.

"Yeah, I offered him my whole birthday money," Jenny said.

Five dollars. Her daughter had offered a perfect stranger five dollars to come protect them from the Wannamacher brothers. She blushed deeply, both at the mortification of her daughter's innocent gesture and at how much an unruly part of herself wished he'd accepted.

"He could work around the ranch. You said we needed somebody," Shawna offered.

"It's not his problem," Carolyn said through a choked

throat. "And I'm sure he has better things to do than..."
She trailed off, not knowing how to finish her statement.

"The girls told me you're being harassed by some people," he said. His voice seemed too deep, and his stillness unnerved her. "You should call the police."

"There aren't any around here," she said, then wished she'd kept her mouth shut; she sounded as if she were asking for his help. "But it'll be all right. We'll be fine. We have family and friends."

He didn't say anything, and Carolyn had the feeling she'd spoken too breathlessly or perhaps a shade too loudly. His silence seemed to mock her words.

"Come on, girls, we've got to get home."

"Is there anything I can do to help?"

Carolyn wished he'd maintained his all-but-taunting silence. His low, graveled and Eastern-accented voice appealed to her and she didn't want anything about the man to touch her in any way.

And she didn't know anything about him, from what he was doing out here to why everything about him rang those alarm bells inside her.

"We'll deal with it," she said firmly.

"How?" he asked softly.

Carolyn had the dizzying sensation of having fallen down Alice's rabbit hole. She was in the middle of the desert, in the cold night of an early spring, talking with a stranger about trouble that had nothing to do with him.

She didn't have an answer. That was part of the problem. She'd called an attorney and asked him to draw up an injunction against the brothers, but without an official complaint on record, he couldn't do as she wanted. And without an official arm of the law in Almost, no complaint had been possible. When the state troopers had come at her request, they'd found no proof it was the Wannamachers who had thrown a rock through her living room window or spray-painted nasty phrases on her bunkhouse. And the Wannamacher brothers had been the very picture of innocence

when the troopers had confronted them. *"Who, us? Why we'd never think of scaring the widow lady."*

"What kind of work do you need done on the ranch?" he asked.

For a moment she longed to simply tell him. Everything needed some kind of touch. The property had been essentially abandoned when Craig's parents died fifteen years before. Craig hadn't wanted to sell it, had even talked about retiring there, but had never made any push to care for it. And fifteen years of Panhandle winds, storms, and the relentless sun had scalded, scorched and eroded the property. The barn needed painting, the house even more and could use some serious trim repair besides. Though only on the place a month, Carolyn thought the hay seemed heavier every day and the muck in the corral got deeper by the minute. The barbed wire fence surrounding the main house sagged in many places and was broken altogether in others.

Neglect and abandonment showed in every piece of wood, every rusting bit of metal. It was no miracle that she'd had a place to come to when the bank repossessed their condominium she hadn't known Craig had remortgaged; the tiny, non-working ranch was more of a curse. But she'd had no where else to go and had arrived, a scant few weeks ago, desperate, broke, and heart sore. And wholly unprepared for either the condition of the place or the Wannamacher brothers' enmity.

"I'm fairly handy," he said, and though she knew what he meant, she couldn't help her involuntary glance at his hands, remembering the way her own had disappeared in his clasp. Her palm seemed to tingle at the recollection.

"Mom...*please?*"

"Yeah, Mom. We *need* him."

"We've bothered Mr. Jackson enough tonight," she said, and wished her words didn't sound as if she intended to bother him more the next day.

"No bother," he said. "And girls, the next time you

decide to disobey your mother, leave a note telling her exactly where you're going and when you'll be back.''

Shawna giggled at the patent absurdity of his statement.

''And when you do skip out, be sure to tether Bratwurst so he can't run off on you when a skunk comes skipping by and some stranger shoots him.''

''Yes, Pete.''

''Okay, Pete.''

A broad hand came out of the shadows and settled on first one girl's hair and then the other. ''You've been a pain and trial. And if I were your mother, I'd sell you to the highest bidder first thing in the morning.''

Instead of taking offence, the girls grinned broadly.

Carolyn found her own lips curving into a wistful smile. She looked up in time to catch the ghost of an echoing grin on his face as well. And his gray eyes on her face, on her lips and then snaring her gaze.

''If you need some help, you know where to find me,'' he said in that graveled voice. For some reason she thought of raw silk, the way it was both rich and scratchy at the same time.

''Thank you,'' she said through dry lips, ''but we'll handle things.''

''All right then,'' he said, stepping back from her.

She couldn't tell him why she couldn't hire him, didn't have the wherewithal to admit she could barely put food on the table, let alone pay someone anything remotely close to a decent wage. If the ranch wasn't paid for free and clear, she literally wouldn't have a roof over their heads—such as it was. And her plans to do something with the ranch were as far away as the stars themselves. And with the Wannamachers threatening her at every turn, she'd more than once considered just packing the girls up and heading out of West Texas forever. The trouble was, there was nowhere for them to go and she had no money to go with.

And she was turning her back on an offer of help.

''He's so big, he'll scare the Wannamachers away just

like *that!*" Jenny said, clapping her hands instead of snapping her fingers.

"Please, Mom?" Shawna said. "I know he'll be able to help us. I just *know* it. Like in my soul or something."

"Yeah. We *know,*" Jenny added dramatically.

Carolyn pushed her daughters into the darkness outside the camp. The stars twinkled merrily in the sky, as if laughing at her panic.

"I accept your offer," Pete said.

Carolyn whirled around. "What offer?" she asked breathlessly.

"Jenny's," he said, striding forward then. "A bonafide offer of employment, I believe."

"Yeah!" Jenny said, frantically digging into her pocket.

"No!" Carolyn said too sharply, too forcefully. Her daughter hesitated, looking up at her in surprise. She seldom raised her voice. She forced herself to a calm she was far from experiencing. "Thank you, Mr. Jackson. Both for caring for my daughters this evening, and for your offer of help. We'll be fine. Now come *on,* girls."

She propelled them the final stretch to the Ranger and ushered them inside. She turned just before boarding herself and found Pete Jackson standing right beside her, his broad hand out, waiting for her to shake it.

She jabbed her hand at his and would have withdrawn it immediately, but he was faster than she and wrapped long, warm fingers around hers. She felt trapped. Caught. And the shock of electricity that seemed to flow between them had everything to do with her panic.

"Thanks again," she muttered for the third time and forced her hand free.

"My pleasure," he said, but she had the feeling he was mocking her again. Or baiting her.

He laid his hand on the hood of the Ranger and gave it a small slap, like he would a sluggish horse. "Good luck," he said.

He stood back from the Ranger as she turned the ignition

and further back still as she circled forward. Her last glimpse of him was as she'd first seen him, a tall, imposing silhouette before a campfire. A solid dark figure in a desert of shadows.

She rubbed her hand on her jeans, not so much to erase his touch from her palm, but to stop the tingling she could still feel.

"Isn't Pete great?" Jenny asked.

"Isn't he funny?" Shawna asked.

"A riot," Carolyn agreed dully.

"And boy-howdy, you should see him shoot!" Jenny said.

"Didn't you like him, Mom?" Shawna asked, her mother's attitude apparently finally impinging her consciousness.

That was the whole trouble, she thought. She *had* liked him. She'd liked a perfect stranger just a little too much. First impressions were inevitably wrong; she knew better than most people one should never judge a book by its cover. Especially a widow alone with two little girls. She'd been down that particularly hazardous road before.

"I liked him fine, honey," she said. "And I'm thankful he was so good to you two. And speaking of which, we need to have a little talk about what you were thinking of, going off the property when I expressly told you not to."

"Aw, Mom…"

"You're just lucky you ran into Pete instead of the Wannamacher brothers," she said, and immediately felt off balance.

"I hope we see Pete again soon," Jenny said. "I *like* him. He reminds me of Dad."

Carolyn couldn't say a single thing to that. Except for his reticence and his height, she didn't find a single thing about him that reminded her of Craig.

She tried seeing him as the girls must have and she half understood. His gentleness with them, his silence when fill-up-the-air words weren't necessary…his banter with them. Those were the things that must remind them of their father.

But instinctively, Carolyn knew that he wasn't the same.

There was something hard in Pete Jackson. She didn't know how she knew that, but she knew it was true. Perhaps it was simply that Craig hadn't been that way, not weak, particularly, but not gemstone hard. And there was some quality that struck her as dangerous about Pete Jackson, something that made her feel breathless and awkward. And there was also the way he'd made her feel when he touched her hand or had brushed against her leg.

No, he wasn't Craig, wasn't anything like Craig. Craig Leary had been a prosecuting attorney, a joiner, a man on the rise in the political arena. This man was a drifter, a loner in every sense of the word. A military man or a recent parolee, by the way he kept his camp and the newness of his clothing. Either way, he had to be diametrically opposite to Craig. One hundred and eighty degrees.

"What do you suppose he's doing now?" Jenny asked Shawna.

He's sitting beside his fire, Carolyn thought, staring into the flames. She didn't know why her mind's picture should bring a feeling of pity, even sympathy.

She lowered her hand to her leg to rub it absently against her jeans, remembering the sensation of his hand wrapped around hers.

Less than fifteen minutes later, their lights arced across the ranch house as they pulled into the curved packed-earth driveway. The graffiti on the front door leapt out in stark relief, looking as if the words had been scrawled in blood instead of red spray paint.

You'll be sorry!

Carolyn was only sorry that she hadn't taken Pete Jackson's offer of help.

"I'm scared, Mom," Shawna said. "I don't wanna go in the house."

"Me, either. What if they're still here?" Jenny agreed, her small hands clutching Carolyn's shoulders. "What are we gonna do?"

"Why didn't you let Pete come with us, Mom?"

Carolyn stared at the front door of the only home left to them and fought the urge to scream in righteous anger. But screaming wouldn't help them. Nor would the tears that pricked at her eyes.

"Is there anything I can do to help?"

After a moment's hesitation, she threw the Ranger in Reverse and sent a spray of gravel across the dried remains of their lawn. When they faced the rutted driveway leading out of the ranch, she put the car in gear and gunned the motor.

"You know where to find me."

"Where're we going?" Shawna demanded, a quaver in her young voice.

"To ask your Pete if he'll come stay on the ranch," Carolyn said grimly, but about a mile down the road she felt a small smile tugging at her lips.

Chapter 2

By the imperfect light of a waning moon and dying fire-light, Pete Jackson slipped a rose quartz arrow point into a small felt pouch. He pulled the bag's drawstring and rubbed the chamois cloth over the facets of the arrowhead inside with slow, careful precision. The perfect arrowhead reminded him of the woman who'd held a gun on him not an hour before.

She'd been right to refuse his offer of assistance. She didn't know anything about him. He was a complete stranger. And if she had known about his past, the things he'd done in the questionable name of right, she'd have kept that gun trained on him instead of trustingly setting it aside.

Pete sighed as he set the small pouch on the top rung of his opened tackle box, alongside some twenty-five similar bags he'd ordered from a jewelry discount house in Philadelphia. That was the last of them, the arrowheads the girls had taken from their pouches to show their mother earlier.

He didn't stop to analyze why packing them away

seemed oddly final, as if he'd ended yet another chapter in his life. There had been too many endings, too few beginnings.

He gave a wry smile, thinking he'd rather enjoyed the novel experience of caring for two little girls all afternoon and evening, though anyone listening to his biting remarks wouldn't have begun to guess as much. The girls had, however. They'd seen through his determination not to give them a single inch and had promptly taken a couple of miles.

He closed the tackle box lid with its many compartments and lifted the mug Carolyn Leary had thrust into his hand when she left the camp. He'd already tossed the cold coffee out into the night, but he studied the mug now as if it held her imprint on it. No lipstick in a semicircle on the rim, no visible fingerprints showed on the glossy enamel surface. And yet, something of Carolyn's presence seemed to linger there, tantalizing him.

In his imagination, he thought sourly.

He lifted the boiling cleaning tin from the grill and poured some steaming water over the cup. He dried it then carefully stowed the mug in his supply chest before sealing the cabinet against the West Texas dust. He surveyed his camp, straightened a few items the girls had knocked out of place, set another twisted log of mesquite on the fire and sat back down on his bed.

And he stared into the flames, thinking he'd never felt so damned lonely in his entire long life. Until Carolyn Leary—and her two overtly wayward daughters—had waltzed in and out of his camp, he been so focused on reveling in his solitude he hadn't given a thought to the narrow difference between alone and lonely. Now he was forced to acknowledge that slim distinction. And he decided too much knowledge and too short an acquaintance was unmitigated hell.

In the pure desert air, the flash of headlights caught his attention long before he heard the hum of a vehicle engine.

As methodically as he would have performed any campsite task, he pulled his .45 from beneath the pillow and tucked it into his belt. By the time he was both hearing *and* seeing the approaching vehicle, he'd reached inside his vest and pulled out a cigarette. He flicked open his lighter and cupped his hand against a nonexistent breeze. He drew heavily on the cigarette and exhaled before replacing the lighter, never once taking his eyes from the oncoming bright lights. While putting his lighter away, he released the safety on the .45.

After ten on-off years of enforced community, he'd taken a buddy's offer to park on his recently purchased ranch for a while. He knew his buddy had ulterior motives, offering the respite as a means of keeping him from bolting from the fold, even to the point of insisting on helicoptering him onto the place so he couldn't make a clean get-away. But he hadn't cared about motives or rationales. The kind of solitude, privacy and sense of utter freedom only a desolate desert could provide was all he, himself, was after. And twice in one day he'd been treated to unwanted company.

The vehicle pulled to a halt outside his camp and he tossed his half-finished cigarette into the fire and set his hands in a falsely relaxed position in his lap, his fingers brushing the cold metal of the .45. He hadn't been allowed the luxury of such a weapon for many years and was re-assured to have one now.

He heard two doors open and stiffened slightly, his hand curling around the butt of the pistol.

He heard boots impacting the sand and drew the pistol to face the headlights. His body tensed and his forefinger encircled the trigger.

"Pete!" a child's soprano voice called out.

What in the hell?

"It's us, Pete! We're back!"

"Mom says we can hire you—"

"Did you miss us?"

"Can you come tonight? There's graffiti on our front door, can you believe it?"

"We're scared to go inside."

"Is something wrong with your stomach?"

Muttering a curse, Pete took his finger from the trigger, reset the safety and shoved the gun beneath the pillow of his camp bed. He told himself relief made his hand tremble while it was mere curiosity that made him frown.

"We're in big-time trouble!" Shawna said, bursting into the light from the fire.

"You're gonna help us, aren't you?" Jenny asked, tumbling a half step behind her older sister. "We need you real bad."

"Really badly," their mother's voice corrected.

"Yeah, *really badly!*" Jenny agreed.

Pete, frozen to his camp bed, decided this was big-time *really bad* trouble all right, and far worse than any that might have been dealt with by a simple slug from his .45.

He'd helicoptered into this desert terrain to gaze into forever, to spend days upon days not seeing another soul. After crowding among the dregs of society, closing his eyes every night to a pocked gray cement ceiling, he'd become convinced that only the desert loneliness would serve as a balm to the bleak terrain that had become his soul. He didn't need or want company.

"I'm sorry to bother you again," the girls' mother said, her voice as velvet dark as the night itself, "but we've had another visit from the Wannamachers and I think we really do need you."

She hadn't said she needed his *help,* nor had she hemmed and hawed around a trumped-up excuse for intruding on his campsite for a second time. She'd simply said they needed *him.* The notion made him feel as if the world tilted sideways suddenly and it filled him with an almost stark ambivalence.

"Please?" she asked.

The fire crackled and three blond heads turned toward

the flames. Pete decided he'd suffered sunstroke and was lying comatose in the desert, conjuring the odd trio in a dream.

Carolyn lifted her gaze to meet his eyes. "Please?" she asked again. "Or weren't you serious? I'm sorry...I'm afraid I have a tendency to take people up..."

She smiled deprecatingly and gave a small shrug that made him feel even smaller.

Pete, lost in her direct gaze, somehow understood that those other men, those lawyers, accountants, men with perfect pasts, would never have heard such a request. If they could have, she wouldn't be out in the middle of nowhere asking a stranger for help.

Jenny coaxed, "I'll give you my birthday money. It's a whole five dollars, remember?"

He remembered that as easily as he recalled Carolyn Leary's low, throaty chuckle. Hearing it again now as she shushed her daughter, he closed his eyes.

"I remember, Jenny," he said.

This woman and her children had taken him at his word? What was that worth anymore?

"Look," Carolyn said, "I don't know why you're out here." She drew a deep breath and added hurriedly, "And I'm not sure I care. All I know is that I need someone on the place. A man, I mean."

Pete could see her fiery blush even in the dim light from the campfire.

"And since you seemed willing to help, to work I mean... I know that sounds lame...but I know times are tough. And it's true that we could use your help. Anyway, it's late, and I'm...well, I'm afraid to go in the house," she finished in a starkly honest rush.

She was afraid? He thought of the past ten years of his life and knew she had good reason to be frightened.

"Listen, this was silly," she said, drawing her daughters closer to her side. "Forget it. I...we'll deal with it. I'll go

stay with my sister-in-law tonight. Doc or somebody will come out with us tomorrow. It's okay. Really.''

If she'd asked him to hike the seventy miles to get the law, he'd have said yes immediately. If she'd asked for his entire arrowhead collection, he'd probably have handed it over. But she was asking for something he didn't have to give: himself.

And yet he'd offered to help her. Strange as it seemed, the words had come right out of his own mouth. Was it so strange to believe she was taking him up on his bizarre offer? He'd meant it, hadn't he? Or had he only been mouthing words, like plane-crash prayers, a last-ditch effort for a salvation of sorts?

"I don't—"

"Please?" Jenny said, and was echoed by her sister.

He would have to be a robot, completely devoid of all human emotions—and desires—to deny the entreaty in the three pairs of bluer-than-blue eyes. And while Carolyn was blushing, she didn't look away. He might have been out of society for ten years but he wasn't dead, and a man would have to be just that to refuse such a woman anything. Anything.

He heard the gruffness in his own voice as he muttered, "We'd better get the girls home before they pass out where they're standing."

"Oh, thank you," she breathed, holding out both her hands to him.

Feeling like a moth caught in a spiraling flame, he stretched his fingers to hers and wondered why she'd said she didn't know why he was out in the desert…and what had made her add that she didn't care.

Pete was still pondering this question a couple of days later. And still questioning why he'd agreed to join Carolyn and the girls at her small ranch.

He rubbed off some of the dirt from one of the panes of glass in the narrow window of the bunkhouse and peered

out at the roseate dawn. Not quite light yet, but no longer pitch black, the flat terrain that made up the Leary ranch seemed to stretch into infinity. From his stance, he couldn't see the main house, the barn, or the largely empty and woebegone corrals. He could only see miles of open graze land, grasses made pink by the cloudless early morning. No wind blew yet, as if it still slumbered, as if the wind, like himself, was waiting for something to happen.

He knew the girls would be up soon and would come tearing out of the house and across the dusty driveway to bang on his door. They'd done so each of the past two mornings and again at least once in the late evenings.

And Carolyn would be standing over the stove in the kitchen, her hair still tousled from sleep, her lush figure enshrouded in faded jeans and an over-size, shabby shirt that should have detracted from her looks but had exactly the opposite effect on him. Her face would be flushed with the heat from the flames. He couldn't have begun to speculate why his own cheeks seemed overwarm just thinking about her.

One of the roosters crowed and a split second later, the loose, creaking screen partially attached to the back door of the main house slammed against the weathered wooden siding. He'd fix that this morning; it wouldn't survive the Leary girls much longer.

"I'm going to get him."

"No, me! It's my turn."

"You got him yesterday."

"Did not! We both did."

His escort had arrived. He thought of how different this escort was than those that had called him for breakfast every day for the past ten years. The contrast was unsettling.

As he let them drag him across the cold expanse separating bunkhouse from primary residence, he asked himself for the fiftieth time what he was doing there. And received an instant answer upon stepping through the back door and

into the heated kitchen redolent with the scent of herbs, a desert harbor warm with Carolyn's presence.

"Good morning," she said, not looking at him.

"Morning," he murmured back, staring openly at her.

She wasn't dressed in her faded jeans and old shirt this dawn. She wore an elegant trouser ensemble that made her look as if she had stepped right from the pages of some ritzy magazine.

Pete wasn't sure he liked it. The silken blouse, the linen jacket and matching pants bespoke a class of woman he wasn't used to dealing with, not that he'd dealt with any kind of female in the past ten years. And where she'd been drop-dead gorgeous in jeans and shirt, lovely in a shabby housecoat, she was flat-out unapproachable in linen.

"Mom's going with us to school," Shawna explained.

"She's our substitute teacher today," Jenny added.

"They only have eight teachers at the Almost School, so when one of them's out, they either double up or see if someone from the area can fill in," Carolyn said as she tipped the omelet pan to slide a perfectly browned concoction to a warmed plate. "I've got a Master's in social psychology, so they're happy to have someone with higher than a high school diploma they can call on. And luckily, they've been calling me quite a lot." She handed the breakfast to Pete.

Not since the first morning had he said anything about eating in the main house. When the girls had rousted him out of the bunkhouse and hauled him over to the main house, he'd been embarrassed and frankly told Carolyn Leary she didn't have to provide him family meals.

She'd stared at him so blankly that he'd been half convinced he'd spoken in a foreign language before she let him know that no one around her place would *ever* be expected to eat meals away from the kitchen table. Except on special occasions, she'd said darkly, and then they would *all* eat in the dining room.

She'd banged so many pots and pans for a few seconds

that Pete had been finally forced into amusement. He'd committed some gaffe of Western etiquette, one that apparently was cause for pot banging. He wasn't the kind of man who had to be told something twice. He'd been in the house and on time for every meal since.

And if she didn't have ten million projects that needed tending to around her place, he would have had to join a health spa just to maintain his waistline; Carolyn Leary whipped together a fine meal—breakfast, lunch or dinner. The "room" part of his hire might leave a considerable amount to the imagination, but the "board" half suited him perfectly.

He waited until both girls and their mother were seated before cutting into the egg, cheese and green-chili omelet. It literally seemed to melt in his mouth.

"The school should call *you* when somebody's sick," Shawna told him, digging into her omelet. "You know lots and lots of stuff."

Pete thought most of the "stuff" he knew would be highly unsuitable for any school, Almost or otherwise.

"Yeah, Mom, did you know that if you pound a nail one time against some concrete or something hard like that you'll be able to drive it into a board easier and it won't split the wood? Cool, huh?"

"Cool," Carolyn said, meeting his eyes with a look that implied shared interest—and pride—in her children. The devil of it was that he *did* feel interest. And pride.

"And did you know that the reason the moon looks so big sometimes isn't because it's close to the earth or anything, it's because the atmosphere is thick with moisture?"

Carolyn smiled at Shawna. "No, I didn't know."

Jenny piped up, "And did you know—"

"That it's time for school? Yes, I did. And you'd better hurry, because I know for a fact that your substitute is a mean old grump and makes tardy kids stay after school."

Both girls giggled and scraped their chairs away from the table. They were out the door and halfway up the stairs

to their bedrooms before remembering their plates. With a noise Pete would have associated with recreation time at a prison, they clomped and clambered back into the kitchen and hurriedly slipped their plates from the table and clattered them onto the countertop.

"Aliens," Carolyn said as they stormed away.

"What?" Pete asked.

"Aliens inhabited their bodies about two years ago. My aunt-in-law says the aliens give our real children back when they get to be thirty or so. Until then, we're forced to live with these strange and unusual creatures passing themselves off as our kids."

Pete chuckled. "They're good kids."

Carolyn raised her eyebrows as she pushed away from the table. "But from some other galaxy. You must never forget that." She carried her own plate to the garbage container—later to become compost, she'd told him that first morning—scraped the remainder of her omelet on top of the muck and set the plate in the sink of cold dishwater to rinse.

It was odd to realize how quickly he'd begun to recognize her morning routine. Breakfast, roust the girls for school, scrape the dishes, set them aside to soak. And sometimes a cup of coffee shared with him.

"I never know when the school's going to call me," she said. "I hope being carless won't be a problem for you."

"I don't see how it could," he said, genuinely puzzled. She turned to stare at him and the color drained from her face only to be immediately replaced by a wash of dark russet.

"I forgot…I don't know what I was thinking…"

And her embarrassment let him understand. Something in the easy familiarity of sharing a kitchen, preparing for going to work, perhaps just because he was a man at her table in the early morning, for a split second, she'd simply forgotten he was a stranger. It was up to him to smooth the

moment away, but he couldn't think of a single thing to say that would do the trick.

He'd been aware of her diffident attempts to get him to tell her about his past, about the reasons he'd been in the Panhandle in February, on the MacLaine ranch without benefit of any means of transportation, but he hadn't wanted to tell her. It was far easier to let her believe him to be a vagabond, a drifter than it was to clue her in on the hell he'd lived for ten long years.

But maybe even telling her that would be easier than watching her shaken reaction now.

"If you ever *do* need the car, you'd let me know, wouldn't you?" she asked, her blush looking painful on her cheeks.

"Of course," he said swiftly, not because he ever meant to take her up on the offer, but because he hated seeing her so uncomfortable in his presence.

"We're quite a ways outside Almost. You don't want to get cabin fever."

Instead of picturing himself isolated, he imagined her Ranger breaking down halfway from Almost and she and the girls stranded out on the lonely stretch of dirt road leading to the ranch.

"I made a lunch for you and left it in the icebox," she said, opening the refrigerator and pulling out three sacks. Pete felt a strange pang on seeing she'd written his name on the sack she left inside. "I'll be going by Aunt Sammie Jo's this afternoon if you need anything."

He looked a question at her.

"Sammie Jo goes to Lubbock every other day and picks up whatever odds and ends she thinks any of us might need. She runs the gas station and local grocery store—if you can call it that. But she keeps track of things her 'special' people like."

"Is she really your aunt?"

"The girls'. She was—is, I guess—Craig's aunt. She's a Leary, but her last name is Spring. She's been really

sweet to the girls, and they're thrilled with her. They'd only met her once before we came here. And they love their new uncle, especially his name...Cactus Jack.''

This wasn't the first mention Carolyn had made of her husband, but it was the first time she'd used his name around him. Pete knew, from the girls, that Craig Leary had died in a car accident a little over a year ago. He hadn't asked questions about their father, some part of him afraid he would bring shadows to their guileless faces, and another part of him afraid he would be tugged into an unwanted pity for their mother. He was in deep enough trouble just being around her; feeling something more for her, even if it was only pity, might ensnare him.

''So, if you have any preferences for anything, just let me know and I'll pass the word on to Aunt Sammie Jo.'' She looked at him questioningly.

He shook his head then reconsidered. ''A pound of ten-penny nails and a hammer that doesn't look as though it came from a kid's play set.''

She flashed him that camera-ready smile that did odd things to his insides. ''Don't like my duct-tape job?''

He thought of the miniature hammer with the head taped insecurely to the handle and couldn't help but smile in response, shaking his head.

''I'm crushed,'' she said, looking anything but. ''Okay, one hammer and some nails to go.'' She yelled up the stairs, ''Girls! *Andale!*'' She turned back to Pete and said softly, ''Spanish lesson, today.'' She again called up the stairs. ''*Andale!* As in hurry up!''

Her generous smile faded when she turned back to him and beheld the twenty-dollar bill he'd fished from his wallet. Her eyes narrowed.

''For the hammer and nails,'' he said.

She flashed him a look of utter scorn and ignored his outstretched hand. ''We'll be back around four-thirty or five.''

She didn't need to bang pots this time; her squared shoul-

ders, firm tread, and tightened lips said everything a slammed frying pan could have.

And with a clatter of feet, a whoosh and crash of the front door and roar of the Ranger's engine, his abruptly adopted family disappeared down the dusty road.

Pete slowly put away the twenty-dollar bill. He'd offended her, that much was certain, but he wasn't sure how. She didn't have any money, she'd said as much and one look around the place made that truth painfully obvious. She'd mentioned a couple of days before that her husband had been a Dallas attorney. What a lawyer's widow was doing hard up for money in the middle of nowhere was beyond him, but he didn't want her feeling embarrassed about it. Hell, she'd said it herself: times were tough.

And, instead of offering him room and board for his sloppy—but improving—attempts at fixing up her place, if she knew even a glimmer of his past, she'd order him out at gun point. And pay him the twenty to speed him on his way.

He lingered at the table, feeling out of place in the silence of the house, out of kilter with the world now that she'd left him alone in her house. He wanted to let her know how dangerous it was to trust strangers. For all she knew, he would clean her out while she was gone.

Of course, for all she knew, he could have killed all three of them in their sleep anytime the past two days. What kind of a woman was she to trust herself and her two daughters to the imperfect care of a complete stranger? And what kind of a man was he to want her to do exactly that and accept him at face value, no questions asked?

He downed his coffee and went to the coffeepot and poured another mugful. Feeling slightly guilty, he opened her refrigerator to withdraw the container of half-and-half she'd stocked inside. In the act of returning it, he paused at the sight of the lunchsack with his name scrawled across the front. He had a picture of her setting out eight slices of bread, sandwich meat, cheese and lettuce. He pictured the

assembly line technique he'd seen her employ for the girls' lunches and wondered why it moved him so that she'd included him in the ritual.

He pulled the ashtray she'd offered him that first morning from its resting place atop the refrigerator. "Good heavens, smoke doesn't bother me," she'd said abruptly. "Watching a person looking as if they might bolt through their skin any second bothers me a lot more."

He'd smiled at the picture her words had conjured then, and smiled now remembering. But she'd been wrong; desire for a cigarette hadn't had a thing to do with why he'd been so jumpy that first morning. Or any morning since.

When he was finished with his cigarette—and with the dishes in the sink as a small apology for a second etiquette gaffe—he slowly and deliberately prowled Carolyn's house. He tried telling himself he didn't feel any pangs of guilt at the blatant abuse of privacy. He attempted rationalizing that since she'd asked for his help he was only trying to find out exactly who he was helping and what resources she had to offer.

At least, that's what he told himself as he opened doors, drawers and cabinets and dipped into boxes she hadn't yet unpacked, closets filled with leftovers of a lifetime spent elsewhere. And with each fresh evidence of her uprooted life, her shattered marriage, he felt more and more an out-and-out cad, a voyeur of her private pain.

The formal dining room off the kitchen had an abandoned, seldom-used feel. It was a smallish, stuffy room with fake wood paneling that made him wonder what was hidden behind the sheets of thin, cheap plywood. The flatware in the hutch still had packing tape around the silver chest, letting him know she hadn't used it since moving to the ranch. Some good pieces of crystal stood upside down behind glass doors but they were layered in dust, a testament to their disuse, though possibly only to the seemingly unceasing West Texas February wind.

The living room struck him as another center of the

house, as if the old building had two hearts: the kitchen and this warm, cozy place. The furniture was mismatched and shabby, but of good-quality oak, despite its worn and out-of-date condition. He suspected the furniture was either recently purchased at thrift shops or had been on the ranch a long time. He didn't think she would have had such furnishings in Dallas.

Navajo blankets dotted the sofas and chairs like brightly patterned, expensive adornments, though they were also old and a bit shabby. A quick check revealed they hid holes and worn spots on the upholstery of the sofas and chairs.

Like Carolyn Leary herself, the rooms and their decorations seemed a dichotomy: riches overlaid by poverty. Or possibly the reverse. In such desolate surroundings and in such a remote area it was difficult to tell the difference. It was hard for him to reconcile the smiling, open-faced woman with the obvious privation he could see at every glance.

And he pictured her keeping her grief and fear to herself, hiding it from the world, from her daughters. From him.

One of Carolyn's living room walls was devoted to family photographs, each of them overlapping one another, a collage of memories captured on film.

Pete studied pictures of Shawna and Jenny in their years from babyhood to perhaps a month before they burst into his camp. He lingered over those of their mother, long hair in college, short fluffy hair while holding two small infants. In another she sported wild curly hair and wore a sad look on her face. One in black and white showed her as she'd been when pregnant with Jenny—heavier, a study in Zoftic lines, lovely, alluring, glowing, a baby Shawna on her lap.

He felt a twinge of something he could only identify as jealousy when his eyes met those of the absent Craig. But the unaccustomed feeling faded as he studied Carolyn's husband. The fair-haired, rangy man looked like someone good to know, like someone he himself would have been friends with once upon a time. In many of the pictures

Craig wasn't smiling, but his eyes conveyed a warmth all their own. And in the ones where his lips were curved into a grin, he seemed to invite a sharing of the pleasure.

Perhaps it was the twinge of jealousy that made him decide there was something weak about Craig Leary, his jaw maybe, or some flaw in his character revealed through his smile. Or perhaps the feeling stemmed from the visible evidence of Carolyn's straightened circumstances. How could any man have left his family so poorly provided for?

But one picture in particular held Pete's attention to the point of complete loss of breath: Carolyn seated on a porch swing, a giggling blond cherub on either side, her blue eyes fixed on a laughing Craig standing behind the swing, obviously intent on pushing it askew a second time. The girls and Craig stared directly at whoever took the picture—meaning they stared into Pete's eyes now—while Carolyn's profile angled so that she looked only at Craig.

The humorous expectation in those three sets of gazes unnerved Pete while the raw confusion on Carolyn's face sent a shaft of unidentified pain directly at his heart. She gazed at her husband as if she didn't know who he was, as if he'd said something utterly incomprehensible and therefore puzzling.

For the first time in his life Pete knew what it was to envy another man. Only a deep intimacy could engender such a look of surprise and confusion on a wife's face. What had Craig said to make her look as if she'd never seen him before?

The fact that the man he envied was dead and buried didn't mitigate the feeling one iota. He turned away from the living room with a grunt that was less an expression of discomfort than one of loss.

He didn't have to go upstairs to the bedrooms before finding what he was really looking for. In the narrow closet beside the front door that opened into the living room he found Carolyn's cache of weapons. The .38 she'd shakily held on him a few nights earlier, an ancient air rifle—the

kind his granddad had given him when he was ten and he was far more interested in the BBs than the rifle itself— and a cumbersome sawed-off shotgun that would take as much trouble to shoot as it would to clean represented Carolyn's full defense.

Pete flicked the .38's chamber open and shook his head even as a rueful smile creased his face. Carolyn Leary had held this deadly piece of machinery on him three nights ago and demanded he give up her children or she would, by God, kill him where he stood.

And all the time the damned gun hadn't been loaded. From what Pete could see, it hadn't been loaded in years.

Carolyn Leary might think she needed someone around her place, but Pete *knew* she did. He took all three weapons into the kitchen, poured another cup of coffee while rummaging through her kitchen drawers and cabinets for items he might need. With such unlikely tools as a barbecue skewer, an old rag and a container of sewing machine oil, he started cleaning the Leary arsenal.

That very afternoon, he vowed, he would start teaching the girls—and their mother—how to go about scaring the living daylights out of a pair of Wannamacher brothers.

And then he would get the hell out of there.

Chapter 3

"So...does he have cute buns?"

"Sammie Jo!"

"Don't look at me like that, Carolyn Leary. You were married to my nephew and he had what women around these parts hail as world-class—"

"Pete shot a skunk and gave me an arrowhead."

"Gave *us* an arrowhead."

"Hear tell he doesn't have a vehicle," Sammie Jo said, slowly filling the cardboard box with the few grocery items Carolyn had picked out. The hammer, nails and half-and-half were still waiting on the countertop.

"I didn't see one," Carolyn said, not bothering to question where Sammie Jo had come by her information. In the short time she'd been in the area, she'd already discovered Almost had an information system to rival any major television network.

She and Pete had decided that it might be better to keep his presence on her place a secret. That way the Wanna-macher brothers could attempt a foray onto her place and

waltz right into Pete's able hands. But they hadn't taken the small population and the Almost curiosity into consideration.

Why she should be so certain that Pete would be capable of rousting the Wannamachers she didn't know. But the certainty was as rooted in her as she knew that West Texas was in the midst of a drought.

"Makes you wonder, doesn't it?"

"What?" she asked.

"What would somebody be doing out in the plains without benefit of car or horse?"

Carolyn smiled and shrugged a little, as if dismissing the notion as unimportant. But she didn't answer, because there was nothing that Sammie Jo could speculate about Pete Jackson that hadn't already crossed her own mind a time or two or seventeen in the past couple of days.

"Yep. Come to think on it, something strange about the MacLaine place, too, that couple coming in here last year, buying it slam-bam-bang and leaving town the very next day. Cactus figures some government survey says there's oil out there."

"Arrowheads," Jenny said. "That's what Pete was digging, Aunt Sammie Jo."

"Suppose there was some survey or such and the Wannamachers got wind of it? Maybe that's why they're after your land so bad, honey."

"That first time they came out to the place they tried claiming the ranch actually belonged to them. They showed me a piece of paper they claimed proved it."

Sammie Jo shook her head. "That's pure bunk, and you know it. My brother—Craig's daddy—bought that place fifty years ago. He went in debt up to his eyebrows to do it. Hard to imagine nowadays, isn't it? But, you should have seen it back then. That was before the drought, you know. Prettiest little ranch you ever did see. Close to three sections. Apples that came from his trees were a treat."

"Treats?" Jenny asked hopefully.

Sammie Jo nodded and handed each of the girls a cookie from the jar on the counter. "What I'd do is call up those MacLaines and see if he has their permission to be on their property."

"He isn't on their property anymore," Shawna observed. "He's living with us."

At Sammie Jo's arched brows, Carolyn felt a blush flash fire across her face. "In the bunkhouse," she muttered, then wished she'd kept her mouth shut.

"Did I say anything?" Sammie Jo asked.

Carolyn chuckled and repeated a family phrase, "The Leary eyebrows speak louder than words."

"Want me to have Doc have a look at him?"

"Aunt Sammie Jo!" Jenny said, highly offended. "Pete's a *man,* not a horse!"

"If that's true, honey, he'll be the first one that's not a big-time combination of both," Sammie Jo said with a broad wink at Carolyn. She punched a button on her cash register and took out a dollar's worth of quarters and handed each of her great-nieces two apiece. "You gals look like you could do with a sody pop."

The girls barely managed to palm the quarters before shooting out the front door of Sammie Jo's minimart and disappearing around the side of the building.

"Seriously, Carolyn, I'm worried about you."

"I'm fine, Sammie Jo. Really."

"Taylor says her boys said the girls told them that you had more graffiti on your door. Why don't you just let Cactus and Homer and some of his friends fill the Wannamachers's backsides with a little buckshot? That'd make 'em think twice about giving you any more guff."

"Homer's in his eighties."

"So? Nothing wrong with his trigger finger a little arthritis cream won't cure. And I picked him up a crate of the stuff just yesterday."

Carolyn chuckled but shook her head. "The police would be more likely to arrest Cactus, Homer and crew

than the Wannamachers. Ten to one those two have an ironclad alibi. Again. And the police don't seem very upset by what they're doing. Neither does the state.''

''Doesn't that just beat all? What is the world coming to when a person can't trust the law to keep a couple of thugs off their property?''

Carolyn sighed. It did seem unfair. She remembered the notice from the Dallas bank informing her that she and her children had exactly ninety days to vacate the condominium she'd shared with Craig. What if she'd hunkered down and refused to leave? Someone would have come to the bank's rescue, that much was certain. Why couldn't some nameless authority come to *her* rescue now?

''Well, I'll tell you, honey, it's got everyone around here hopping mad. Pretty poor welcome to give you when you went to the trouble of bringing your daughters home to us. Taylor's the maddest of all, I think. All those buddies of Doug's and no one doing anything to stop her sister-in-law from being harassed.''

Carolyn didn't want to point out the obvious, that if it were Taylor being harassed, those buddies of a fallen officer would have rallied around immediately. And, in all honesty, she hadn't asked her sister-in-law to intervene on her behalf. She didn't know any of them well enough yet to really feel an inside member of the Leary clan.

''Maybe Pete's just being on the place has stopped them. We haven't seen hide nor hair of them since Pete got there,'' Carolyn said doubtfully. ''Besides, a little spray paint hasn't really hurt anyone.''

She didn't have to lie to Sammie Jo. The older woman knew full well the effect a ''little spray paint'' could have on a woman and two small girls.

''And what if they don't stop at spray-painting, sugar? What are you going do then?''

Carolyn shook her head. ''That's why Pete's on the place.''

Sammie Jo's graying eyebrows raised and lowered as she hefted the hammer and bag of nails. "And he's just fixing up a few things to wile away the hours between Wanna-macher visits?"

Carolyn shrugged again.

"You know, sugar, Cactus and I didn't want to pry into your affairs, but we've talked about it plenty. Craig's being a lawyer and all should have set you and the girls up pretty well, but Taylor doesn't think that's true. Neither do Cactus and I." She held up her hand. "Now let me finish!"

"We're fine, Sammie Jo," Carolyn said repressively, and was unable to meet her aunt-in-law's eyes as she told the lie. Craig had been one of those people who believed that death would never come his way. And he'd trusted far too many people with what little resources they had, which as a prosecuting attorney hadn't been much to start with. And then she'd been too trusting herself.

The bottom line, after his funeral, was that she and the girls had the aging ranch and enough to live on for another six months if she was very, very careful. That they'd also apparently inherited the Wannamacher brothers was a complication she hadn't counted on.

"We don't have a whole lot, you know, but what we've got you're welcome to," Sammie Jo said gruffly, setting the hammer and nails into the box.

Unexpected tears stung Carolyn's eyes. Sammie Jo and Cactus were in their late sixties and relied on the small gas station and minimart as their sole means of support. Since both operations seemed to run more as a kindness to family and friends than as a going concern, Carolyn knew she'd never take them up on the offer. About all she had left was her pride, and she wasn't going to turn her back on that now. "Thanks, Sammie Jo, but really, we're doing just fine."

"I mean it, now." The older woman held up the container of half-and-half. "This how you're paying your fellow?"

"He's not *my* fellow," Carolyn protested. He was only a stranger out of a desert night, a quiet man who for some inexplicable reason had decided to take pity on a helpless widow and her two little girls. She felt like squirming at the damning truth.

As if reading part of her niece's thoughts, Sammie Jo asked, "Why is he doing this, Carolyn? Why would a man agree to work on a falling-to-bits ranch for nothing more than a little girl's birthday money, three squares and some half-and-half for his coffee? Oh, don't deny it. The girls told Taylor's three all about it and they told me. So, what's he doing out here? What's he want with you and the girls?"

Carolyn could only shake her head. She didn't have any answers and her aunt-in-law knew it.

Sammie Jo dusted her hands on the back of her jeans as she abruptly changed the subject. "Don't forget that Saturday the Almost Over-Sixty Club's having their annual shindig over at the Catholic Church. We use a different one of the churches every year so God won't think we're trying to play favorites. And of course, seeing as how I'm the head honcho this year, I'm putting out the word for mandatory attendance. It's five bucks and all you can eat. The girls'll love it. It'll rain, of course. Does every year, but we just eat as fast as we can then all move inside or go home to nap. Besides, we could stand some rain. It's as dry as the Sahara this year. Farmers would probably pay us to hold our picnic."

At her next words, Carolyn realized she hadn't shifted the topic one iota. "You bring your Pete with you when you come. No sense pretending everybody around here doesn't know he's out at your place. Wannamachers included. *And,* it'll give everybody a chance to look him over. Outside opinions never hurt anyone. Besides, there's a few folk around here you haven't met yet yourself."

Carolyn took her box of groceries and turned to leave.

"And bring your deviled eggs, sugar. Nobody makes

'em like you do. Swear I put on two pounds just looking at them.''

Carolyn pushed the screen door open with the box.

"And Carolyn?"

"Mmm?"

"Just remember that there are some things that are far worse than loneliness.''

Carolyn wasn't entirely certain what Sammie Jo's warning implied, but she knew it sent a shiver of reaction down her spine.

And the warning made her think of Pete's rare but warm smile.

Pete was waiting for them when they pulled onto the ranch. He'd set up a target range on the far side of the barn.

"Do you know how to shoot, or just point?" he asked her, a lopsided grin on his face.

She blushed as he held out Craig's old .38 pistol to her.

"Point," she answered truthfully. She'd been city raised and the gun only meant worrying about the girls possibly getting hold of it.

His grin broadened. "I'm teasing you. One look inside the chamber and I knew it hadn't been fired in years.''

She couldn't help but smile back at him and it gave her a strange feeling of familiarity and brought on a wistful sensation. She realized that it simply felt good to smile at a man and have him smile back. Too good, perhaps.

"Can we learn, too, Pete?" Jenny asked.

"Please, Pete, can we?" Shawna begged, subconsciously adding a feminine entreaty to her request by leaning against him, gazing up at him with wide, innocent eyes.

"We're all going to give it a try," he said, leading the way past the barn.

"Is this really necessary?" Carolyn asked after he'd shown them the targets he'd apparently designed employing the girls' crayon collection. Seeing the brightly colored targets had sparked a couple of questions in her mind: one,

when had he found the crayons...not to mention the guns, and two, what else had he come across during his obvious search through her house?

But the thought that made her feel the oddest was picturing him sitting at the kitchen table drawing circles with her daughters' crayons, then slowly, carefully coloring them in. Like a kid would do. Like a dad might.

"I think so," he said.

"What?" she asked, forgetting she'd asked him a question. His simple acknowledgment had sounded too much like an answer to her inner thoughts.

"I don't know too many bullies who won't back off at the sight of a gun. You managed to scare the living hell out of me the other night and the damned thing wasn't even loaded."

"I was scared," she said defensively.

"That's why you want the gun loaded and want to know how to use it. Even if you just fire in the air, it'll get the message across," he said.

She was struck by the realization that Pete Jackson wasn't any hired hand. He was talking to her as if he were the man of the house, the boss, the head of the family. And he was talking as if he knew very well what a report from a gun could mean.

She risked looking directly at him only to find him staring at her quizzically.

"What?" she asked.

"I thought all Western women learned how to shoot before they could walk."

"That's in the movies," she said tartly. "Besides, I was raised in Dallas. We don't have many skunks and rattlers in the big city. And I don't know if I like the idea of Jenny and Shawna being around guns. They're only eight and ten years old. They might—"

"They might be able to defend themselves," he said calmly. "And they won't get hurt if they know how to handle a gun. It's the inexperienced and experimental, cu-

rious-because-they-know-they-shouldn't-touch-it kids that get hurt just touching a weapon.''

She wasn't entirely convinced, but let him lead her toward a line he'd scuffed across the dust.

''Now, the first thing you want to do is plant your legs—like this—right, spaced apart.'' He demonstrated what he wanted the three of them to do.

Carolyn had a sudden flash of gym class a thousand years ago. Different clothes, different times. And had Pete been a different man, someone she was close to, she might have shared the memory of the dreadful gym clothes.

''Bend your knees a little. Yeah, that's right.''

He showed them how heavy the gun really was—and Carolyn wondered if the new weight came from the bullets and withheld a shudder—and gave them tips on using the left hand as a support and extra sight for aiming the weapon.

''Keep your right arm straight. That's it. That's good.''

And later, a chuckle as he repositioned Jenny. ''No, sweetie, don't close your eyes. It's hard to see the target that way.''

Between the noise of the guns, the kick of the shotgun and the dust blowing in from the west, Carolyn could see that the target practice was less than even a qualified success in Pete's eyes. But after the girls had finished their wild shots and complaints about the way the noise hurt their ears, and their mother had managed to literally and embarrassingly hit the broad side of a barn—some fifteen feet away from the targets—Pete stepped behind her and lifted her arms.

If electricity had jumped from his body to hers, she would have felt no less shocked. ''What—?''

''Like this,'' he said.

She could feel the heat radiating out from his body and touching hers. She told herself that he was doing nothing more than showing her how to hold a gun. She even tried telling herself that it was *Craig's* gun, one he'd insisted on

keeping in the closet of their condo in Dallas because his Dad had given it to him as a boy. Why hadn't she just gotten rid of it when they moved? Then she wouldn't be standing here in Pete's arms wondering why her legs were shaking and her insides felt like liquid fire.

She attempted the impossible, scrunching her skin to avoid contact with him. That her efforts were futile was obvious, but she felt the need to shrink into herself, to try not to feel the contact, because then she wouldn't have to face the simple, stark fact that she was attracted to the man.

If only he weren't so tall, so broad chested. And if only she weren't so conscious of the way her hips nestled naturally into his loins. And if only his warm breath didn't play against her ear, inciting a riot within her. And if only his muscled arms didn't rest along hers, propping her, his large hands cupping her own.

And if only the dusk wasn't coming on and the February wind blowing cold and his body didn't provide such a barrier against the chill then she wouldn't have leaned into him as if she were welcoming an embrace instead of a simple lesson in firing a weapon.

"That's it," he murmured into her hair.

He was lucky she didn't shoot him.

"If you have clear title to the ranch, those boys can't really believe they'd have a chance to get it from you," Pete said over coffee that night.

Carolyn knew he had no idea how alluring it was to share something so simple as a cup of coffee after the children had gone upstairs for the night.

"I don't know what they're thinking," Carolyn said, resting her elbows on the table and cradling her warm mug in both hands. She felt too aware of his presence, too jolted by the feelings she'd had that afternoon in his arms. *Nothing personal, ma'am, just target practicing.* But it had felt like a prelude to a kiss.

"How long was this place empty before you moved in?" he asked.

Carolyn shrugged. "Fifteen years or so. Since Craig's parents died."

"But it was always in your husband's family?"

"Yes, and when Craig's parents died, he and his siblings all inherited it. But Taylor didn't want it, and no one could get hold of Allison—who had moved away right after the funeral. So Craig and Taylor went through the process to have it legally transferred to Craig's name only."

He gave her an odd look then and his lips quirked in a smile.

"What?" she asked.

"Nothing," he said, but his grin broadened.

"Okay...what?"

"I just like the way you talk," he said. "Slow and soft. Like the vowels are all blurred somehow."

She didn't know what to say to that. She liked the way *he* talked, crisp and clean and as if many of the consonants were actually vowels. The only thing she didn't like about it was the way it made her skin feel tight and tingly. She met his gray eyes with—hopefully—imperturbable composure.

"And Craig had full rights to the land? Water, mineral, the whole gamut?"

"According to the papers we—I—have."

The smile had faded from his lips and it was obvious he was thinking about something else.

"The Wannamachers could have had access to it all those years?"

"The years we weren't here?"

He nodded.

"Anyone did, I guess," she said. "It was here. Empty."

He lit a cigarette before asking, "How close would you say we are to the Mexican border from here?"

"Two hundred miles?"

He frowned.

"What are you getting at, Pete?"

"I don't know," he said. But she knew he was lying. He was thinking something. Something important.

Then she saw what he was after and shook her head. "The Wannamachers wouldn't be smuggling in illegal aliens through here," she said. "No profit in it. I've read about the border troubles and, for the most part, the people dealing with human flesh get those poor people just inches across the border then ship them directly to where they can be hired. There aren't many farmers in this area who could even afford extra help, no matter how inexpensive."

"Maybe they just haven't met the right man," Pete said, not meeting her eyes. His lopsided grin lifted his full lips.

Carolyn felt a blush creep up her cheeks. Had she? The question leapt all too neatly into her mind. Like him, she had to look away before he read the thought, caught it in the confusion in her gaze.

Nevertheless, she had to acknowledge his statement. "Men who work as hard as you do, and for nothing, are rare," she said.

"Oh, it's not for nothing," he said slowly.

And when she raised her eyes to his in quick surprise she saw he wasn't smiling anymore. His eyes were on her, and he looked dead serious.

Her heart jolted once and then seemed to race. She felt a curious pull in the pit of her stomach. She didn't know what his words meant exactly, but she could guess. And if she'd been unable to accomplish a speculation, the look in his eyes was explicit.

He wanted her. More than that, perhaps. Something about the way he steadily regarded her, without smiling, without shifting his gaze to her lips, simply, straightforwardly letting her know that whatever he felt about her was nothing casual, made her weak with desire so long suppressed she was nearly shocked by feeling it again.

She needed to ask him why he'd been on the MacLaine property, how he knew them, what he'd really been doing

out there—how he'd gotten there—and what it was that made him agree to come to her place. But all she could think about was that his gray eyes had darkened to a rough steel blue.

Had he even needed a job? She didn't think so. Nor did she believe him an itinerant. And judging by the quality of his clothing and the caliber of his camp equipment, he didn't appear to be hurting for money. And he was looking at her as if they'd known each other years before and had come back together again.

So, why was he willing to come to her place at nothing more than a request and a five-dollar bill from an eight-year-old? And why wasn't she breaking the shocking link with his eyes, why wasn't she frightened, running scared?

Caught in his gaze, she knew he could see her questions. Could he understand that she didn't care what his reasons might be for being on her ranch? She needed his help. The Wannamacher brothers hadn't shown their faces during the entire time he'd been on her place.

But she knew what he was really seeing was the strength of her wanting him, the depth of the longing to be held again, assured that things would be okay. That she could trust him to keep her safe.

"It's all right," he said. But his words were oblique. What did he mean by them?

"What is?" she rasped. She had to ask.

He looked away then and drew a deep breath and let it out slowly. He crushed his cigarette out in the ashtray she'd given him that first morning and said, still without looking at her, "That they know I'm here."

That he'd ducked the electricity between them made her nearly sag with relief. She didn't know him; didn't really know anything about him. She was a fool to have been fantasizing about trust and safety. She'd never had that luxury with someone before. Certainly not Craig. She couldn't pretend this stranger would be any different.

"What do you think they'll do next?" she asked, but she

was wondering what she herself was likely to do if Pete held another shooting lesson.

"If they're bullies—and believe me, I think that's all they are—they'll back off once they realize you're not alone out here."

"And if they're not?"

"If they're not your garden variety bullies," he said, "then they want something specific. Not just your land. Let's get real, this land hasn't been worked in fifteen years no matter what they're claiming. And from what you've told me about the place, the good land was all sold off to pay debts and taxes."

"But what?" she asked. "What could they possibly want?"

Pete looked at her pointedly.

She shook her head again. "It's not me. I mean—maybe now, but this war of theirs started before they ever laid eyes on me. It's this place they want."

But when she met Pete's gaze she could see that he didn't have the same restrictions—or motivations—the Wannamachers did.

"I don't know," he said, his gray eyes moving away and lighting on the coffeepot. "But there's something here they want. And getting you off your property is the only way to get it."

She remembered Aunt Sammie Jo's speculation about some kind of survey that revealed something wonderful buried beneath the surface of the old ranch. "Are you thinking they know something we don't?"

"I think that's probably a given," he said.

"Why?"

"Because if they'd just left something here, buried it in the cellar or whatever, they could simply take it when you aren't at home. Everyone around this place must know when you substitute-teach. They could duck in here the second you're not at home and nab whatever they've stashed."

"Drugs...treasure...?"

He shrugged but his lips lifted in a smile that caused a minor earthquake inside her. "I haven't met them," he said. "Somehow, they don't sound like the treasure type. And I'm afraid the notion of buried treasure is a little pat."

"So you think there's something else?"

For a split second she questioned why she was asking him. Then she wondered why she hadn't understood before. She sought his advice because he seemed a man who might know answers. That hard edge she'd instinctively seen in him was a reality.

He'd been on her property for a few days, but looking at him now, she felt she was seeing him for the first time: he might not talk about himself or offer any information about his past or his present, but he was a man to whom command came easily, readily. Was this the key to him, then?

"Maybe," he said.

He had the oddest way of allowing a pause to fall into nonresponse before answering a question, she thought. And to appear to be responding to her unvoiced thoughts. "Maybe...what?" she asked.

"I think they're after something else," he said. "I don't know what, but you being completely off this place is what they want. What they're after."

And you? she wanted to ask. *What are you after?*

He looked down into his empty mug as if reading tea leaves. Why did she know that something was bothering him?

"What?" she asked.

He half chuckled, but didn't meet her eyes.

"Really...what?" she asked.

He raised his gray eyes to meet hers. "It's not about the Wannamachers," he said. "I...it's been awhile since I had a shower..."

She felt immediately chagrined by the realization that the bunkhouse had only a toilet and sink, nothing more. She'd

asked him to come to her place, asked him to help her solve a problem no one else seemed willing to tackle and she'd never even considered his personal needs.

And she felt ensnared by her sudden mental image of him in a shower she didn't even have. "Upstairs," she said. It felt like she croaked the words. "But we don't have a shower. Only a bath. You'll have to use the tub."

"Fine," he said. "If you don't mind…would tonight be okay?"

"Fine," she said, unconsciously echoing his words. "You'll need towels."

That lopsided grin made an appearance. "One will do."

"Right. Well…I'll just go get them. It. I'll get the towel for you," she said.

"I'd appreciate it," he said.

She left him sitting in the kitchen, staring into the empty coffee mug, while she raced upstairs for a clean towel and washcloth.

It wasn't until she'd handed over the linens that she wondered what on earth she'd done. She'd invited a perfect stranger onto her property and now that perfect stranger was about to take a bath in her house.

His need was mundane. His want was simplistic and necessary. A man needed a bath. Anyone did.

So why did his taking a bath in her tub make her hands tremble and her heart thunder?

"Thank you," he said, accepting her gift of the towel and washcloth.

"The hot water's really hot…" she said, then trailed off at the look on his face.

"I can figure it out," he said.

She was very sure he could.

Chapter 4

Pete leaned back in the huge claw-footed bathtub, idly rubbing a sweet-smelling bar of soap across his chest as he listened to the distant low, sad cry of a nighthawk and the harmonized giggling of two little girls down the hall in their room.

In the short time he'd spent in the West Texas desert he'd learned the high plains were a study of sharp contrasts. And on this strange night, only seventy-some miles from Lubbock, ninety miles from Amarillo and a whisper from Carolyn Leary's bedroom, he felt those contrasts to his very soul.

He'd taken all three of the Leary women out to a make-shift target range he'd set up on the far side of the barn. He'd been pelted with more questions than bullets had hit the hay bales that held up the paper targets he'd drawn with the girls' crayons.

"Why's it so loud?"

"Can't we use a silencer like they do on the movies?"

"Why don't you lean your head over sideways like they do on TV?"

"Why does it want to push me backward when I pull the trigger?"

Target practice had been an unmitigated disaster. Of the four of them, only he hit any of the targets, Bratwurst the horse had complained bitterly, and the girls had been more concerned with covering their sensitive ears and closing their eyes in anticipation than worrying about where they *shouldn't* point the gun.

And Carolyn had eyed the guns as if they were live snakes. She was tough as nails when the guns weren't loaded, but put a little ammunition in them and she started shaking like a kid in a thunderstorm. Except she hadn't started trembling until he'd wrapped his arms around her, had she?

And she'd felt so very right in his arms. Her body curved into his in perfect harmony. He'd felt her stiffen, felt her try to avoid touching him anywhere, and had been unable to resist the urge to press closer. He'd used the target practice as the excuse, but it was the need to feel her that made him step into her, draw her closer, slowly ease his hands down her arms.

And then there was the way her eyes met his when they were downstairs drinking coffee. There was a candor and fresh honesty about Carolyn that he'd never encountered before. She wore her vulnerability on the surface and apparently had no idea what a strong aphrodisiac it was.

Pete sighed and stirred the warm water.

On the one hand he'd never been made to feel more welcome anywhere. On the other, he knew the face-value Pete Jackson they welcomed was like some killer iceberg, the kind that only had the tip showing while the base could rip apart huge ocean liners. Couldn't Carolyn feel the murky depths inside him? What kind of woman was she that she could give trust so easily, so readily? And why did

that very trust both warm and frighten him at the same time?

Upon first consideration, it had seemed he might just scare off a couple of thugs and make the lives of three Leary blondes a little happier. But just a few days in close proximity and he knew the Leary trio was like a vortex that would, if he lingered or strayed too close to the center, suck him in.

As with many older homes, insulation in the walls proved virtually nonexistent, so, from his vantage spot in the old iron and enamel tub in the bathroom at the apex of the stairs, he could hear everything transpiring in the house. The girls were playing some board game—and by the sound of it, Jenny was cheating—and Carolyn had mounted the stairs singing some love song Pete almost recognized.

He'd have much preferred a quick, curtained shower but the plumbing in the place didn't run to such modern conveniences. He hadn't said anything when, after questioning her, Carolyn handed him a large, stiff, line-dried towel and washcloth, but he'd been all too conscious of the blush on her cheeks and the warmth in his own. Had she been picturing him leaning back in the tub as he was now, his legs crossed and sloped against the far wall? Had she thought, as he did now, that with his legs where they were, the tub was definitely large enough for two?

Maybe her mind didn't run to such thoughts. Maybe it was only him who, after looking at the ancient hulk of a tub, pictured her long limbs dewy with moisture, her naked form blurred by eddying water and soap bubbles, her hair pulled up from her damp face, her eyes closed in bliss.

He ran the washcloth over his face as if to erase the image. It might have worked if another part of his anatomy hadn't bought the picture wholesale.

A sudden rap on the bathroom door made him jump guiltily and slosh a good gallon of water onto the tiled floor. "What?"

"I gotta go, Pete," Jenny's voice piped urgently as she

punctuated her need in staccato knocks against the thin door. "Let me in!"

"Hang on a second," he said even as he hauled himself out of the old tub, losing another gallon or two, and grabbed at the towel that didn't seem nearly so large once it was wrapped around his middle. He fumbled with the lock and had scarcely drawn the bolt back before the door slammed into him and Jenny burst through it, already tugging at her jeans.

Clutching the towel and rubbing his bruised forehead, Pete ducked out of the bathroom and swiftly closed the door behind him. If he'd had any intention of staying, he would install a shower in the bunkhouse even if it would have killed him. Which it might well do since he didn't have the foggiest notion of how to go about building a shower stall.

He raised his forearm to the doorjamb and rested his bruised forehead against it. "What am I doing here?" he muttered. "I've got to be insane."

"Oh my God!"

He stiffened and turned slowly to meet Carolyn's wide eyes. She was wearing a shiny, loose nightshirt that did absolutely nothing to hide her curves or her shapely legs. And she had a pair of ridiculous slippers that looked like happy-faced raccoons on her feet. A thick terry robe dangled uselessly from one limp hand.

"Jenny had to go," he said, and tried to grin. But her parted lips and the hand pressed against her chest—in what should have seemed a melodramatic gesture but wasn't—didn't help his attempt to be casual.

"I—I'm sorry," she whispered, and her eyes dropped to the puddle of water at his feet and skittered back to his as if determined not to see anything else. Or afraid of doing just that.

The bathroom door jerked open, almost causing Pete to lose his footing, and Jenny shot out and under his arm, zipping her jeans. "Thanks! I almost didn't make it!" She

skidded a bit in his puddle and giggled as she caught her balance, ducked around her mother and skipped into her room.

"You were right! He's got hair all *over* his body!" she said before the bedroom door slammed shut.

While the comment should have made him feel more self-conscious than ever, Carolyn's reaction to it saved the day. She closed her eyes for a moment and her lips moved in an obvious oath. Without opening her eyes, she pivoted and said aloud, "Aliens. Just think *aliens.*"

Staring at her back, the lush curves, the long legs, the bent blond head, Pete had to fight the urge to walk up to her and wrap his arms around her as he'd done earlier that afternoon. In reassurance, he told himself, but knew his desire ran far deeper than that.

He wanted to do a lot more than simply hold her, he thought, dragging his eyes away from her. He stepped back through the bathroom door and into copious amounts of cold water on the floor. He stared at the tub half-filled with what was sure to be tepid water.

But a slow smile took hold of his lips. The Leary household didn't have any more notion of safety than literal babes. Fine. He would make certain they all knew how to shoot one of their weapons and *then* he would leave.

He reached over and wrenched on the hot water faucet and grinned before dropping his towel onto the wicker clothes hamper and stepping back into his interrupted bath.

When she heard the door snick shut behind her, Carolyn felt as if two tons of lead weight slipped from her shoulders. Her heart still beat too rapidly and her fingers shook in a contrapuntal rhythm. But at least he wasn't standing there any longer, too tall, too lean, too muscular...and too nakedly wet.

His eyes had seemed more silver than gray in the dim light from the hallway. And his wetted hair had seemed almost black. Droplets of water had clung to the thick mat

of hair on his broad chest and riveted down the coarse hairs of his long, sturdy legs.

She'd wanted a brawny man out where the Wannamachers could see him so they would understand she wasn't helpless, wasn't desperate. She'd wanted his sheer size parading around the place to let the Wannamachers know she had one tough hombre on hand for protection. But when she came out of her room to see what Jenny's commotion was about and saw Pete instead, mostly naked, *wet,* leaning against the bathroom door, holding his towel around his waist, she hadn't spared a single thought to any notion of mere protection.

The sight of him had completely robbed her of any semblance of rationality. Her heart had scudded in her chest, then seemed to stop for a wild moment. Her first need had been to repress the groan that had instinctively risen from deep inside her. Her second had been to slip away without letting him discover she'd seen him.

But before she could do either, he'd shifted position, propping one elbow against the doorjamb and resting his head on his forearm. He'd looked like a Michelangelo statue come to life and she'd involuntarily made some sound. He hadn't whirled around, he'd only stiffened and turned his head, as if in slow motion, arm still against the door, his eyes panning the hallway to meet hers.

She'd wanted to sink into the floor…or into his arms. She wanted to dry his brow, wipe the moisture from his back and legs; dear heaven, she'd wanted to press against that damp mat of hair on his chest and feel his hard, taut body melt into hers.

She leaned her overwarm forehead against the woodwork surrounding her bedroom door and closed her eyes. He had to have seen every vestige of her want in her gaze.

"Carolyn Leary, you are a complete idiot," she murmured.

"Mom?"

She didn't move. "You're dead. Both of you."

"Why?"

The voice of total innocence. The voice of complicity and deviltry.

Carolyn sighed but she had the feeling that someday, perhaps when she was eighty or so, she would be able to laugh about the situation. "The next time, if Pete's taking a bath, you either *wait* or figure out some other solution."

The girls were wise enough not to argue or ask about alternate solutions.

"And you do not, on pain of death, discuss Pete's body, do you understand me?"

"Yes, ma'am."

"Yes, Mother," Jenny said too sweetly.

"Good night."

"Good night, Mom."

"See you in the morning."

"We love you."

"Yeah. We love you."

"I love you, too," Carolyn said, but at that moment, she couldn't for the life of her think why.

All she could think about was Pete's naked, muscled form sprawled out in her bathtub. He was too tall to fit easily, she thought. He would have to stretch his feet far up the wall if he wanted his back anywhere near the water. In Dallas, Craig had used to splay his legs on either side, but somehow Carolyn couldn't picture Pete doing the same.

No, Pete would find a comfortable spot near the corner and cross his legs, his arms lightly resting on the sides. A king at home. A big cigar in one hand and a glass of champagne in the other would complete the picture.

Especially if he was beckoning her to join him.

The mental image actually made her ache.

Only after she'd heard the bathroom door open and his quiet footfalls on the stairs and the subsequent closing of the back door did she leave the safety of her bedroom. And, when she saw the single wet footprint near the corner of

the wall, some three feet above the faucets, she understood why she'd come in the room.

After splashing a little cold water on her face, she went downstairs to perform the routine locking up of doors. She fumbled her way into the darkened kitchen.

"Don't turn on the light."

Her heart seemed to leap into her throat. Pete had spoken the words too softly to be anything but a warning. A nearly hysterical part of her wanted to ask if he'd been waiting for her. And her hands trembled in immediate reaction.

"Get out of the light from the living room," he murmured.

He'd been waiting, but not for her. The realization made her both relieved and oddly disappointed.

"Why? What's wrong?" she whispered, edging around the kitchen table. Her eyes hadn't adjusted to the abrupt change from light to dark, nor had her body adjusted to the notion that Pete Jackson was somewhere in her black kitchen.

"I'm not sure," he said softly.

She hesitated then inched toward Pete's voice. She had both hands stretched out before her and she jumped a little when her fingers poked his rigid shoulder. She wrapped her trembling hand around his broad arm then jerked back from his heat.

"What's wrong?" she managed to repeat.

"Someone's here," he said.

By now she could make out his silhouette against the opened curtain on the back door. His eyes weren't on her but on something outside. He raised his left hand to cover hers and pull her behind him a bit.

She was reminded of the night she'd found him in the desert with her daughters, the way he'd pressed them behind him as she got out of the Ranger.

She leaned into him a little, feeling his back against her body, drawing strength from him. Tall as Craig had been, she'd never felt this sense that he'd been a fortress, a bul-

wark against danger. The realization stung her a little, as if she were betraying Craig's memory by merely thinking of their differences.

"I saw the headlights of a car as I was starting for the bunkhouse," Pete murmured.

She leaned forward to look around him and pulled back as she felt him stiffen and realized she was pressing her breasts against the back of his arm. She shifted to cease the contact and was sorry. "Where? I don't see any car."

"By the barn. In the shadows."

She could see it then, now that she knew where to look. It was a low-slung, older model Chevrolet. "Wannamachers," she said.

"You're sure? Is that the kind of car they drive?"

"It has to be them!"

"But have you seen that car before?"

"No...I don't know."

"Shh...someone's outside the car."

"What are they doing?"

"I can't tell from here," he said.

Immediately Carolyn thought the worst, imagining the barn suddenly bursting into flame. "Bratwurst's in the barn tonight! I made the girls put him in because the weather report said we were getting down to ten degrees or so with windchill!" She instinctively moved around him, reaching for the door.

His hands grasped her shoulders and pulled her back against his chest before she could wrench the door open. "Wait," he breathed in her ear. And even as she felt the jolt of fear-induced adrenaline coursing through her veins, her knees seemed to quaver at the sensation of his hot breath playing against her skin.

"Wait here," he murmured, and she could feel his lips moving at her temple.

He released her shoulders and she heard him moving swiftly away. She sagged against the doorjamb, not know-

ing if she was afraid of what waited for them outside or
how the stranger Pete made her feel.

He was back in a matter of seconds. "Stay inside," he
growled, gently pushing her out of the way and silently
turning the knob. "At least I got that damned squeaky
screen door fixed," he said as he pulled open the back door
and pushed on the screen. It swung out and wide and then
screeched like a banshee.

Carolyn scarcely noticed Pete's muttered oath as she
heard two other higher-pitched swears and the sudden slamming of car doors. She realized several things in the split
second that Pete leapt out of the door: one, Pete was armed
with Craig's old .38 pistol, and two, the vehicle she hadn't
even heard idling was already pulling away.

Pete was well into the driveway and taking aim at the
car before Carolyn could even draw a breath. But he didn't
fire. He stood, legs parted, knees bent, arms straight forward, gun hand resting in the other for accuracy. Then he
abruptly raised the gun heavenward and dropped his left
hand as he straightened.

A completely irrational part of Carolyn's mind thought
how much the girls would have appreciated this particular
sight; for a moment Pete had looked exactly like one of
their heroes from the movies. Then she burst out the back
door, not even feeling the starkly cold night.

"Why didn't you shoot?" she demanded.

He turned as if surprised she were there. He glanced once
at the distant taillights of the disappearing car and back to
her. "Could have been kids looking for a place to park."

"Are you kidding?" she asked angrily. "We both know
who it was!"

"Do we? I like to be a little more certain before I shoot
somebody. Let's go in. It's cold, Carolyn," he said.

He didn't seem to notice that he'd used her name. It was
the first time since they'd met that he'd called her anything
at all.

"Get inside," he said.

"We've got to check the barn."

"You've got to get inside. *I'll* check the barn."

"I want to see what they did."

"They're gone. There's no sign of a fire in the barn. *I'm* freezing my ass off and I'm dressed more warmly than you are. Now *get inside.*"

Pete had only been with them for a short time, granted, but this was probably the longest speech he'd uttered in her presence since his arrival. And the fact that he said it with absolute command made a frisson of unknown reaction ripple through Carolyn's body.

She'd always had to be the strong one in her marriage. Her husband might have come outside to investigate a prowler, but he would have asked her what they should do next.

Pete swore then and strode forward to take her arm and not so gently lead her back to the porch and up the steps he'd mended only that afternoon. "If it makes you feel better, I swear I'll check the damned barn as soon as I get my shoes on!"

The warmth of the house was palpable as he shoved her inside and shut the door behind them. Carolyn shivered then, unaware in her fear and anxiety that she'd been standing outside in subfreezing temperatures in nothing but a fake-satin nightshirt and a pair of heelless raccoon slippers her daughters had given her for Christmas the year before.

At least she'd had slippers on. Pete's feet must be excruciatingly cold. She wanted to say something to that effect, but his back was to her as he pulled a chair out from the table, all but slammed the pistol to the surface and reached for the hiking boots and socks he'd obviously cast aside when he heard the car outside.

Why was he doing this for them? There wasn't anything in it for him. No money. No promises. No nothing.

She had to ask him. "Why are you doing this for us?"

He didn't answer as he pulled on his socks and hiking boots in sharp, rough jerks and tugs.

"I really want to know," she said softly.

He remained silent as his hands flew in the process of tying a fierce knot in his boot laces.

"Pete? What do you do for a living? Why were you out in the desert?"

He stood abruptly and took a long stride toward her. He was no more than a single inch away from her. She could feel the cold from the outdoors wafting from his clothing and the heat that burned underneath.

"I thought you said you didn't care why I was out there."

"I—I know I said that."

"But you didn't mean it."

"No, I did, but…"

"But you've reconsidered?"

Why was he so angry with her? Because she'd snapped at him? She thought it was something more, something she hadn't even triggered, something caused by the sight of strangers on her property. And her questioning him had simply been a final straw of sorts.

"No, I just…I'd just like to understand why you're doing this for us."

"Jenny's birthday money and three squares a day."

She wanted to smile but couldn't. He'd said the words without a vestige of humor and the explanation was patently absurd.

"The real reason you came here, Pete. Please tell me," she said softly. "Please."

"Okay," he growled. She could feel his exhalation of air, the soft play of his breath against her hair. "You," he growled.

"W-what?"

"You."

"I don't understand."

"Yes, you do, Carolyn. Nobody's that blind."

She shook her head, but wasn't sure what she was negating—his words or his proximity. The truth in his words.

"You want it spelled out? Okay. I agreed to come play handyman and bodyguard because of your laugh. Your smile. Hell, I don't know, maybe the way you said 'please.'"

"I d-don't understand..." she began again but trailed off as his ice-cold hands grasped her shoulders.

"Don't lie to me, Carolyn. I can see through a lie at a hundred yards. And I'm nowhere near that far away," he said.

"I think you'd better—"

"I think so, too," he said, and slid his hands down her arms only to encircle them and roughly pull her against him as he lowered his full, very warm lips to hers.

Chapter 5

The slow fire he'd started when he'd been standing all but naked and wet in her hallway upstairs burst into flame as his hands slipped into her hair and he cupped her face with the heels of his palms, drawing her even closer.

His tongue, hot and tasting vaguely of creamed coffee and a hint of tobacco, swept into her mouth, strong, demanding, a raw exhortation for her to respond. His hands trembled slightly and his body was rock hard against hers, no longer cold now, but hot, seemingly on fire.

She couldn't withhold the moan that escaped her as his hands dropped to her waist and pulled her against him. Her thin nightshirt felt nonexistent and her legs quivered as she leaned into him.

This was wrong, she thought, she didn't know him. He was a stranger and a mystery. But how could anything that felt this good be even remotely wrong? Like hot fudge sundaes, lobster dipped in melted butter, filet mignon... wonderful delights, but they were bad for you... Was he bad for her?

And as his hands began a slow, deep caress of her back, her bottom, and then raising to cup her aching breasts, she ceased to think at all. Wrong or right, she arched against him, granting him greater access, clinging to his broad shoulders and meeting his lips with a fevered kiss of her own.

"Oh, Carolyn," he groaned as he released her lips and pressed a trail of liquid fire down the line of her jaw and onto her sensitive collarbone. "You're so beautiful it hurts."

His words seemed to release her fragile hold on reality another notch and she dropped her head back as he arched her even further and nuzzled her rock-hard nipples through the flimsy nightshirt. He blew hot breath against them and grazed her lightly with his teeth. His hands lowered and cupped her rounded bottom and slowly rotated her against him, letting her know a measure of the extent of his desire for her.

She felt liquid, molten, and every part of her body seemed to tremble and quake with unvarnished need, with a longing so intense it was nearly agonizing.

Pete knew he had to let her go, to call a halt to this utter luxury. But he would have to have been made of pure steel, totally lacking in emotion and passion and devoid of the glorious sense of touch in order to release her now. And he lacked none of those feelings...not one of them.

He could scarcely tell where her satin nightshirt ended and her skin began, so soft and silken was her exquisite body. The hollows beneath her chin smelled of the soap he'd used in the bathtub and her lips tasted of peanuts and raw heat.

The feel of her body melting against his roused a demon in him that made him forget the past, the future, everything but her velvet touch, her ragged breathing. He felt nearly mindless, his entire being was focused on her, on her ragged breathing, her soft inchoate murmur of acceptance and possibly denial, not of him but of what they were doing.

"Mom? Are you downstairs?"

He heard the words, even registered them in some deep recess of his brain, but it wasn't until Carolyn went perfectly still in his arms that he understood them, understood the implications behind them.

With the greatest reluctance in the world, he slowly pulled away from Carolyn, still holding her but stepping back a pace. He could feel her entire body trembling and he thought she might slide to the floor if he released her fully. Somehow the very notion made him feel powerful and he ached to pull her back against him.

"Mom?"

He half smiled as she cleared her throat before she answered, "Yes, Shawna, what is it?"

He wondered how she could tell which of her daughters was speaking. Was it a mother thing or would he know if he spent enough time around them?

His smile faded from his lips. He wasn't going to be spending time around the Leary women; he was going to be leaving before what happened tonight progressed to other levels. They had been granted a reprieve even if, at the moment, it felt like a curse.

He realized that Carolyn didn't know how lucky she was her daughter had called at that precise moment. Like a guardian angel, the little girl had rescued her mother from a colossal mistake.

"I forgot to do my math homework."

Carolyn straightened even more and turned slightly, freeing herself from his grasp. He shoved his hands into his pockets, his fingertips tingling with the remembered feel of her skin, the weight of her breasts.

He closed his eyes when Carolyn breathed a short curse. She'd done the same thing in the hallway; apparently she didn't swear aloud around the children. "Will you have time to do it in the morning?" she called. She ran her hands through her hair and tugged at her nightshirt as if it would lengthen by such a maneuver.

"There's so much I'll *never* get it done!" Shawna wailed.

Carolyn looked at him then, a tentative flickering glance that exposed her candid vulnerability, her lingering desire, and something else, a barrier, a guard that hadn't been there two minutes before.

"I'm sorry," she said.

Pete frowned. "I'm not."

She frowned then and Pete knew he hadn't understood what she meant, nor had she known what his words implied. He wanted to ask but knew it wasn't the time, nor—because the kitchen remained dark and she remained alluring and Shawna was waiting—was it the place.

"I—I'll see you in the morning," she said, but her words hung between them not so much as a statement but as a question.

"Lock the door after me," he said, nodding, thinking it sounded as if he were telling her to lock him out. Maybe he was.

She nodded as he crossed to the table and hefted the .38. He turned it around and handed it to her grip-first. He felt odd pressing the cold steel into her hands. "Put this back in the living room closet. On the top shelf. You don't come out of that door tonight—or any night till this is all over—without it in your hand, okay?"

He stepped around her and opened the back door, letting a blast of cold air blow through the kitchen.

Carolyn gasped behind him and he slipped through the door without looking back at her.

"Pete?" she asked, halting him in the act of shutting the door. He felt a tentative touch against his shoulder blade.

"Yes?"

"I—nothing," she said.

Whatever she'd been going to say could wait until light of day, until dawn made this madness in her dark kitchen seem like nothing more than a dream, he thought.

"Good night," he said, pulling the door shut. The icy

February air slapped his face and clawed at his shirt. He drew a deep, thankful breath and pushed the screen door that didn't make a single sound gently back into place. He heard the click of the dead bolt Carolyn slid into place and laid his hand against the door frame as if he could feel her through the wood.

"Good night," Carolyn whispered to the empty kitchen, resting her forehead against the cool doorjamb.

"Mom?"

"Coming, Shawna," she said wearily.

"Can I stay up, too?" Jenny called out.

"Not a chance," Carolyn said as she left the kitchen. Her legs shook as she mounted the stairs and her hand, when she took Shawna's math book, trembled so noticeably that her daughter took it back.

"Are you okay, Mom?"

No, she thought. She was *far* from okay. A thousand miles from all right. She'd come very close to surrendering to a complete stranger on the floor of her own kitchen.

"Mom?"

"I'm fine, sweetie." She shook her head a little as if shaking the memory of Pete's impassioned kisses from her mind.

"There's twenty-five problems!" Shawna said in an aggrieved tone.

"When you do one, there will only be twenty-four. And then twenty-three."

"You'll help me, won't you?"

"If you want every answer wrong, sure," Carolyn said, dropping her arm around her daughter's slender shoulders and guiding her down the hall to her own bedroom.

She tried to feel comfortable with the notion that Pete was *outside* while she was *in* but all she felt was restless and out of sorts. Her lips burned and an unfamiliar sensation of an elevator falling at least four floors gnawed at her insides.

Shawna settled at the old desk in the corner of her moth-

er's bedroom and Carolyn stood over her as she opened the math book and took out a folded paper with only one answer on it.

"Twenty-four problems to go," Shawna said, and sighed.

Carolyn looked out the window and down at the lighted window in the bunkhouse. She felt her heart jolt as Pete's shadow crossed between the lamp and window only to stop, a solid silhouette. She could almost feel his stare at her own lighted window, her own shadowed form.

"How much is sixteen times one-half?"

"One half of what?" Carolyn asked absently.

"Oh, Mom!" Shawna giggled.

Jenny spoke from the doorway. "I'm scared in there all alone. Can I sleep in your bed while Shawna does her homework? I won't say a word, I promise."

Carolyn sighed and turned away from the window. This was the reality, two wonderful daughters in a ramshackle old farmhouse. What happened in the kitchen had been nothing more than an aftermath of fear and the accidental chemical reaction of two lonely people. That's all it was...and all it ever would be. It would never happen again because she wouldn't let it.

What if Shawna had come down the stairs before calling out? Worse, what if they hadn't been interrupted?

She pulled back her covers and motioned for Jenny to hop in. She was rewarded with a blinding grin that brought a smile to her own lips.

"Why are you shaking, Mom?" Jenny asked.

Why, indeed?

Pete waited until all the lights were out in the house before donning his heavy sub-zero parka and a pair of work gloves. He carried a can of white paint to the side of the old barn. Muttering a string of highly improbable threats to the absent Wannamacher brothers, he slapped a coat of cold-thickened paint over the spray-painted scrawl.

Get Out Or Get Dead!

"I'd like to spray a couple of phrases on you two," Pete growled. "With mace."

Damnation, it was cold. Whoever thought the desert southwest wasn't cold in the winter hadn't been painting over a threatening message in the dead of night in February.

When the words were covered with the sluggish paint, he stepped back to survey his handiwork. The new white paint stood out in sharp relief against the dirty, weathered barn's original coat.

Pete shook his head, but a grin lifted one corner of his lips. Now he'd have to paint the whole damned barn. That would take him at least a week. Or more. The other side of his mouth lifted.

He glanced up at Carolyn's darkened window. He'd done a thousand things in his life that he could regret, but coming to Carolyn's ranch wasn't one of them. She needed him. The girls needed him.

And he desperately needed to be what they wanted him to be.

They might not be getting a paragon, but at least they wouldn't be getting much more grief from the Wanna-machers.

Those two boys—men—were cowards, he thought derisively. Bullies who sneaked around in the middle of the night spray-painting threats on a widow's property. Like all bullies, what they needed was a lesson in who was tougher.

Pete replaced the paint can lid and drove his heel down on it to seal it closed. That's what he'd do to the Wanna-machers, Bubba and Jimmy. He'd grind his heel in their faces until they were crying for him to let them go.

For the first time since he came to Carolyn's ranch, he knew the why behind the why he'd agreed to join her. She was the reason he'd said yes, but the reason he'd come and stayed was simply because he could do what no one in Almost seemed able to: he could face down a pair of bullies with one hand tied behind his back.

He'd done little else for ten long years.

He'd show those Wannamachers what "get out or get dead" really meant. He had plenty of experience in the latter.

Carolyn was sure breakfast the next morning could have been an exceedingly awkward affair, but two things stopped any uneasiness cold in its tracks.

The first was the delivery of five kittens by Ralphette, the barn cat. Ralphette, a Siamese cross with one battered ear and a complaining disposition, announced the arrival of the new mousing team after the first rooster's crow. Pete was still pulling on his boots as he hopped along behind Shawna and Jenny, each of whom had a portion of his parka in their hands, propelling him forward.

Carolyn, watching from the kitchen window, chuckled a little at the sight of Pete's ungainly progression across the track between the bunkhouse and barn. Ninety-eight percent of all men would have told the girls to wait and the other two percent would have grumbled at them to get lost. Not this man.

She may not know where he came from or anything about his past, but she knew that, at his core, Pete Jackson was a good man. No man so kind to two unruly girls could be anything else.

As a former social psychologist who had specialized in prison parolees, she knew her logic was specious at best. Prisons were filled with men and women who were good with children and still capable of murder, rape, theft and a host of other aberrant behaviors. Because someone hopped on one foot while trailing a couple of eager children didn't make him a superman. It only made him human.

All too human, she thought, remembering the hot satin of his tongue, the forceful pull of his hands at her back, the electricity that sparked so effortlessly and so tremendously between them. And so mysteriously and terrifyingly.

Just as she was tensing up again, anticipating his exit

from the barn and his walk across the grounds to the kitchen door, the second tension-reducer occurred in the form of Doc Jamison.

Though she'd gotten to know him well during their month's residency, largely thanks to the acquisition of Bratwurst and Ralphette, she'd become acquainted with the Almost veterinarian many years before, while visiting Almost with Craig. Still, for all that their relationship went back some ten years, he'd never driven his mobile clinic van onto their property before the sun was even over the horizon.

She slipped on a jacket hanging near the back door and stepped out of the house at the same moment Pete slipped out of the barn. She was shocked to see he carried a gun in his right hand. Not *Craig*'s gun. Something entirely his own, an extension of his hand. Something deadly.

"Doc!" she called loudly, running down the porch steps to greet him. Doc was looking at her so probably hadn't seen Pete's potentially deadly welcome nor his rapid disappearing act.

"Hey there, Caro," he said, unknowingly using her hated nickname. He threw his truck into Park and hopped down from the cab. "How's life in the fast lane?"

"What on earth are you doing out this way so early in the morning?" She meant the words sincerely, but she heard the accusations hang on the air: what are you doing checking up on me? Who asked you to do this?

If he hadn't blushed ten shades of scarlet, she might have believed any excuse he might have offered. But his discomfiture gave his mission away. Craig's salty aunt, Sammie Jo, had sent him to check out Pete Jackson.

"It's cat and horse day," he said, lying through his teeth.

"Is it really?" she asked. "So soon?"

Doc had given all her critters, feline and otherwise, shots and teeth-cleanings only two weeks before.

"Prevention…you know," he said.

"I know," she answered dryly, then smiled to take away the sting. "You want some coffee?"

"You bet," he said. He cast her a commiserative look of mingled apology and regret.

The girls pelted out of the barn.

"Doc!"

"Ralphette has five baby kitties!"

"Come see! Come on!"

Jenny and Shawna skidded to a stop just shy of bowling Doc down.

"Pete says Ralphette's in-dis-criminate," Shawna said.

"Will that hurt the kitties?" Jenny asked anxiously.

Doc met Carolyn's eyes with a grin in his before turning back to the girls. "Not that I ever heard of."

"Come see, Doc. Make sure they're okay."

Each girl took one of the vet's hands and dragged him toward the barn. At least he already had his shoes on and wasn't being pulled by his sheepskin jacket, Carolyn thought, watching him go with the girls.

Why couldn't Doc Jamison set her heart racing the way Pete did? She knew Doc. She respected him. The whole town did. Like Pete, he was good with her girls. And he, as she suspected of Pete, had a good heart. He was good-looking, taller than she, and had an easy manner around humans and animals alike. He was smart, funny and always ready to lend a hand to a person or critter in need. And he had to be lonely, having just become a widower about the same time Craig died. So why couldn't it be him who made her knees turn to jelly and made her forget every single cautionary rule? Why did she have to feel this way for a virtual mystery man?

However reticent Pete might be with her—despite the inherent eloquence of his lips—he appeared to have no difficulty with Dr. Charles Jamison. Before they even tossed their jackets onto the pegs by the back door, she could see that some kind of click had taken place between the two men.

"...some twenty years now and sometimes I think I'm still considered a newcomer," Doc was saying as he wiped his feet on the mat.

"Mom, one of the kittens looks just like that weird yellow cat over at the Greathouse's farm."

"Yeah, and another one is all black but has one white paw. I'm naming it Paintbrush 'cause it looks like it dipped its paw in the paint on the barn."

"What paint?" Carolyn asked.

"You can't name all the kittens!" Jenny insisted. "I'm naming the Siamese-looking one...*Beatrice.*"

"Beatrice?" Shawna asked, sounding horrified. "Why?"

"Why not?" Jenny rebutted.

"What paint?" Carolyn asked again, only to be ignored by everyone present.

"Boston man, aren't you?" Doc asked, and at Pete's nod, he grinned broadly. "I'd recognize the accent in my sleep."

"Harvard?" Pete asked.

"To my shame," Doc said, and grinned. "My father never could understand why I went to a big-name school only to come practice in a backwater desert. You?"

"Not so ritzy. Boston City."

"Business or law?"

"And one of the kittens has a big splotch of brown in a perfect circle on her butt. Her tail sticks right out of it. It's *so* funny, Mom. Pete named her BB for brown butt. Can you believe it?"

"Hush, girls, you're interrupting," Carolyn said, wishing she'd issued the reminder earlier...if she had, she wouldn't have missed Pete's low-voiced answer to Doc's question.

He'd been in their house how many days now and she hadn't even guessed he was from Boston, hadn't suspected he'd attended college, let alone in either business or law. Law? Like Craig? Impossible, and yet business didn't seem to fit at all.

This time she missed the prelude question. "What can I tell you?" Doc asked. "They think they're cowboys, that the 'code of the West' is carrying a can of spray paint and scaring people to death," Doc said.

He went on. "Trouble with the Wannamacher boys is that their daddy had more money than anybody around here knew what to do with. I take it from what people say about them, they never had to really do a day's lick of work. They were in and out of trouble as regular as other people change their socks, but never spent a night in the hoosegow because their daddy always knew the judge, the marshal or the D.A."

Pete apparently noticed the silence in the kitchen about then and looked from Doc to the girls. The message was clear to Carolyn, and apparently to Doc, for the veterinarian looked at Carolyn suddenly and asked if the offer for coffee was still on.

She blushed and turned for the mugs. She had forgotten all about coffee or breakfast.

"Do we have to go to school today?" Jenny asked.

"It's not every day Ralphette has kittens," Shawna pitched.

"Can we take them for show-and-tell when they get older?"

"Give your mother a break," Pete said suddenly, and a little gruffly, causing every Leary female to turn startled eyes in his direction.

"Yeah," Doc agreed. "It's only dark-thirty. And she hasn't had any coffee yet."

Carolyn turned her face away from the group in her kitchen and stared at the full coffeepot in her hand. A ridiculous grin hovered on her lips. When was the last time anyone had thought about her, her needs, her wants?

A long, long time, she thought. Too long.

"I'll get the cream," Pete said, right behind her.

For some odd reason, she felt like the cat that had already eaten the cream.

Chapter 6

Pete lit a cigarette and the chilly February breeze snatched away his exhaled cloud of smoke and melded it with the predawn murkiness. He half wished he could disappear as easily. The whole setup on Carolyn Leary's ranch was getting to him in a host of ways.

Carolyn accounted for some of his uneasiness, as did her daughters. And the unexpected sharp pang of loneliness he'd felt after encountering them that first day. And the sense of displacement he'd felt, that sense of being really out in the world for the first time in ten years.

He'd been on the Leary farm just shy of a week and already they seemed to accept him as a member of the family. It hadn't been so tough when the girls went to school and a whole lot easier when Carolyn had joined them, substitute-teaching the last few days. But today was Saturday, the first day all three would be around the place all day. No school. No escape.

He reviewed a list of projects he had in mind for the day, things that would keep him busy and out of sight of the

house—and its occupants—most of the time. The list was so extensive he knew he would only get half done, but thinking about it kept his mind from the thought of Carolyn inside all day, working on school papers perhaps, or stretching out on her bed for a deserved nap.

Repair the lintel over the barn door and set the double doors with spring hinge. Paint the backside of the barn, completing his cover-up of the Wannamacher brothers' work. See what he could do with the defunct rototiller in the machinery side of the barn. Carolyn had mentioned something when Doc Jamison had come around about the Farmer's Almanac saying planting could start on March 28 this year.

Why should he worry about that? He would be long, long gone by then. Like the proverbial ill wind he would simply blow away. Still, it would be a rather helpful farewell gift, readying Carolyn's garden. Something about the notion gave him a sense of inner peace, as if by preparing the soil for her garden, he was giving her a bit of himself that would last beyond his departure. The vegetables she would harvest in the summer and fall would be there because of him.

From habit, he carefully excised his cigarette, twisting the hot coal from the filter, then pocketed the spent paper before stepping off the short porch at the bunkhouse. That unfamiliar grin spread his lips as he thought about the work facing him. The labor around Carolyn's place had been therapeutic in a strangely satisfying way.

For the past ten years he'd been forced to literally wallow in the negative side of man. At every turn, he'd been confronted with the pressing awareness that the positive elements in society seemed to be falling apart. Television newscasters touted violence as a plague; prisons burgeoned with misfits, bullies, violence-driven sociopaths.

But out on a small ranch near Almost, Texas, each board replaced, each strand of wire tightened and straightened, the muck cleared from the corral and the stock tank cleaned

and refilled, all became tasks that seemed to address a basic requirement for order in his life.

At the end of every project, large or small, Pete felt the satisfaction of having restored a measure of symmetry to an out-of-sync world. His hands ached and his shoulders were stiff with the unaccustomed physical labor. And his mind felt curiously quiet, as if at rest.

It was only his heart that seemed to question why he lingered at the Leary ranch. The longer he spent there the harder it would be to leave. And he would have to leave. Once Carolyn knew about his past, however justifiable the things he'd done, she would want him out of her daughters' lives. And she would want him out of hers. And, even if she didn't, he wouldn't drag her into the morass that represented his past.

But just hearing the girls giggling made his own lips curve into a grin. Day by day, the grin felt less unnatural on his mouth and every question they asked seemed to loosen his tongue a tad more.

And just seeing their mother made his heart thunder in his chest and his loins tighten painfully. Sometimes when her eyes took on a faraway look and he knew she was thinking about what she'd lost, was remembering something Craig said or did, he had to fight the urge to draw her into his arms and comfort her. And had to face the knowledge that comfort was far from what he really wanted to offer her.

The Wannamachers hadn't returned since their spray paint foray two nights before. Carolyn had suggested that the Wannamachers had discovered that she and the girls weren't alone on the place any longer, that the thugs had found out about Carolyn's new handyman. She seemed relieved and the girls appeared to have forgotten all about the Wannamachers.

Pete hadn't forgotten them nor was he relieved. Bullies as bold as the Wannamacher boys didn't give up at the first

sign of opposition. His presence on the ranch simply represented a new challenge, a new opportunity for mischief.

They knew the land wasn't theirs; if it was, they'd go through normal channels. Pete still had no idea what it was they truly wanted, but suspected they didn't even care about the property as such. He'd seen their type too many times before. Deep down he knew what the Wannamachers wanted was simple: they wanted to terrorize Carolyn and her daughters. If they succeeded in driving her from her land, they gained the ultimate prize. They had time, incredible nerve and a total lack of conscience on their side.

They would be back. He knew that as surely as he knew the sun would rise in the morning and set again at night. But the Wannamachers would be in for a little surprise: Carolyn Leary's new handyman would be waiting for them.

The rooster crowed and seconds later the screen door banged against the side of the house—but didn't make a single other sound—and his morning escort pummeled across the dirt driveway.

"We're having pancakes for breakfast!" Jenny said, skidding to a stop at his feet.

"We always have pancakes on Saturday."

"Nuh-*uh*. Sometimes we have waffles. And sometimes—"

"And Aunt Taylor's bringing the boys out so they can ride Bratwurst," Shawna said, ignoring Jenny's interruption. "They don't have a horse."

Jenny abandoned her litany of alternate Saturday breakfasts. "They're triplets. Dentical ones."

"Aunt Taylor's Daddy's sister. Her husband died, too. It was so sad. He was a state trooper, you know."

"Uncle Doug. But we didn't know him very well. They lived here and we lived in Dallas."

"Yeah. You know what? Jacob Sanderson—he's a boy in our school—says there's a curse on the Leary women. You don't think that's true do you, Pete?"

"No," Pete said, angry at the unknown Jacob Sanderson.

"Good, 'cause that would mean me and Jenny would be cursed, too."

"Don't believe it for a second," Pete said.

"That would be cool if we were like cursed with magic or something," Jenny said.

"That's silly," Shawna said from her superior age.

"It isn't, either," Jenny said, but her heart wasn't in the argument. "Our cousins are okay," she added as if she weren't too sure about it. "I can tell them apart now. Mostly. And you know what? They have a dog named Elephant."

"Is he big?"

Jenny giggled. "No. He's about the size of Ralphette's kittens!"

Pete shook his head, grinning, and followed the girls to the main house.

The sight of the tall, smiling man stepping through her back door literally took Carolyn's breath away. She felt a strange catch in her heart as she watched him take the girls' jackets from their outstretched hands and hang them on the pegs. Her daughters seemed unaware they'd conscripted Pete to do this simple task for them.

"When we get a dog, I'm going to get a great big one and name him *Mouse,*" Jenny called out, cackling at her own joke.

Pete ruffled her hair gently and guided her around his long legs to her place at the table. He made certain both girls' chairs were pushed in before moving to the one he'd taken as his own.

It was only then that he looked over at her. Something raw and hungry flashed in his eyes for a moment, something deeper and more complicated than mere desire. Then he smiled.

"Good morning," he said softly. Roughly.

"Pete," she said by way of greeting, and was sure his name came out as a rasp. She set his coffee mug on the

table, taking care not to brush his fingers with her own. But she might as well have rested her hand on his; his proximity alone made her tremble.

The pancakes were perfect—fluffy, light and stuffed with pecans gathered, she told him with some pride, from her aunt's trees. The coffee was dark and rich and the warmth in the kitchen seemed a mere extension of the man seated at her table.

A certain awkwardness had existed between them since their impassioned kiss in the dark a few nights earlier...the night the Wannamachers had paid their visit, the night Jenny had interrupted Pete's bath.

She wondered if he was as sorry for the tension as she was, but she was nonetheless somewhat grateful that he seemed to have difficulty meeting her eyes and so carefully, studiously, avoided her touch. His diffidence made it easier for her to do the same and made it easier to believe that whatever it was she felt about him wasn't going to make her do anything crazy.

When finished with breakfast, the girls all but threw their plates into the sink and dashed off to curry Bratwurst before their cousins arrived. Pete took his plate to the dishwater, also, and would have left following the girls' dust trail, but she stopped him before he could make his escape.

"Why were you out in the desert, Pete?"

He turned to meet her frowning gaze.

She blushed a little. "I know I said I didn't care, but—"

"But?"

She looked away from him and fidgeted with the button of her blouse. She risked a glance at him and found his gaze on her hands. She dropped her hands, suddenly aware of her unconscious body language.

"It's not really any of my business," she said slowly.

"Of course it is," he said, leaning back against the old enamel sink and folding his arms over his chest. "I'm living in your bunkhouse, eating my meals with your family. I'm taking my baths in your house, for God's sake. Whose

business is it, if not yours? You want to know what kind of man you brought in here.''

Halfway through his words, her eyes had flown to his and widened. In his list of things he did within her family, he hadn't mentioned kissing her, molding her to his body, running his hands over her glorious curves. But he might as well have shouted it, for it hung between them like a palpable presence waiting to be acknowledged.

"Is that about the size of it?" he asked.

Carolyn nodded, feeling as if his question had totally robbed her of the ability to speak. He'd pegged her concerns so accurately she felt a combination of shame and fear strive for equal billing.

While it seemed he understood her need perfectly and had even disagreed with her avowal that it was none of her business, she could see that her questions had hurt him in some way. And she thought of how she'd melted into his embrace only a few nights before, remembered how she trusted him to hold her in his arms, believed he wouldn't hurt her, how she'd had a complete faith in his sure touch. Before that kiss had been the time to ask questions. Before bringing him into her home, into her life.

"Call the FBI," he said with a slow, bitter twist marring the line of his lips.

"What?"

"Run a check on me, Carolyn."

"No...I only—"

"Ask them to tell you everything they have on one F. Peter Jackson."

"Oh, Pete...I didn't mean..."

"I could tell you everything about me, but you still wouldn't know if it was true or not. Call the FBI...if you want the truth, Carolyn, go to the source."

He was the source, she thought incoherently. Surely he was the true source. She wanted to tell him she would believe him, would believe anything he had to tell her. She needed to tell him that, but her tongue seemed frozen in

her mouth and the bitterness in his raw-silk voice left her feeling as if she'd stumbled across a land mine.

He pushed away from the sink and didn't look at her as he crossed the room, retrieved his parka—his *new* parka—from the peg beside the back door.

Her mind seemed a maelstrom of chaotic thoughts. Why would he say "FBI" with such a bitter twist to his lips? Why would he look at her so pointedly? Oh, dear God, what had Pete done?

What had she done?

"Just do me one favor when you call them, will you? Don't tell them where I am." He pulled the door closed behind him and, while it had no more than clicked shut, the sound echoed in her mind like a slam.

Or a slap.

She washed the dishes without the slightest awareness of having done so. It was only as she was wiping off the breakfast table and happened to glance out the window in time to see Pete coming out of the barn with a can of paint in one hand and a brush in the other that she realized she'd been in the kitchen for thirty minutes or more actively engaged in desperate denial of Pete having committed any transgression big enough to involve the FBI.

A person could have the FBI after him if he evaded taxes, if he committed mail fraud…or if he made bombs, sold drugs, murdered people, committed treason, shot at presidents, ate all meals with subversives, or wrote threatening letters to movie stars.

There were a host of reasons a man would be known by the FBI. A host. And a lot of those things could be perfectly innocuous. But most of those things wouldn't bring such a bitter twist to a pair of lips that had incited hers to riot only a couple of nights before.

Don't tell them where I am. Only a man on the run would want to stay hidden. Was there any other interpretation she could place on his words? Was that why he'd agreed to

help her? Was that what he'd been doing in West Texas in the first place?

She'd known somehow, that first night in the desert. That's why she'd said she didn't care what his reasons for being out there might be. She'd known. His neat camp, his lack of a vehicle, his utter solitude. Oh, dear God, she'd known and she'd still brought him into her home, folded him into her family.

As protection.

She watched his slow, steady strokes that were transforming her barn into a seemingly different structure and saw his head turn as both her trusting daughters rounded the side of the barn and asked him something. He nodded at the house and his eyes seemed to connect with hers though he couldn't possibly have seen her with the eastern light bearing directly at the door's window and screen.

The girls pelted across the driveway, and they were calling for her permission to help Pete paint before they ever hit the porch.

"Old clothes," she said as they opened the door.

"Thanks!" they both cried, running for the stairs, as if she'd granted them permission to ride in a spaceship instead of wield a paintbrush.

They were layered in a couple of Craig's old shirts—which caused her a momentary pang—and back outside in less time than it would have taken her to tell about it. She couldn't help but smile at the long-suffering expression on Pete's face. But her smile disappeared as he pulled two paintbrushes out of his parka's pocket and solemnly handed one to each of her daughters. He'd known they would want to help. He'd prepared for it. And as he shrugged out of his parka and tossed it across the fence, she realized he was more than prepared...he *understood* the girls.

What would the FBI want with a man who had enough savvy to take off his new parka while painting with two pint-size helpers? Why would the FBI be after a mountain-size, openly grinning Tom Sawyer?

As the morning progressed and the temperature rose, she kept her eye on the barn-painting campaign and saw at a glance that Pete would have had the project done in half the time without the eager aid of his two assistants. Half a dozen times she'd reached for one telephone or another to dial information assistance to get hold of a number for the FBI. And then she'd see the gamin grin on Jenny's face or the shy adoration on Shawna's and she'd remember how infrequently they'd giggled and laughed during this first year without their father.

Did it really matter what Pete may have done in his past? Didn't what he was doing now count for more? He'd helped her immeasurably and for no remuneration of any kind. Was her repayment to be an FBI check on his past?

Doc had seemed to like him. But that didn't necessarily mean anything; Doc was one of those people who found the good in everyone. Shawna and Jenny accepted him completely, but then children tended to like anyone who liked them. Adults, too, for that matter, she thought, remembering how she'd leaned into Pete, aching for the feel of his hands on her body.

As she set down the phone receiver for the tenth time, she told it she wasn't going to call anyone. "I didn't ask him to marry me, for heaven's sakes. He's just helping out for a while until the Wannamachers forget about wanting our little piece of ground."

Besides, she told herself—and the hapless receiver—who better to roust a couple of thugs than a bad guy? Unless the FBI knew about him because he'd been in trouble over children... What about that one, Carolyn?

She shook her head. A lot of things she might be able to swallow about Pete Jackson, but harming a child didn't fall into any possible category. Not Pete.

The honk of a horn made her jump away from the telephone guiltily, as if her sister-in-law might know what she was thinking. She went to greet Taylor and the triplets with

both relief—which she hoped didn't show—and genuine pleasure, which she knew would.

The boys were already out of the minivan and inspecting the barn before she even reached the back porch. Five blond heads caught the sunlight and as they chattered, their mobile eyebrows seemed to drift on their young faces. Cousins.

Taylor joined her on the porch steps and stood for a moment in the warmth of the midday sun to watch Jenny and Shawna showing the triplets how much fun they were having painting the barn.

"The weatherman said it's going to rain today," Taylor said. "In fact, the phrase he actually used was 'come a gusher.' That would be such a blessing for the farmers."

Carolyn glanced from the congregation at the barn to the sky. She hadn't noticed it was darkening in the northeast. It hadn't rained since she moved to the ranch. The thought of rain now made her feel strangely hopeful.

Pete left the scene for a few moments and came back with a second can of paint and three more brushes.

"He's nobody's fool, is he?" Taylor asked.

"No," Carolyn said, a self-conscious grin on her lips. She was, but he certainly could never be labeled with that tag.

Taylor studied Pete for a few minutes. "He reminds me of Craig," she said. Was it wistfully?

Carolyn murmured an acknowledgment, if not an agreement. She felt both vaguely uncomfortable and somewhat relieved to hear Craig's only sister talking about Pete. "He's different though," she said finally.

Taylor gave her long, steady and utterly neutral look before turning her gaze back to Pete. "I hope so," she said flatly, her tone falling somewhere between condemnation and acceptance. "But how do you see him as different?"

"I don't know, exactly. He just is," she said, turning to find her sister-in-law studying her intently.

"You know I loved Craig. Who didn't? But I'm no fool.

I know full well he wasn't the world's perfect man, Carolyn,'' she said seriously.

Carolyn flushed. Of anyone, Taylor might know some of Craig's less than stellar qualities. Or, she thought, if she was to be totally fair, Craig's bad side was completely the same as his good: he was an equal-opportunity taker. Or perhaps it was more fair to say that Craig just *leaned* on people. He needed others' support the way most people simply needed air.

From his endearing, gamin give-me-a-hand smile to his faith in a myriad of get-rich-quick schemes, Craig seemed to drift from one crisis to another to the point that Carolyn had decided that crises appealed to him. And he always trusted his friends, his givers, his supporters to bail him out.

Unlike Pete, who seemed to trust no one. Nor need anyone. The notion made her feel vaguely sad. People should need others, not as dependents but just as human beings.

One of the famous Leary eyebrows rose on Taylor's expressive face. A question or a supposition?

"What?" Carolyn asked defensively, fighting the heat rising in her cheeks.

Taylor shook her head, but her smile spoke volumes before she changed the subject. "I brought a batch of Sammie Jo's fudge."

Carolyn grimaced. Much as she was growing to love Sammie Jo, her ineptitude in the kitchen was notorious throughout the Almost countryside.

Taylor chuckled. "This is the worst of all. It's fat-free fudge. Luckily, Sammie Jo's not kitchen proud so she sent along some store-bought cookies, too. And, of all the strange things, a pint of half-and-half cream."

"Oh, that's for Pete," Carolyn said, standing back to let Taylor inside the house.

"I see," Taylor murmured, her eyebrow flexing a little.

Carolyn only shook her head.

"But at least I can tell Sammie Jo that he's got cute buns. That was her biggest question."

"He can be wanted by the FBI, but if he has cute buns, he's okay in Sammie Jo's book," Carolyn said.

"Is he?"

"Is he what?"

"Wanted by the FBI?"

Carolyn hadn't realized she'd verbalized that statement with quite so much doubt. She shrugged, tried a smile and shook her head.

"Seriously, do you know anything about him? Doc says he's pretty closemouthed about his past. Want me to have one of Doug's former buddies run a check on him?"

Since Taylor's husband had been killed in the line of duty, there weren't many of his former buddies who wouldn't do anything for his widow.

"No!"

Taylor's eyebrow lowered as her brow creased. "You know, Carolyn, checking up on someone doesn't mean the end of the world. It only means you're being smart. Don't be like Craig."

Carolyn smiled ruefully. "Yeah, I know. But it seems low-down, somehow. He came here at my request. He's working for free. All I'm providing is a leaky bunkhouse—"

"Since it hasn't rained in over a year, that's not terribly problematic," Taylor interjected.

"It's supposed to rain this afternoon."

"So he can sleep in the house."

The thought stole Carolyn's breath.

"What else are you doing for him?" Taylor asked.

Carolyn smiled self-consciously. "A little half-and-half for his coffee—"

"While everyone else in the county makes do with milk."

"He's practically transformed the place."

"I did notice the screen door didn't scream to high

heaven and your mailbox down at the junction was actually standing erect.''

''So it seems kind of unfair to sneak behind his back and run a security check on him.''

Taylor made herself at home, unknowingly sparking a pang of envy in Carolyn; Taylor was at home anywhere she went, whereas Carolyn wasn't even comfortable in her own sister-in-law's presence, let alone her house.

Taylor poured herself a glass of sun tea and fought an ice tray for a couple of cubes. ''I get it. Bad guys are bad all the way through. No good sides. No ponies in them anywhere.''

Carolyn smiled. ''Okay, point well taken.''

''After what happened to you, I'd think you'd never trust anyone again. Losing your life savings and every scrap of your husband's insurance money would make more than a Leary cautious of trusting anyone.''

Carolyn looked at her sister-in-law with shock. She'd never told anyone in Almost, let alone Craig's family, the whole truth, and Taylor had just casually recited the bare-bones facts as if she'd known them all along.

Taylor held up her hand as if in self-defense. ''I was a cop's wife, what can I say? The only consolation in being made a widow in your thirties is that you come into a pile of cash. And you didn't. The family wondered why.''

The family, Carolyn thought with a tinge of bitterness and a ton of wistfulness.

''So, I did a little checking.''

Carolyn's sister-in-law carefully didn't meet her eyes as she pulled at a stray thread on her sweater's cuff.

''And you found out we trusted our accountant a little too freely with our investments.''

''That's a kind way of describing a nest of snakes.''

''They weren't all snakes.''

''No, one of them managed to scare up about ten grand for you and the girls. Enough to bury Craig and get you

three to Almost. When, let's face it, you should have been on a Dallas easy street.''

Carolyn nodded self-consciously. She didn't like anyone knowing how badly she and Craig had been duped. Especially since the accountant had been a close personal friend. A trusted friend. A friend she had introduced to Craig. And he'd only been one of a good baker's dozen, each owning more of their lives than they had.

''And after that, you're still willing to put yours and the girls' well-being out on the proverbial line?''

Carolyn was spared the necessity of answering that difficult question as five pairs of undoubtedly paint-covered feet hit the back porch with the force of a tornado.

''Stop right there!'' she called, racing for the door and holding it closed with her body. ''All shoes off! Any piece of clothing saturated with paint is to be discarded on the outside of the door. I don't care if you're buck naked. No paint is coming inside this house!''

All five of the cousins giggled and laughed as they happily got rid of shoes and various sweaters and smocks.

''Well, if they're going to be buck naked, you'd better hope your Pete isn't among the rabble on the porch,'' Taylor said as Carolyn opened the door.

Did she feel relief or dismay that he wasn't standing on the other side of the screen?

''Can we ride Bratwurst now?''

''You said we could later. Is it 'later' yet?''

''It's really hot outside, Aunt Carolyn, can we go swimming in the stock tank?''

''Whoa,'' Taylor said, coming to Carolyn's rescue. ''No, you can't go swimming. It may be seventy degrees now, but it was below freezing this morning and will be again tonight. But,'' she added, forestalling the five groans of disappointment, ''if Carolyn says it's okay, you guys can wear out old Bratwurst.''

Carolyn gave her permission and all five kids scooted

upstairs for alternate jeans and shirts and were back down and shod in less than ten minutes.

"Why can't they move that fast on school mornings?" Taylor asked.

Carolyn realized that her daughters had been up with the dawn every morning since Pete arrived. She hadn't once had to nag them about getting dressed or collecting homework or the myriad little chores they performed on a daily basis. Why? Was it just the novelty of having someone else around the place?

Or was it deeper than that? Was it some of the same underlying reasons that she'd been getting up just a mite earlier herself, had been making a whit more elaborate breakfasts, setting prettier tables and taking the time to wash her face and comb her hair, even daub on a little lipstick before putting on the coffee?

"Whatever you're thinking about, I'd like to have some," Taylor said with a sly grin.

Chapter 7

Pete withheld an urge to jump in Carolyn's Ranger and head for the nearest hills when five Leary-related children, ranging in age from eight to ten years, came barreling out of the house and headed in his direction.

What he knew about saddling a horse could be summed up in a single word: nothing. What he learned in the ensuing fifteen minutes served as apotheosis of the Biblical notion that "a little child shall lead them." Five voices, pitched at varying soprano high-decibel levels, took him through each stage of accomplishing the monumental task.

By the time Carolyn and the Aunt Taylor he hadn't met made their way to the corral, Pete knew how—despite sudden attacks of giggles by assorted members of the cousin quintet—to sling a two-ton saddle over a totally placid but quirky-humored mount. And he knew how to reach beneath the beast and grab hold of the strap and to choose a seemingly endless selection of notches in which to place the buckle's tongue.

And *then*, he learned, ignoring the two women who had

come outside and were now leaning against the corral's top rail, that he was supposed to shove his knee into the horse's ribs two or three really rough times in order to expel the horse's excess gas and air. This, it was explained to him by at least four of the five cousins, would ensure that the rider wouldn't find him or herself upside down beneath the horse's belly still clinging to the saddle horn.

"You wouldn't want that to happen to me, would you, Pete?" Jenny asked, unable to stifle all her giggles.

Pete had been conned a few times in his life and generally knew a con when he saw one. And this had all the high-water marks of a world-class scam. He shifted his gaze to Shawna, the shy one, the more sensitive of the two girls, and met her blue, guileless eyes with what he hoped was desperate faith.

"You're telling me that if I lift my knee and start slamming the side of this horse, old Bratwurst won't suddenly turn into Grizzly, the Wild Desert Pony?"

All five kids laughed out loud. And he heard two contralto chuckles chime in.

From her position of safety behind the corral fence, Carolyn leaned against her sister-in-law, convulsed with laughter. Pete decided there was something in the Almost water, for Taylor Smithton was damn near as gorgeous as Carolyn.

"I've been had, right?" he asked Carolyn with a lopsided grin. He could drop a man with a look, but he'd broken into a sweat just thinking about kneeing a horse.

"No," Carolyn chuffed. "It's true." She put a foot on the lowest rail of the fence and vaulted over. The graceful motion did something odd to Pete's insides.

Still chuckling, she crossed in front of him and took hold of the girth strap. "Watch."

She stood back a pace and let fly her knee into Bratwurst's midsection. Pete winced in sympathy as the horse gave a seemingly startled "oof" and Carolyn tightened the cinch a couple of notches. She repeated the process, achieving the same results, then locked the girth strap through the

cinch and deftly wrapped the excess strap length around the exposed cinch buckle into something resembling a Windsor knot.

"We do that so the rider's leg won't get scratched by the cinch or possibly undo it," she said, giving the strap a last tug. Pete assumed it was the awed look on his face that made her chuckle again when she finally turned to face him.

A strong gust of wind swept through the corral, lifting her hair and making it dance on the air. Pete's fingers actually twitched with the urge to tame that mane of wheaten silk. He didn't know what showed on his face, but the smile on hers froze for a moment, then slowly slipped away.

"Me first," one of the triplets said.

"No, me."

"All of us," the third said.

Taylor spoke for the first time. "Jenny and Shawna first. It's their horse."

Pete felt a pang of some hitherto unknown emotion as Jenny positioned herself in front of him and raised both arms straight above her head and said, "Please?"

The eight-year-old girl, an infant delivered some thirty-six years after he'd arrived on the earth, seemed to weigh less than a bag of Bratwurst's oats. Like an elf in a fairy story, the child seemed to spring into his hands, a thistle-weight, a feather. The second his fingers touched her waist Jenny knelt and sprang from the ground, a graceful, seemingly choreographed leap of faith into his arms. Up, over and into the saddle.

"Now me," Shawna said, holding up *her* arms.

The same strange transmutation occurred as Shawna lifted her arms to him, flew up into the air at his touch and landed perfectly and neatly on the saddle—right behind Jenny—on Bratwurst's back.

"Now...*Mom!*" the girls called.

Pete suddenly felt as if the day were far too warm and the company far too close.

"I don't want to ride today," Carolyn said. But Pete

knew what she didn't want to do was have his hands around her waist.

"Please...Mom...please?"

Carolyn flicked a coltish glance his way and cocked her head as if asking his permission. He stretched his arms toward her and his fingertips seemed to tingle with anticipation. Like her daughters, she would raise her arms and leap into his hands, faith and trust absolute in their purest forms.

"Would you give me a leg?" she asked.

He'd give her every functioning part of his body, he thought. "A leg?" he asked, perplexed.

Carolyn half smiled, but she felt disconcerted. Her daughters were waiting atop the horse, her sister-in-law was leaning against the corral and Pete was looking at her legs.

"You have to kneel and I'll step on your leg," she said, and, for some unknown reason, blushed.

He looked from her to the horse and back again. "What's wrong with the way Shawna and Jenny got on?"

"Nothing," she rasped. Nothing at all. "B-but they're little and I'm—"

"Raise your arms," he said. A little, strangely wistful smile tugged at his lips.

"I'll have to put my hands on your shoulders," she said, as if warning him against a dire fate.

He couldn't even smile. His hands encircled her slender waist as she lifted her hands to his shoulders. "Ready?" he asked softly.

"Yes," she said, and it seemed to Pete that she agreed to things unrelated to his lifting her to the horse's back.

She felt like pixie dust in his hands, magical and ephemeral, ready to fly at his touch. Like the girls had done, she gave a little spring into his hands. For a moment, a split second of time, she poised above him in the air, a dancer, beauty taking flight, and then in a fluid motion she swung her leg over the horse and shook back her hair as she drew her fingers from Pete's shoulders.

And still he held her waist. For a long, seemingly endless breath, he ached to pull her back down from the horse, down and into his arms.

He was conscious of dark clouds building in the sky miles behind her, providing a backdrop for her pale hair and accenting her blue eyes. If he could paint, he would immortalize her thus on canvas. If he could compose music, he would capture the way her hair danced on the wind in a melodic and haunting phrase.

But he was only a man, confused by the violence in his past and lured beyond rational thought to the woman he half held in his hands. It seemed to him then that if he let go of her he would be letting her go altogether.

She started to lean down to him and her hand brushed his forearm, a light, almost affectionate, caress. "Thanks," she said finally, releasing him from the unusual spell.

"You're welcome," he said hoarsely, forcing his fingers to release their hold. He reluctantly stepped back from the horse.

She sat just behind the rear lip of the saddle, holding on to Shawna, who held on to Jenny. They walked, then trotted and eventually cantered around the corral, then, amid clamoring from the triplets, slipped down from the horse's back to allow the boys a turn.

Carolyn adjusted the stirrups for the boys' legs and helped them up on the horse. "They'll be fine," she said, dusting her hands off on her jeans and joining Pete and Taylor by the gate. "If one of them gets hurt, we'll be able to hear it from the house. Let's go get some coffee."

She stepped through the gate, flashing Pete a smile that seemed half-shy. He thought his own answering nod might be rueful. Longing. Hopeful. He didn't know. He wasn't sure what he was feeling; he'd never felt anything remotely like it before.

He knew he should dream up yet another task around the place, was fully aware that any proximity to Carolyn was tantamount to encouraging his desire to linger at her

Almost ranch. But he could no more have resisted the chance for more of her company than he could have lifted his knee into old Bratwurst's ribs.

She solemnly introduced him to her sister-in-law, and Pete was disconcerted by the direct, seemingly probing, stare Taylor gave him. He could read a warning and a message. The warning was clear: don't you hurt her, buster, or you'll be sorry. The message seemed less formed, a rather global plea to stay, to take care of her extended family.

He released her hand after a small pump. She nodded as if he'd agreed to something, and smiled. Pete smiled, too, not so much in response to Taylor's grin, but to the look of relief on Carolyn's face. What had she thought he would do?

Pete felt that stab of uneasy peace as the three of them walked together to the main house. Walking beside Carolyn, his stride matching hers, her head at his shoulder's height, he was conscious of a rightness in being there.

The relief of getting in where it was silent and wind free made all three of them groan in unison.

"I hate spring in West Texas," Taylor said.

"How long does the wind blow?" Pete asked, pulling out a chair for her.

"Until all the topsoil's in Arkansas," she answered, flashing him a smile for the courtesy and trying—and failing—to surreptitiously shoot Carolyn a raised-eyebrow look.

"Those dark clouds in the Northeast—?" Pete asked.

"A much promised rain. I'll believe it when I see it," Taylor said. "It hasn't rained since last September. Although the weatherman is really excited about this storm. He's already issuing flash-flood watches and the whole bit."

Pete saw Carolyn's quick, concerned glance out at the corral. Apparently Taylor saw it, too, for she added, "Oh, it won't be here for hours. But if those clouds hold and the

wind doesn't blow them on south of us, we could really have one of our famous Panhandle storms."

"What are they like?" Pete asked, smiling.

"Everything from drizzle to tornadoes."

"Tornadoes?" Carolyn asked.

"Oh, sure. But don't worry, this house has been standing a hundred years. I don't think it's going anywhere. About the most we'll have is that on-and-off storm—high winds, a little rain, more winds, and if we're lucky, more rain. Wild temperature changes. And lots of lightning and thunder. You have candles, don't you?" At Carolyn's nod, Taylor continued, "And your cell phone is juiced up, isn't it? Because we usually lose phone service during a storm."

Carolyn nodded again and Taylor patted her hand reassuringly. "Nothing to worry about."

Pete couldn't have said why he instantly liked Taylor. Perhaps it had something to do with the way that she appeared to accept him even as she openly regarded him with a measure of suspicion. Carolyn's doubts about him lay on the surface, but he knew she fought them, making her a target for hurt.

God knows he didn't want to hurt Carolyn, but just staying near her would do the trick.

Carolyn turned her back on them and poured out three mugs of coffee as Pete retrieved his half-and-half from the icebox. He didn't say anything as he reached around Carolyn to take a mug and add a dollop of the cream to the hot brew. She glanced at him and flashed him a brief, somehow knowing, smile. He couldn't help but smile back in response. It was as if they kissed. He turned to find Taylor eyeing him with curiosity. She'd taken in the intimacy that they had inadvertently, oh so accidentally, settled into in such a short time together.

"The girls told me about your husband," Pete said after they'd exhausted a second review of the Almost weather, touched on the Almost politics and dismissed the current situation in the Middle East. "I'm sorry."

"Thank you," she said, staring into her coffee mug.

"Good cops are hard to come by," he said.

She smiled a little wistfully as she nodded. "You sound as if you know."

"I do," he said, but didn't elaborate.

Her eyes shifted slightly to connect with Carolyn's in some unspoken message, then returned back to his. "What did you do before Carolyn and the girls dragged you onto the ranch?" she asked point-blank.

Carolyn felt her breath catch in her throat. She watched as Pete directly met Taylor's eyes and wondered if her sister-in-law was as aware as she that something in his eyes made it clear that whatever was to come out of his mouth wasn't going to be the truth.

"This and that," Pete said.

Taylor smiled. "I have a degree in 'that.'"

Carolyn smiled in relief as Pete grinned his appreciation. "Minored in 'this'?" he asked.

"Yes, but I never went back for my certification."

Carolyn shook her head at their nonsense but was aware of Pete's tension—and her own—and was conscious that Taylor's mobile eyebrows were expressing her curiosity and her doubts about the taciturn stranger at the table.

When Taylor offered to take Shawna and Jenny with her back to Almost, Carolyn felt a momentary stab of panic. She'd been on the ranch alone with Pete before; the girls had gone to school without her the first couple of days he'd been there. But that had been before she'd seen him nearly naked in the glow of the hall light. That had been before he kissed her and before she kissed him in return. That had been before his eyes took on that glitter whenever he looked at her, before he'd told her that *she* was the only reason he'd come to her ranch.

"We'll catch up with you at the picnic. Though it will probably be rained out. Just like it is every year," Taylor said. "You are coming, aren't you?"

In all honesty, Carolyn had forgotten about the Almost

Over-Sixty Club's annual picnic. She had agreed to bring something...deviled eggs.

"I kind of hate to leave the ranch," she said. "It seems like every time we do, the Wannamachers show up."

"Damn those two. If only we could prove it was them."

"They're clever, I'll give them that," Pete said. "The other night when they were here—if, indeed, it was them—they'd even taken the trouble to hide their license plate number. And Doc tells me they don't have a Chevy of that make or model."

"It doesn't seem fair that they can get away with the stunts they pull," Taylor said with some heat. "Just because we don't have a marshal anymore doesn't mean we should have to put up with those two's shenanigans."

"What happened to your marshal?" Pete asked.

Carolyn answered, "Essentially, the state decided having a full-time law enforcement officer in Almost was a waste of money. And except for people like the Wannamachers, I'd probably tend to agree with them. There's not that much in the way of crime around these parts."

"I'll stay on the ranch. You go to the picnic," Pete said.

"No," Taylor said. "You ought to come. Meet some of the people around here. You've already met Doc, so you'll know at least one person, and, of course, you'll know me and the kids, so it'll practically be old-home week."

"No," he said. "I think I'd better stick around."

Carolyn felt torn. Pete hadn't been off the place in nearly a week. Surely he was getting a little cabin-feverish. But at the same time, maybe he had a very good reason not to want to show his face. *Call the FBI...don't tell them where I am.*

She did an abrupt about-face. "I really would feel better if someone was here," Carolyn said, ignoring the speculative look on her sister-in-law's face. To Pete she added, "I won't stay long."

"Stay as long as you want," Pete said, pushing back from the table and taking his mug to the sink. He shook

Taylor's hand and murmured appropriate words of departure, nodded at Carolyn and went out the back door, shutting it quietly. The room suddenly seemed twice the size it had been seconds earlier. And twice as cold.

"Well, at least he's house-trained," Taylor said.

Carolyn smiled, but her thoughts were on the man who had just left. Did he *want* her to call the FBI? Was it some kind of a game?

"He's polite. He's well-spoken, even if he doesn't volunteer much information."

"He's good with the kids," Carolyn said.

"And he's good with the kids. Yes. And he's got cute buns."

"Taylor!"

"Oh, admit it, Carolyn. You're attracted to the man. And he's equally smitten."

Carolyn couldn't lie about that no matter how much she wanted to.

"It's all right, you know. People who have lost someone are allowed to feel an attraction to someone new. It's in the widow's almanac somewhere. Page 350, I think."

Carolyn lifted one corner of her mouth. "He told me to call the FBI and ask about an F. Peter Jackson."

To Carolyn's surprise, Taylor chuckled. "The man's got a sense of humor."

"Sense of humor?"

"Sure. You remember that big prison riot back East a few years ago? The one demanding real meat instead of soy patties, and a host of other prison benefits? Well, the supposed ringleader was one F. Peter Jackson."

"Oh, God," Carolyn said.

"Well, this Pete can't be that Jackson, because that guy was in on a first-degree murder charge and serving about a hundred consecutive terms. He wouldn't—couldn't—be out."

Carolyn felt her blood boil a little at Pete's joke. And

she'd been worried all morning about him. And she'd felt sorry for him.

"I'll take you up on your offer to take the girls," Carolyn said. "And, I wouldn't miss the picnic for the world."

"There you go," Taylor said, rising to her feet. "Though I should think staying out here with your Pete might prove a temptation."

"Not a chance," Carolyn said firmly, deliberately avoiding her sister-in-law's quizzical gaze.

With the girls off with Taylor and crew, the ranch should have seemed silent, forlorn even, but it didn't. To Carolyn, the storm threatening in the eastern quadrant of the sky seemed to be making its tension felt on the ground. The day was hot, unseasonably so, and the air that had been wildly blowing earlier was still now and oppressive. The calm before the storm.

Carolyn could hear the steady pounding of Pete's hammer as he worked on the corral fence. He'd been there most of the time since Taylor left. Carolyn poured a glass of sun tea over ten or twelve ice cubes and set a couple of deviled eggs on a small plate.

She almost stopped and turned back for the house when she saw that he'd stripped his shirt off and was a study in rippling, sweat-glistened muscles.

He had his back to her, but something must have told him she was there, for he lowered the hammer slowly and turned around. He glanced at the small plate of deviled eggs and the tall glass of iced tea.

"Thought you might be thirsty," she said.

"Thanks," he said, taking the tea and draining it in one long swallow that made Carolyn wish she'd brought tea for herself, for her mouth was unaccountably dust-dry.

He popped one of the deviled eggs into his mouth, and his eyebrows raised and a smile quirked at his lips. "These are good," he said thickly, reaching for the second one. "First-rate."

Carolyn knew people liked her deviled eggs, she even liked them herself. So what was it about the way Pete seemed to enjoy them that took her to an entirely different place?

He took one of the ice cubes from his glass and ran it over his forehead and cheeks. "Damn," he said, unknowingly echoing her own oath.

The electrical storm building beyond the corral and barn was nothing compared to the one threatening to flare between the two of them. Water dripped from his eyebrows and he shook his head. Carolyn was vaguely aware that Bratwurst was shaking his dark head, also.

She hadn't realized she'd been standing stock-still with the empty plate still half held out to him until he reached for it and took it from her numb fingers. He balanced it on a fence post and set his drained glass atop that.

Carolyn watched his motions, knowing he was putting the objects down so that her hands would be free, so that she could respond when he kissed her. She *knew* that and yet she didn't move an inch. She knew she should say something to stop him but was completely unable to think why she would want to. Her eyes traveled his muscled torso, broad shoulders and down his tawny arms. The hair, so dark on his chest, was lighter colored on his arms, longer, silkier. Alluring. Enticing.

He had a tattoo on his right forearm, red and black and deadly looking, a glowing-eyed skull inside a cowled robe. It wasn't a finely executed tattoo; in fact, it looked as if it had been carved into his skin with a piece of broken glass. She'd seen something like it once, but couldn't think where. It made her shiver a little since it was another thing she hadn't known about him, didn't know about him still.

He turned back around then and came to within an inch of her.

She tried to forestall him. "I...we...shouldn't—"

"The hell with 'shouldn'ts,'" he growled, cupping her face with his hands and lifting her to his lips. His mouth

was cold from the iced tea but his tongue was hot and tangy and knowledgeable. His fingers splayed across her face and into her hair, caressing, exhorting, drawing her closer and deeper into his kiss.

She raised her hands to his velvet arms and moaned a little when he dropped his hands to her shoulders, gripping them tightly for a second, then gentling, rocking her to him. And she sighed into his kiss as his hands lowered still further, gripping her waist, her rounded buttocks, her tight thighs.

Carolyn sighed as he pulled his lips from hers with an agonized groan and she trembled as he dragged at the warm desert air like a man who was drowning, and grasped her body to his as if seeking a life preserver.

"You have no idea," he said but didn't continue. Somehow she seemed to know what he meant. He had no idea, either. Like her, he couldn't understand how a single touch could spark a flame of such intense light, such remarkable heat that she couldn't begin to think let alone resist.

His touch was a spell and his lips the magic that carried her into another dimension, a place where FBIs and doubts didn't matter and where trust and faith were promises that could, someday, come true.

As he freed her lips yet again and trailed a series of burning, searing kisses down her neck and collarbone, she gripped his forearms as if for dear life.

Pete didn't say anything, lowering his lips to her outthrust breasts.

"Please...?" she asked, but wasn't sure what she was pleading for. She turned her head to press a kiss to his shoulder, savoring the tangy taste of his moist, sun-warmed skin. *Do me a favor...*

His hot breath played against her breasts and as his fingers swept her buttons free, exposing her to his avid gaze, she ran her own hands down his solid torso, reveling in the rippled muscles on his back, the rock-hard taper of his waist.

Don't tell them where I am.

She realized suddenly that she was with him regarding his not wanting anyone to know where he was. She didn't want him gone. She wanted him right here on her ranch, holding her in his arms, kissing her, tasting her, making her shiver with want, ache with need.

Her knees seemed to buckle and she knew in a moment she would slide to the dusty ground. He turned her then, pressing her against the corral. She felt the top rail of the fence bite into her shoulder blades and moaned aloud as he gave a sharp tug to her brassiere, freeing her completely only to capture her with his lips.

She heard a thud and the sharp tinkle of breaking glass but didn't look to where the plate and glass had been. She could only close her eyes and shudder as wave upon wave of sensation rippled down her body, inciting a riot of reaction. Cold, then hot razor-sharp spikes of desire warred within her.

She trembled and ached and whispered his name. He raised his head and stared at her with glassy eyes, a gaze tortured with longing, blank with the fire that raged between them.

She knew her own gaze to be heavy lidded, her breathing ragged and uncertain. And she knew little more than that she wanted this man, this stranger. She raised her hand to his chest and felt his heart thundering beneath her shaking fingers.

She could read the question, the plea in his face and half wondered if it was echoed on her own.

"Carolyn..." he murmured, leaning closer, pressing against her hand.

She raised her free hand to his face and had to close her eyes against the raw supplication in the kiss he turned into her palm. He brushed her hair back from her eyes and whispered her name again, a question and a seeming answer in his gentle touch.

Kissing him, feeling the quickening in her body, the deep, tortured ache in her soul, she rested her forehead against his broad shoulder, her eyes on his velvet skin, the

taste of him in her mouth, the longing for him making her shiver, making her feel as if heady wine coursed through her veins now. Now that he'd touched her.

Seeking any excuse to stay the moment, to delay what felt to be an inevitable union, she lowered her eyes to his tattoo. "Did it hurt?" she asked, trailing her finger across the gruesome image. It was both strangely beautiful and incredibly dark.

"Yes," he said. "In more ways than you'll ever know."

From beneath a cowled hood, the glowing eyes of the darkened skull seemed to meet hers. A flex of Pete's muscle seemed to make the eyes glow redder, a baleful, evil stare.

He lowered his lips to hers again, blotting out questions, thought, erasing futures and yesterdays, creating a moment out of time, out of space.

The storm building behind them seemed an extension of the want that flared so dramatically between the two of them. She clung to him because, without clinging, she would have slid to the ground. And she arched against him because she could do nothing else.

Mindless, caught by a wave of desire so strong, so insistent that any thought was impossible beyond savoring his taste, she inhaled the scent of his salty skin and moaned at the feel of his roughened hands on her own body.

"Carolyn," he mouthed against her collarbone. And murmured her name again as his hot tongue laved an aching, turgid nipple.

And suddenly, without warning, Carolyn remembered where she'd seen the death's-head tattoo before. An exiting parolee had told her about it years ago, had drawn a picture of it so she'd know it in the future. She just had forgotten. Touching Pete, kissing him, feeling his skin against her own had erased all thought, all memory.

The death's head tattoo was a prison symbol of honor. Honor among murderers. It signified one thing only: killing someone inside prison and getting away with it.

He pulled back from her a little, his eyes focusing on her

now, the desire not ebbing but shifting to a wariness. "What?" he asked.

"Nothing," she said. Why hadn't she seen his tattoo in the hallway outside the bathroom? Because she'd been looking elsewhere, desperate not to see too much of his naked body.

Because she hadn't been looking for it.

"No, there's something," he said.

What could she say? *You killed someone in prison?* She'd known better than to bring a stranger to the ranch. She'd known better. And yet she'd trusted him with her ranch, with her children. With her own unbridled passion.

"Tell me, Carolyn," he said gently, though his tone implied command.

"I worked as a social psychologist in Dallas," she said. In the face of his stiffening silence, she added, "Primarily with exiting parolees."

She felt his fingers digging into her shoulders, felt his chest harden beneath her hand. "And?" he asked softly. Coldly.

She couldn't meet his gaze and couldn't lower her own back to that dreadful evidence of his past. "And I know what your tattoo means."

"I see," he said.

He said it so carefully she had to look at his face. "Do you?" she asked.

"I think so," he said. There wasn't so much as a nuance of inflection in his even tone.

Carolyn drew a deep breath. She had to tell him to leave. It was the only right thing to do. For her daughters' sake. For her own sake. Whatever she'd conjured in her imagination about his past—thievery, tax evasion, fraud, all of those could be condoned on some bizarre level, but murder...never.

"So," he said, pulling away from her and turning his back to her. "What happens now?"

Still limply draped against the corral railing, she lifted numb fingers to readjust her bra, to attempt fastening her

blouse. She made sorry work of it. "I don't know," she muttered. She did know though. He had to go.

"What about the Wannamachers?"

Carolyn closed her eyes. A known murderer versus two known thugs. A man who had murdered someone and gotten away with it versus two bullies who terrorized a widow and her daughters and got away with it. A man who was kind to her daughters, afraid of hurting an old horse... versus two terrorists who didn't mind frightening two little girls and their mother half to death.

Pete grabbed his shirt and shoved his arms into it. He didn't reach for the buttons. With his back to her, he stood perfectly still for several seconds. What should have appeared defeat or despair merely seemed a cautious, poised waiting.

Finally he asked, "You didn't call the FBI, did you?"

"No," she said.

"Why not?"

What could she possibly tell him? *I didn't call the FBI because doing so would have seemed a violation of trust...he had to know as well as she did that murder was the greatest violation on the face of the earth.*

"I don't know," she whispered.

He turned around then and met her gaze with his own sad, tortured eyes. "I do," he said, lifting a hand to her face.

She didn't flinch, though a part of her wanted to do exactly that, to duck from a truth too stark and too harsh to face. A stronger part fought the impulse to lean into his rough caress.

He lowered his lips to hers in the briefest, most sorrow-filled kiss she'd ever known.

The first drops of rain splattered onto her upturned face and felt like cold tears against her cheeks.

Chapter 8

Pete packed his gear swiftly. Angrily. As furious with Carolyn as he was at himself.

She hadn't asked him to leave. Why not?

He could have told her the truth days before, he thought. He could have wiped the doubts from her face with a clean, simple explanation. All he'd had to do was open his mouth and tell her that the tattoo on his arm had been his sole means of protection while behind bars.

He knew he'd taunted her with his elliptical challenge to call the FBI. A part of him had wanted her to do just that, to have the truth out in the open. And a part of him exulted in the fact that she hadn't called them, had apparently decided to accept him on faith, to trust him despite her lack of knowledge.

That damnable trusting nature of hers unmanned him. No one should be that trusting, that vulnerable. And yet, it was her very ability to give such unwarranted trust that had made him agree to come to her ranch, made him long to clean up her difficulties, to set the world right for her.

He could tell her now, he thought, simply halt the confusion in her lovely face by just spilling the sordid details of an even more sordid ten-year confinement in hell. But what would the telling solve? He didn't know what the future held. He couldn't make her any promises, though God knows a part of him wanted to do just that.

The rain had already stopped, but the storm in him raged on. Even as he shoved what few items he'd unpacked in the bunkhouse, he wondered why he was so angry with her. For accepting him without needing proof of his good intentions? For leaping to a conclusion that anyone would? For being more afraid of the Wannamacher brothers than she was of a confirmed murderer?

Or was it far more complicated than that? Was he angry, not at her, but at himself, for believing in the trust, for needing it to the point of duplicity?

"Damn," he said, looking out his window in time to see her placing a covered tray on the back seat of the Ranger. He leapt for the door of the bunkhouse, but was too late to do more than call out her name before she slammed the door of the Ranger, threw the vehicle in gear and roared out of the driveway.

The picnic. He'd completely forgotten about that picnic. He stood in the cooling afternoon watching Carolyn disappear down the road and tried to understand her motivation for leaving a known murderer in charge of her ranch.

Either she was the biggest fool this side of the Missouri river...or he was.

Since he could still feel every nuance of her in his arms, the sensation of her skin beneath his fingertips and the silk texture of her lips lingered upon his own, he knew he was the fool. By not telling her, by not giving her a measure of the trust she'd offered him, he'd thrown away the only possibility of happiness that he'd been offered in ten years.

"I'm sorry, Carolyn," he said aloud, but there was no one there to hear him. There was no one besides a restless

horse and a mother cat to know how deeply he meant the apology, how many years it had been since he'd made one.

Thunder anew rumbled in the sky and echoed in his soul.

Everyone in Almost, Texas, except the bedridden and Pete Jackson, attended the Almost Over-Sixty Club's Annual Spring Picnic...including the Wannamacher brothers.

Of a town comprised of some six hundred pleasant, familial people, the Wannamachers couldn't have been more affable, more considerate, and more helpful to those in need of a paper cup filled with pineapple punch or a plate loaded with beef ribs or a variety of the homemade tidbits brought by the Almost citizenry.

If she hadn't known better, if she hadn't been faced with their dirty dealings at a personal level, she easily could have been led to believe Bubba and Jimmy Wannamacher were two of the nicest old boys the county had to offer.

It had taken her two days to get Pete to tell her what their latest spray-paint message had read. The fact that he'd wanted it withheld from the girls had warmed her heart and had made her feel protected, safe.

But seeing the Wannamachers now, knowing they'd tried terrorizing her with *Get Out Or Get Dead!* she felt nothing but cold revulsion. And a wish that Pete had come with her.

Wannamachers...Pete. Thugs and murderer.

Thunder rumbled ominously and all eyes looked up, but no rain fell.

"And what can we get you, little lady?"

Carolyn looked from the dark sky into the squinted, mocking brown eyes of Bubba Wannamacher. At six foot two and weighing some two hundred and sixty pounds, he seemed to tower over her, a caricature of Texas size and structure. When she didn't answer, he used a forefinger to push his expensive gray felt hat back on his head. Unbelievably, he reached his other hand between his legs and pulled upward at his crotch.

"I don't believe this," she muttered, furious but none-theless exceedingly disconcerted. She was grateful to see Sammie Jo and Cactus approaching from her left and Doc Jamison from her right.

"What?" Bubba asked, his voice the very sound of truculent innocence. "If you don't want anything, you just have to say so."

"I want you to leave us alone," she said coldly, forcing herself to meet his eyes. If only Pete were here, she thought, and tried to dismiss the notion.

He smiled, an unctuous, oily insinuation in his glittery assessment of her body. "And what if I was to say I couldn't do that?" he asked, his voice pitched too low to be heard by the nearly deaf old-timers sitting less than five feet away.

"Then I'd say you're staring at a stalking charge," Sammie Jo said, not nearly as quietly as he.

To Carolyn's disgust her hands were trembling and her stomach knotted painfully. Cactus dropped a hand on her shoulder.

Bubba Wannamacher laughed aloud. "Is that so?" he asked. "And how are you gonna prove that, huh, Miz Spring? Me and Jimmy ain't been hide nor hair near the widow's place."

"Did you know that authorities can test for spray paint residue on your hands just as if you'd fired a gun?" Cactus asked coldly.

Carolyn had no idea if that was true or not, but the sudden flattening of Bubba's features made the assertion worth the uttering.

"Why don't you do yourself a favor?" Bubba asked, menace clear in every word. "You can't work that place by yourself. Word has it you don't have enough money to even run one old mama cow and her calf, let alone a herd. We can use it right well. We need it, you might say. And we'd really consider it a favor if you'd just pack up your pretty little family and clear the hell out."

"It's my property and my home," Carolyn said, striving to sound collected. Cool. She knew she sounded as scared as she felt.

"We've worked that place for ten years without getting a single dime from you or yours. I reckon we earned the rights to it fair and square."

"You should have been paying us to lease the land all these years," she asserted.

He snorted. "Hell, lady, we was doing you a favor. Everyone 'round here knows it, too."

"What do we know?" Doc Jamison asked, stepping up beside Bubba.

The elder Wannamacher brother turned to glance at Doc. Carolyn couldn't wholly read the expression on Bubba's face, but underriding her relief at Doc's presence she felt a pang of pity for her old acquaintance.

"Everybody knows what a good rain can do for the land around here. I was just telling the little lady how lucky she was it rained a mite today."

"Is that right?" Doc asked.

"He was threatening her," Sammie Jo said, leaning closer to Carolyn, who, while conscious of feeling safer with her friends, was also aware this feeling was nothing remotely like the way she'd felt when Pete pushed her behind him. Or when he held her in his arms.

Bubba pulled back in mock horror. "Threatening her? Me? Hell, I think you been in the sun too long, Miz Spring. Tell her, Doc, old Bubba wouldn't hurt a fly."

"Old Bubba better not," Doc said with a friendly smile on his face. He reached down and took Carolyn's hand to pull her to her feet.

Now that she was standing, Bubba didn't seem nearly so oppressive, nearly so massive.

"Taylor was asking after you," Doc said. "Something about staying out at the ranch with you awhile," he said. "But I told her that your new hired hand was more than a match for any trouble that might crop up."

Carolyn gave him a grateful smile.

Bubba, apparently recognizing he'd been beaten at his little game, tipped his hat and ambled away, stopping at one of the chefs-of-the-day to inquire after her health.

"I thought it was time we let the Wannamachers in on the fact that Pete Jackson's out at your place," Doc said.

Carolyn didn't say anything; she wasn't sure if Pete would even be there when she got back. She knew he'd seen the farewell in her face, heard it in her voice. And he'd known why he had to go.

What he didn't know was how very sorry she felt.

Taylor had been right: the storm circled back and hit with a vengeance of thunder, lightning and seemingly torrential rain. Pete didn't stop to consider anything beyond his need to help Carolyn get the girls from the Ranger into the house without getting totally soaked. And he thought about the need to tell her the truth.

In the couple of hours she'd been gone, after his bags were packed and his arrowheads secured, he'd made the nearly astonishing discovery that he didn't want to go.

It had nothing to do with protecting her and the girls. Nor with what other reasons he had for having come to this desolate part of the country. It had to do with something inside him, something she was changing.

No, he didn't want to leave her. Not this way. For someone who had made his living by living a lie, he suddenly had a burning need for Carolyn to know the truth about him. Dark as it might be, something told him that, of all women, Carolyn had it in her to understand.

He tucked his head against his shoulder and ran for the vehicle, holding up his arm against the glare of the headlights and frowning against the onslaught of cold, driving rain.

He was rounding the front of the car before he saw it wasn't Carolyn's Ranger. And the heavyset cowboy de-

scending the cab of the double-cabbed, half-ton pickup didn't resemble Carolyn in the slightest way.

"You the new hired hand?" the man asked.

Pete didn't answer. He'd seen the passenger door open and the rear door, as well. Two more men jumped out into the rain. One, obviously the brother of the cowboy inches away from him, began moving toward the front of the pickup while the other man, still in shadow, rounded the rear.

Pete took a couple of steps backward, his arms going out from his sides in classic fighting position. "I don't want any trouble," he said.

"You hear that, Jimmy? This here hired hand don't want any trouble."

"I heard him, Bubba. I reckon he's asking for it though."

"Why he surely is. We politely ask the lady of the house to get off our property—and from what I hear tell, old Craig was well paid for it—and instead of listening to us, she goes right out and hires herself a bodyguard," Bubba said. He moved toward Pete with slow menace. "'Cuz that's what you really are, ain't it? A *bodyguard.* Have to admire you for that, pardner. She's got a body I wouldn't mind guarding."

The third man stepped out from behind Bubba. "All this talk isn't necessary," he said softly, with such a slight accent that Pete couldn't place it at first. "Let's just leave our message and go, eh?"

A Canadian in West Texas? Pete frowned heavily. Drugs. His buddy had been right in his speculation. And the notion fit what was transpiring on the Leary place. It had been empty for years, easy to use as a drop spot. And then Carolyn and the girls had moved in, thwarting the runners.

He'd stupidly run out into the rain without a weapon, doing the very thing he'd told Carolyn *never* to do. Living in prison, without benefit of a gun for ten years, he'd mo-

mentarily forgotten that in the real world, the outside world, a painfully etched tattoo didn't guarantee him any more than a shocked understanding from a widowed psychologist.

Here in the dark, in a torrential rain, facing three fairly good-size men, his tattoo was of no more help to him than a bouquet of flowers would have been.

"Like I said, I don't want any trouble," Pete growled.

"Well, way I figure it," Bubba said, moving in with the force of a derailed train, slamming his fist into Pete's stomach, "you don't have a hell of a lot of say about things."

Pete got in a couple of swift punches, making Bubba swear, not at Pete but at his brother to grab Pete's arms. "Damn it! Do I have to tell you everything? Hold him! Son of bitch cut my lip!"

The third man jumped forward and grabbed Pete on the right as Jimmy moved in on his left.

Pete struggled to break free and succeeded in shaking Jimmy off for a moment so he could drive his left fist into the Canadian's face. Despite the fact that he was right-handed, the punch connected squarely with the man's nose and he dropped his rough grasp on Pete's arm with a surprised yelp of pain.

Bubba yelled something at Jimmy and Pete kicked out at the solidly built cowboy, striking him just above his knee. Bubba screamed and crumpled to the muddy ground at the same time his brother rushed Pete again.

"That's enough," the Canadian said in a low, furious voice and in a tone of complete command.

Whereas Pete was capable of ignoring him, the surprise on Jimmy's face made him whirl around to face the Canadian. The man stood with a handkerchief pressed to his obviously bleeding nose and a larger-than-life .347 Magnum trained on Pete's chest. At that range he would not ⬚⬚⬚ Pete, he would probably take Jimmy out, as well.

⬚⬚⬚'t be stupid," the Canadian told Pete somewhat

thickly. He waved the gun a little, from Bubba to Pete. "I don't think he'll fight you now," he said.

Pete winced, knowing what was coming. Bubba and Jimmy would beat the living daylights out of him as a message to Carolyn. And he would have to take it, because it was a lot better that Carolyn bring her daughters home to a beaten message, not a dead one.

Bubba slung the first punch with relish and Jimmy followed with a couple of quick jabs to Pete's ribs.

He'd been in fights before. Plenty of them. But none where he was held at gunpoint and forced to take the hits without benefit of striking back. He hated the helplessness with a gut-wrenching fury. He tucked his arms close to his body and his fists against his face. He hunched down, gritting his teeth at the rain of pounding fists against his back, his kidneys, his shoulders.

"I think that's sufficient," the Canadian said, after the Wannamachers had driven Pete to his knees. "Now, whoever you are, tell Mrs. Leary that her husband was well paid for our rental of this property. And paid in advance. We don't want her presence here now and would very much appreciate it if she would pack up her pitiful things and go back to Dallas, or anywhere else on earth for that matter."

"What's to stop her from calling the police?" Pete asked with difficulty, for his lips were cut and bleeding freely.

Bubba kicked him in the side, making him bite back a groan of pain.

"Because she knows the brothers here?" the Canadian asked.

Pete didn't answer. He was busy trying to figure out a way of leaping to his feet and wresting the gun from the man. That he didn't stand a prayer in hell of doing so wasn't the reason he didn't try; it was the thought of the horrified expressions on two little girls' faces when they found him dead in the mud.

"If Mrs. Leary chooses to go to the police, I'm very

much afraid she'll be sorry. She can't be with her daughters every minute of the day. Tell her that what the Wannamacher brothers did to you, they can very easily do to her daughters. Or to her. And Bubba, I believe, likes the lady, don't you, Bubba?''

"You bastard," Pete said.

"Exactly. Now, will you remember our little message and pass it along for us? Let's be generous, however. She can take two days to pack her belongings and clear out. After that, her daughters are fair game. Do you understand?''

Pete didn't say anything. He understood all too coldly and all too clearly. But for all the talking that Magnum in the man's hand was doing now, that gun wouldn't protect him from Pete for long. The man was going to regret every threat, every nuance of a threat made to Carolyn and her daughters.

"Finish it," the man said, and Pete felt movement to his right. Even as he tried throwing himself to the left something with the combined weight of an anvil and the force of a sledgehammer slammed against the back of his head.

The girls...and Carolyn...were going to find him dead after all, he thought as he slumped down. He never heard the Wannamachers and their cohort leaving. He didn't hear anything at all.

Carolyn flinched as lightning carved a jagged fissure across the thundercloud-darkened sky. A half a second later the Ranger shuddered under the impact of the thunder.

She gripped the steering wheel with both white-knuckled hands. Rain, something as rare as black diamonds, was coming down with a fury, slamming into the windshield with enough force to rock the car and almost wholly obscuring the road.

Since the entire county had been locked in a drought for some four years, she'd assumed the light shower that af-

ternoon was the rainfall of the season. This torrential downpour was, as the weatherman had predicted, a true gusher.

She'd already flipped the Ranger into four-wheel drive,
in the event that the sudden downpour turned the dirt and
gravel road into a mud slide. She drove slowly and carefully, but the lightning and thunder, the rain and slippery
road beneath her vehicle, escalated a tension that was already overly high.

She'd left the girls to stay overnight with her sister-in-
law, ostensibly because the girls would be less frightened
of the storm with the triplets to constantly distract them.
However, the real reason she'd left them with Taylor was
because she needed time—without her daughters' influ-
ence—to decide what on earth to do about Pete. On the off
chance that he hadn't disappeared during the afternoon.

The farmer she'd bought Bratwurst from had told her the
horse was scared of thunder. She should have known that
was why he was tossing his head earlier. But then she'd
only had thoughts for Pete Jackson and Bratwurst's jet
black hair lifting to the still air had somehow seemed an
extension of Pete's mood, their mutual passion.

A dim part of her hoped he'd already realized he needed
to put Bratwurst in the barn with Ralphette and the kittens.
But, without knowing about the recalcitrant horse, why
should he so much as wonder about the animal?

She shook her head. The day had turned into an unmitigated disaster. First she discovered the tattoo on Pete's arm,
the death's head representing murder. She'd followed that
choice bit of information with finding out she was the prime
object of curiosity at the Almost Over-Sixty Club picnic.
Her prize-winning deviled eggs were of much less interest
than the mystery man staying on her ranch.

Then she'd had the uncomfortable encounter with Bubba
Wannamacher. He'd left the picnic early, he and his gap-
toothed brother. And his insolent tipping of his hat and
knowing smile in her direction as he departed had made
her skin crawl.

She'd been thankful when the thunderstorm broke up the picnic, sending people scattering in all directions, some for the church hall, some for their cars, others dashing down the street, heading for their homes, carrying pots, casseroles, and sheet-cake pans filled with melting Jell-O salads.

Some sixth sense, perhaps born of the day's tensions, the combined worry over the Wannamacher situation and the deeper, more problematic concern over what to do about Pete Jackson, kicked in as Carolyn pulled into the muddy driveway. She automatically lifted her foot from the accelerator and lightly pumped the brakes, turning the wheel into the slithering slide.

Though everything looked as it should on a stormy, cold and rainy evening in late February, she knew without any uncertainty that something was terribly wrong.

Her headlights strafed the barn, then the house, sending the lights' reflections back at her from the darkened windows. Some fifty yards from the house, she came to a full stop, her heart unaccountably thundering in her chest.

The house and bunkhouse were dark, the barn a black mass to the far right. Bratwurst didn't appear to be in the corral; he'd either escaped in his panic or Pete had put him in the barn. Even as she took in this seemingly simple evidence that Pete had stayed around her place and she felt a weight lighten from her shoulders, she frowned, staring at a spot some ten yards in front of the bunkhouse, a darker shadow on the ground. A puddle? A blanket?

But she knew what it was. Who it was.

She jumped the Ranger several yards forward and slithered to a muddy halt. She threw the vehicle in Park and left it running, the headlights illuminating the still form lying face down in the mud. She leapt from the rocking car.

"Pete!" she called, sliding through the wet clay, and jumped across a pair of deep tire-induced ruts filled with water to reach his side.

She had no way of knowing how long he'd been lying

there, but his clothes were thoroughly soaked and his body had served as a dam for the water pouring down from the northeast. His skin was cold to the touch and his face was streaked with mud and rain.

And blood.

"Oh God, Pete..." she murmured, stroking the water and mud from his face, probing gently to discover where the blood was coming from. She found that easily enough; a darker wet spot on the back of his head revealed a large knot and an open wound.

She refused to even consider the notion that he might be dead. He was too vital, too powerful. He'd kissed her that afternoon as if there were no tomorrow. She gulped back a sob, ruthlessly forcing the natural progression of that thought to the back of her mind.

Even as her fingertips gently shifted his hair, he moaned aloud, low and strong. A living, breathing curse against her touch.

"Can you hear me?" she asked. "You've got to get up. I can't lift you."

"What happened?" he asked.

"I don't know," she answered perfectly honestly, though she had a few guesses. The deep ruts flanking his body could only have been made by a heavy vehicle, and not all that long ago, for they weren't overflowing with the heavy rain yet. Though she was no expert in tire tracks, ruts this deep and this wide could only have been made by a large car, a half-ton pickup, perhaps. The kind the Wannamacher brothers had jumped into before leaving the Almost picnic.

She tried assisting Pete as he struggled against the mud and his own pain for a few seconds, though she felt totally useless, and worse, a hindrance. Finally, between her tugging at him and his oath-ridden pushing, he achieved a shaky-kneed stance. He looked like a wounded bear, and seemed all the more dangerous in his vulnerability.

"We've got to get you in out of the rain," she said.

He didn't argue with her, but he seemed to be without

use of his legs for several seconds as he leaned his weight against her and shoved against the unresisting mud. His eyes, as they passed over her, seemed without recognition, without anything but that shocked, sharp pain.

Craig, who had been the kind of man who would complain about a paper cut for three days or more, would have been close to tears and begging for her help. This man, who bore a death's head tattoo on his arm and a bleeding open wound on his head, was preternaturally quiet and his suffering seemed strangely larger because of his silence.

"Come on," she encouraged, rocking him upright, looping an arm beneath his and gripping him around his back.

Though the bunkhouse was closer, she steered him toward her home, thinking only of the warmth, the water and the bandages in the bathroom cabinet.

He balked at the steps, pulling back a little. "No," he muttered, gripping her arm in a painful clasp. "You've got to get out of here. Take the girls and go."

"Don't be ridiculous," she said, pushing him toward the steps. "You're hurt."

He didn't argue further, but stumbled up the steps, nearly crushing her with his weight.

She fumbled with the door and guided him to the kitchen table. He sank into one of the chairs with a bitten groan. He rested his forearms on the tabletop, smearing the clean surface with red mud and then laid his head down on his wrists.

"I'm going to be sick," he said.

Carolyn shot to the kitchen cabinet for a pan, telling him to hold on. She flicked on the overhead light before setting the kettle on the floor beside his dripping and muddy feet.

His face was a sickly shade of gray and his lips were liberally coated with mud. The wound on the back of his head was still sluggishly oozing blood. She couldn't tell if his eyes were dilated or not, for they were closed now, but his shallow, labored breathing frightened her.

The mud on her own boots caused her to slip a bit on

the linoleum as she flew to the sink to make a warm compress to use in cleaning his wounds.

"What happened?" she asked.

"I was careless," he said clearly.

She gently pressed the warm, wet cloth against the lump on the back of his head, wincing as he swore aloud when she touched him. "I thought it was you coming back," he said. "I went out without my gun."

Carolyn knew why he'd gone outside without a gun. He'd been planning to talk to her, ready to explain the tattoo on his arm, the reason for its presence.

"They didn't say much," he said. "Just jumped me and lit out."

"The Wannamachers?" she asked.

"They didn't leave their calling cards," he said. "Except on my head."

"But you saw them? Big fellows, stocky? Cowboys?"

"There were three of them."

"Three? But..."

"Three. Bubba, Jimmy...and a man I think is a Canadian. Ring any bells?"

"No."

It was only then that Carolyn realized that mud wasn't solely responsible for the marks on Pete's face. His full lips were even fuller now, bruised and dark. A cut trailed from the side of his lips that often lifted into a grin. He wasn't grinning now.

One of his eyes was already blackening and a semicircular matching cut showed how closely he'd come to losing vision in that eye. She wished she could kiss the pain away as she did her daughters' hurts.

She lightly, gently washed the mud from Pete's face. She didn't know which of them winced more, she at the sight of his pain, or he at feeling it.

"We need to call the state police," she said, grimacing. "I think this is proof enough."

"What you need to do is go out, get in the car and drive

you and the girls as far away from here as possible. Until this is settled.''

"It's my land," she said.

He sighed and worked his bruised fist open and closed. "They're not playing games, Carolyn," he said. His tongue gingerly touched his torn lip. "They can be stopped, but not while you and the girls are in danger."

"They beat you up as a message to me, didn't they?" she asked, nearly rhetorically, for she instinctively knew it was the truth.

He nodded, absently, she thought.

"And threatened to hurt me or the girls if we called the police."

He gave the merest ghost of a smile. "You're quick," he said. "So, go get in the car and get the hell out of here."

"And what about you?"

"I'm staying," he said softly, evenly, but something in the tone sent a shiver of fear down her spine.

"I can't leave," she said.

"You have to," he growled as he took her wrist. His battered face shifted upward and his eyes met hers with fierce intensity. "You *have* to go."

"I can't," she said, then added, before he could argue, "I don't have anywhere to go to. Nor the money to do it with. This place is all the girls and I have."

"I'll give you the money," he said, releasing her wrist. "You and the girls hole up somewhere—"

"The girls, yes. Okay. I'll have Taylor keep them—"

"That's not good enough. The Wannamachers will look for them there first. They've got to be taken out of the area completely. Are you listening to me? I don't want those bastards to so much as *look* at Jenny or Shawna." He fumbled with his pocket and finally managed to get his battered hand in the slot. He winced as he withdrew his wallet. He handed it to her. "Now will you get in the damned car and go?"

"The girls are with Taylor," she said, not accepting the wallet.

"Oh. That's why they're not here asking a thousand questions."

"Yes," she agreed shakily, feeling an odd desire to chuckle at the thought.

He bit back another oath as she brushed the cloth over his cheek. Another cut came to light with the removal of the mud. It carried the same semicircle shape.

Bubba Wannamacher always wore his high school class ring. It could easily produce this kind of cut, she thought.

Carolyn didn't try to analyze why she felt guilty, she simply accepted it. She'd been the one to bring Pete onto their ranch. She'd been the one who left him there. And she'd been the one, with Doc, to let the Wannamachers know Pete was alone out there. And she'd been the reason why Pete had gone out to meet them without a weapon, because there had been too much left unsaid between them.

Pete gently pushed her hands away from him and used the table as a crutch to rise to his feet. Unsteadily he crossed the kitchen to the sink and turned on the water. He ran his muddy hands beneath the warm stream and lowered his head to the faucet. When he raised back up, Carolyn could see the shiver ripple down his back.

"You're freezing to death," she said. "We've got to get you out of those wet clothes."

He ignored her. "They said they'd give you two days. I don't want you to take even those. I mean it, Carolyn."

"It's not just the lack of money. This is my home, damn it, and I'm not walking out on it. Not without a fight."

Pete smiled crookedly. Or perhaps he grimaced. "These boys fight dirty," he said, leaning heavily on the counter-top.

"What do they want so badly?" she asked.

"My guess is drugs. They've been using your place as a drop site. Probably a connection point."

"What's that?"

"A distribution center. A place where a large stash is separated into several smaller caches and dispatched. Usually by small planes. This would be a perfect site. It's largely unpopulated, close enough to a bigger city to have airports, fuel, even trucks, but far enough from civilization that small planes wouldn't be noticed."

"But why this place? The Wannamachers have their own ranch. Why not right on their own land?"

"Probably because that would be too close to home. Literally. Your place has been empty for years. Piece of cake to use it," he said, but he no longer was looking directly at her. She had the feeling that he knew something and was leaving it out. Some other reason why they would use her place.

"We have to call the police. They'll give us protection. They have to know about this."

"No," he said uncompromisingly.

Appalling her, she remembered his words only that afternoon. *Don't tell them where I am.* Surely that wasn't his consideration. She thought of the tattoo on his arm, the suggestion that she call the FBI.

"I'm not leaving, Carolyn," he said.

Strangely, at that moment, his leaving was the furthest thing from her mind. "You've got to get out of those things," she repeated.

"I mean it, Carolyn. You're getting out, but I'm not." His broken lip lifted in a half grin. "I'll stop them. Trust me."

Her breath caught in her throat.

He turned to the countertop and leaned forward, propping his body on his hands, and while the position should have struck her as weary or even weakened, it seemed to her that he was holding in a wild fury.

"Come upstairs," she said. "I'll run a bath for you. And there are dry clothes in my closet." Craig's clothes, items she hadn't been able to throw away. They would be somewhat small on Pete but would do. She didn't know why the

notion of Pete wearing her husband's clothes should rattle her, but it did.

"I mean it, Carolyn. I'm not leaving." He was caught in the broken-record cycle of shock, repeating his strongest, most pressing concern. That it should be about her touched her deeply.

"I'm not asking you to," she said softly.

He turned then and met her gaze squarely. She didn't know what he could read in her eyes, didn't even know what she was feeling. But what she read in his was a combination of scarcely banked anger and a shockingly deep determination.

Carolyn had the clear knowledge that the Wannamacher brothers had messed with the wrong man. And on the heels of that thought she realized the power exuding from him at that moment acted on her like a splash of freezing water even as it thoroughly heated her.

"C-come upstairs," she said raggedly.

He nodded then and pushed away from the sink. Slowly, carefully, he made his way past the kitchen table and through the door. She placed her hand on his arm as he passed her and she felt his muscle flex in response, though he didn't say a word.

She followed him up the stairs and went on down the hall to her room as he entered the bathroom. She could hear the water running in the tub and fought the shaking in her hands as she gathered a fresh towel and the largest sweater and pair of jeans she could find.

Oddly, though she still had many of Craig's clothes, she couldn't seem to find underthings. Why would she have kept the outer wear and gotten rid of the rest? Holding Craig's clothing in her arms, she realized she felt no attachment to them, couldn't remember Craig ever wearing this particular blue sweater, couldn't imagine him pulling it over his head, his blond hair ruffled afterward. But she could picture Pete running his hand through *his* hair, a lopsided grin on his battered face.

She lightly tapped on the bathroom door and, when he didn't answer, hesitated before turning the knob. It was unlocked and opened silently at her touch. Cautiously she peeked around the door. And froze in place.

Pete had already shed his wet things and was lying back in a cloud of steam. His eyes were closed and his hands were resting on the curved sides of the large tub. One long leg was stretched up the wall and the other was bent and resting against the side of the bath.

His chest sported a few bruises though it was his muscled stomach that had taken the worst abuse. The cut beside his eye and the one at the edge of his lip seemed to stand out in relief against his pale skin. He'd already rinsed the mud from his body and hair and he resembled nothing so much as a knight back from the wars.

As if he could feel her staring at his naked body, he opened his eyes and met hers. He didn't smile. Nor did he move to cover himself.

"H-here are some clothes," she stammered.

"Thanks," he said, and closed his eyes again.

Did he have a concussion? Should she leave him alone? What if he slipped into unconsciousness?

She set the sweater and jeans on the hamper and hesitated beside the tub, trying not to stare at him, unable to do anything else.

"Can I get you anything?" she asked, carefully shifting her gaze to the window above the tub.

"No." His answer was uncompromising and definitive. She didn't know why it flayed her and made her feel as if he were shutting her out, pushing her away.

"Sure?"

He didn't answer and she quietly left the bathroom, pulling the door closed behind her. Through the wood barrier she heard a sudden smack of his hand against the water before he shut off the faucets. She leaned back against the door, unashamedly eavesdropping, worried that he would get sick, that he would drift into sleep.

She heard him mutter something to himself and again heard a splash. And in a flash she understood. He was angry. Embarrassed and angry. He'd come to her ranch to drive off the Wannamachers and had been brutally beaten because of it. But he was furious that he'd been caught without a weapon in his hands, livid that they'd gotten the better of him.

And embarrassed that she knew about it.

Oddly enough, this understanding of his reaction eased Carolyn's mind. He wasn't drifting into unconsciousness, he wasn't suffering a concussion. He was simply, starkly furious.

Carolyn pushed away from the door and went down the stairs. It wasn't until she saw the disaster of mud in her kitchen that she remembered she'd left the car running with the lights on.

She grabbed a jacket from one of the pegs and, accidentally slamming the door closed behind her, dashed out into the sleeting rain and after only a slip or two, managed to reach the Ranger. She left it where it was, merely cranking the key to the left to turn it off. The lights doused with the dying engine and she raced back to the house.

She collided with a dripping, naked Pete as she reentered her kitchen. He grabbed her shoulders and held her back from him. "Damn it, Carolyn, you can't go out there without a gun."

She didn't—couldn't—say anything. She only stared at him, the heat rising in her cheeks.

"You saw what they did to me. For God's sake, sweetheart, what's to stop them from coming back a second time? You think they won't rough you up, as well? Or worse?"

The battered condition of his face and body and the look of stark horror and shock in his eyes robbed his words of real rebuke, but sparked a rush of tears to her eyes anyway,

not because he'd expressed himself with anger, but because it was so obvious that he cared for her.

And cared deeply.

Chapter 9

At the sight of tears springing to her eyes, Pete swore softly and slid his hands down the slick, wet sleeves of her icy-cold parka.

"Ah, don't, Carolyn. Please," he said.

Her tears and the fact that he'd been the cause of them made him want to strike out at some inanimate object, yell at the night...or drag her into his arms to cradle her against his body, holding her forever.

"Carolyn," he said again, and even to himself her name sounded ragged and harsh on his lips.

If she had looked away from him, if she had pulled back even a step, if she had done anything signifying that he should release her, he told himself he would have complied. Surely he would have.

But she didn't look away. A film of tears washed her blue eyes, making them seem larger, even more luminous than he'd thought possible. And she half smiled, a tremulous, partly apologetic lifting of the corner of her lips.

That she should apologize to *him*...

A single tear snaked a trail down her cheek, carving a path in his heart. She lifted a shaking hand to the bruises at his ribs. "They hurt you so badly," she said.

"Don't cry," he whispered. He felt incapable of vocalizing anything beyond begging her to melt into his arms and felt he couldn't utter such a plea...so said nothing more.

She closed her eyes then and another tear raced for freedom. He rubbed it away with his thumb. And another ran free and he caught it, also. It seemed to tremble on his thumb like some rare gem seen only every couple of hundred years. The hot tears on his skin seemed to burn him, to reprove him for chastising her after she'd done so much for him that night. Every night since he'd come to her ranch.

In some mysterious fashion, she and her daughters had pried open a doorway deep inside him, a door he'd thought closed forever. He had the sensation of a warm, scented wind blowing through him now, and it both terrified him and made him ache for more. But not at the expense of hurting her. Never that.

If she'd moved, turned, even sighed, he would have been able to resist kissing her. But she held perfectly still, a rain-drenched butterfly snared by his harsh words, caught in his rough grip. Her face was slightly upraised and her lips parted slowly, unconsciously, he thought. And he had to touch her, had to feel the satin of her skin, had to taste the tears on her face, needed to erase her sorrow with a kiss.

Or perhaps it was his own pain he needed to assuage.

And then he didn't care about rationales or reasons. He lightly, almost nervously pressed his mouth to hers. Her lips trembled beneath his own and he both heard and felt her quick intake of breath. The cut at the side of his mouth stung for a second then was forgotten as her tongue lightly, hauntingly connected with his own.

He could taste the salt of her tears and perhaps a measure of the fear she'd felt for him earlier. And he could taste an

indefinable hunger, a want that may have been his own darker taste, his own need of this woman who trusted too easily, gave so readily. He remembered the feel of her hands gently probing the wound on his head and felt dizzy at the wave of sharp desire that coursed through him.

He knew he should have felt awkward standing in her fully lighted kitchen, naked and vulnerable to her, but he didn't. He felt strangely tender and perhaps a bit dazed, but strong and oddly empowered by her quivering response to his touch.

He pushed the jacket from her unresisting arms and understood it slid to the floor and knew neither of them cared where it fell. He stiffened when her cold hands tentatively touched his waist...and held his breath as she lifted them away...only to touch again, as if unable to resist the lure of caressing him.

As unable to resist as he.

Cupping her face with his hands, he pulled her more deeply to him, plunging into her mouth, telling her a thousand things words could never begin to express. And she opened fully to him and moaned into his breath, her fingers pressing deeply into his sides, exhorting him to explore even deeper.

A frantic, desperate need swept through him and he dropped his hands from her face to the small of her back, dragging her to him, needing to feel her body pressed sharply to his, aching for her, craving the knowledge that she desired him as much as he did her.

Stunning him, she arched into him, then slowly, deliberately, slid down and rotated upward, pressing against him in pure, womanly enticement. Not only was she with him on this journey, he realized, she was independent and strong enough to take a leader's role. She was letting him know, in the sweetest and most primal method possible, that she wanted him, too.

Oh, but she didn't know what fire she played with, he thought. She surely couldn't know.

Her hands, no longer tentative, swept up his back and across his shoulders. He shuddered in reaction and groaned an oath into the warm curve of her neck. She gave a small, choked laugh that made him grasp her to him and match her kiss for stroke.

The beating he'd taken was forgotten, her kisses healing wherever they landed, whatever they touched. He was suddenly and vibrantly whole again, revived, resuscitated in both body and spirit by the simplicity of her hunger for him.

He sensed her knees buckling before he felt her languorous slump against him. He caught her easily, eagerly, and held her tightly against him, aware, in amusement, of his nudity and her far-too-clothed condition. Unable to tear his lips from hers, he held her with one arm and used his free hand to tug her blouse from her jeans.

When she raised her shaking hands to her shirt buttons and released them with a deft expediency, he wanted to bless her, and did so by following her fingers with a trail of kisses. She arched back, leaning heavily on his arm, granting him full access to her splendid body.

For half a second, transfixed by her beauty, he could only gaze down at her. Her face tilted up to him, lips parted, eyes closed, and seemed the embodiment of longing. Her breasts, full and ripe, beckoned him from behind the wispy lace of her bra. Part of him wanted to gentle her, to slowly ease her full, dewy breasts from their prison, and another, baser part wanted to yank the brassiere down, rip it open, exposing her to him completely.

He compromised by nuzzling her through the lace, smelling her delicate, intoxicating perfume, tasting her skin despite the wispy barrier. She leaned further back, granting him even greater purchase, and one of her damp, jean-clad legs slowly, sinuously raised along the side of his own bare limb until she hooked the backside of her leg about his hips and drew him sharply against her.

He was both shocked and enchanted by her innocent

wantonness and couldn't resist the urge to press himself against her apex, reveling in her immediate response. He lowered his hand to her raised leg and hitched her even closer as he grasped her other leg and lifted her from the floor.

Straddling him, straining against him, Carolyn tried telling herself that what they were doing was wrong, that they didn't know each other well enough for such rough, stark intimacy, that such chemistry couldn't be allowed to reign so out of control. She tried, but miraculously failed.

For a split second she worried her weight would be too much for him, that a man who had been beaten and left for dead in the mud couldn't hold a well-rounded woman of nearly six feet in height. But she lost even that modicum of self-consciousness as he turned around, as if dancing with her, carrying her seemingly effortlessly, holding her tightly against his gloriously naked body, kissing her deeply, his tongue warring with hers, his need as strong as his muscled arms, his want as pure and sharp as her own.

When she would have slid from her mounted straddle, he held her in place, his large, strong hands keeping her aloft, his kisses shifting in intensity from exhortation to raw demand. She wasn't conscious of his moving until she realized the room was dark, and understood he'd carried her from the kitchen into the dining room.

At the stairs, he allowed her to slip from him, but only so that he could strip her remaining clothing from her. He followed his hands with his lips as he tugged the dampened jeans down her legs. He pulled off her wet and muddy boots with a groan that spoke more of his desire for her than any difficulty in removing them. And her jeans he cast aside without so much as a glance. Her shirt followed the boots and pants into shadow and her bra seemed to melt away at his touch.

Naked on the stairs, a single step above him and placing her at exactly his eye level, she shivered in the sheer awareness that she was so very wanted by this bruised, beautiful

man. She knew what he was, a man who had murdered in prison, a mystery, a danger to everything she held sacred, and yet she'd never wanted anyone more than she did this man, this moment.

His skin was velvet and hot to her touch. His wet hair teased at her breasts and his hands played a torturous melody on her thighs and back.

He was a *murderer*. And a battered message from criminals. And, sweet heaven, she wanted him like none other on earth.

Some inner murmur suggested that it wasn't too late to call a halt to their passion, but another, much louder voice begged her to continue on the route to what seemed an inevitable union.

As if he heard her unspoken thoughts, Pete stilled his roaming hands and met her eyes directly. "We can still go back," he said, his voice as harsh and rough as her own inner thoughts.

"No...we can't," she said, and sighed, knowing it was true but, for some strange reason, feeling she might be lying to him.

He stood perfectly still, with his hands at his side as he unknowingly echoed her thoughts, "Carolyn...I've never wanted any woman as much as I want you."

The unvarnished honesty in his face, evidenced in his grainy, impassioned voice, told her far more clearly than elaboration ever could have done that he spoke nothing, absolutely nothing, but the truth. And his truth made her knees weak and her arms languorous and heavy.

And, perhaps naturally, made her want to say something light, something humorous, something that would bridge the gap between passion and humanity.

"I'm so glad," she said, smiling. She was half stunned to find she could flirt with him at such time. "Because I'd hate to be standing here naked with you and find out you really had other things in mind."

For a second he looked shocked, as if she'd suggested

he go out and saddle Bratwurst for a midnight ride, then his lips quirked into that lopsided grin that did such wonderful things to her insides. The cut marring his lips didn't hide his relief or his smile. When he chuckled, a low rumbling thunder, she couldn't help but join him.

"Not much chance of that," he said both brokenly and pointedly.

"I'm glad of that, too," she said, wholly serious now.

He reached for her then, lifting her from the stairstep and into his arms. He whirled her around, pressing her tightly to his chest. "So am I, Carolyn. Oh, God, so am I."

She couldn't have said how they got upstairs. She supposed they walked, though some part of her remembered floating about six inches above the steps and another portion recalled stumbling, bumbling and giggling as if she were a teenager again. But by some miracle they reached her bedroom.

As though in unspoken agreement, they hesitated on the threshold of the doorway to her room. His eyes linked with hers and she could read the question inherent in his gaze and was sure he could read the myriad of doubts and uncertainties in hers.

In some inexplicable manner, she felt they were linked, already conjoined.

They were both naked and both aching for that moment of total connection, and yet stepping through the threshold of her bedroom door took on the weight of crossing the proverbial Rubicon. On this side of the door they were interested, surely, and vibrantly, vitally aware of each other, and they were still somehow innocent, strangers playing at intimacy. On the other side of that door lay a measure of commitment, promise, doubt, potential regret, and the possibility of fulfillment.

She had asked him to come to the ranch as protection, as safety, so perhaps it was only natural that it was Pete who stopped her from stepping through the doorway with a single word. "Protection?" he rasped.

"What?" She honestly couldn't comprehend his question. Then, at the nearly amused expression on his face, she understood. "Oh, heavens...I hadn't thought...I don't know—"

She broke off, not in embarrassment, for she was vaguely pleased, even flattered that he would remember such an intimate need when she had totally forgotten. And dismayed because she didn't have a clue where such protection might be found in the middle of the high plains so late at night.

"Stay here," he commanded. It wasn't a plea or an attempt at play. His words were a simple, straightforward demand that she remain exactly where she stood. He held up a finger as if impressing the point before whirling and dashing back down the stairs.

She frowned, puzzled, them smiled ruefully. She had worked with exiting prisoners. She knew better than most that one essential parting gift was a box of condoms. Dear Heaven, what was she doing?

She leaned against the doorjamb of her bedroom, waiting, certainly, and suddenly aware of being alone, nude, faced with decision.

He was back before she had time to dive into the deep well of second thoughts and she could feel the heat radiating from his body as he stopped beside her. She leaned into him as if drawn by a powerful magnet. And at his touch, at his kiss, the well receded and she forgot what scared her only moments before.

The doorway to her bedroom suddenly seemed less a barrier than a welcome and it was less painful to cross that threshold than to deny what lay beyond it.

The old comforter on her bed, repaired a thousand times or more to keep the goose down from escaping, beckoned and looked seemingly new again. And the old cotton sheets, nearly threadbare, became the purest silk satin.

But it was the touch of his skin, the way he smelled—tangy and, somewhat naturally, of the soap she herself pre-

ferred and he had used earlier—the way he felt against her, and, most of all, the way he made *her* feel that allowed her to sink and then swim into a mating so intense, so passionate that heart, body and very soul were intertwined in both giving and taking back.

As if he understood that the time for doubts, for questions, even for possible answers, had come and then gone, he drew her close to simply hold her for a long, tantalizing while, lying still as if drawing energy, though probably, more likely, to hold back the moment.

"There are a thousand things I want to say to you," he said, but didn't.

"You don't need to," she said honestly, the driving need in her supplanting the wish for knowledge about him. And, truthfully, at that moment, she didn't want to know more. She'd resolved, within the confines of his embrace, to think only of the moment, of the time they had together.

Battles with criminals, worry over his past, those things could wait. For now, for tonight, with a miraculous rain pounding against the roof and unable to tell whether it was his heartbeat or her own that she felt thundering at her breasts, she was firmly and irrevocably locked in the present.

Secure in his arms, his body pressed to hers, his long legs encircling her own, she couldn't see his death's-head tattoo, couldn't feel it…could forget it. Tonight the girls were safe elsewhere, the Wannamachers had already done their damage for the evening, and she could allow reality to slip away.

"From the moment I saw you," he said cryptically, but she understood.

"And I…you," she whispered, teasing his lips with her tongue.

He groaned aloud and rolled her over so that she lay sprawled on top of him.

"Am I hurting you?" she asked, remembering his bruises, stroking them gently, reverently.

"Not even close," he murmured before capturing her lips again.

The kiss was long and deep and she felt they somehow melded together, linked forever in a joining as old as time itself.

She could feel how much he wanted her and found a profound grace in that knowledge. She reared up and back, relishing the feel of his callused hands upon her legs, her waist and, as if staving off the best until last, her breasts.

He uttered a low, nearly agonized moan as his hands took the weight of her full breasts, his thumbs and forefingers meeting to capture her hard nipples.

It's been so long, she thought, and perhaps said aloud. He muttered something in reply, some oath or maybe a simple agreement. Who are you? she wanted to ask. How can you make me feel this way?

But she felt no need for words, only for the expression of feelings. And as he growled her name, he rolled her over and onto her back. Her legs parted naturally, easily, and she arched to meet him only to find that the man she'd brought to her place for protection was engaged in protecting her in yet another way.

Anticipating him, she sighed at the precise moment she heard the final slap of latex, and felt off balance when he didn't rise above her and take what she was so readily offering.

"Pete?" she asked, raising a little, opening her eyes, seeing him clearly in the undimmed room.

He sat at the end of her bed, his jaw tight, as if angry, but she knew, by the look in his eyes, that he was snared by passion, by a longing so intense that it burned through him and literally took her breath away.

"This is important," he said.

She frowned for a moment, wondering what he was trying to tell her, and then she thought she understood. "Yes," she murmured, holding out her hand.

Their union, this connection *was* important. Perhaps one

of the single most important things she'd ever done in her life. Significant. Portentous. Meaningful. So very, very *important.*

He took the hand she'd held out to him and raised it to his lips to press a kiss first on the back of her fingers, then turning her wrist, to her palm in an oddly tender tribute. Something in his manner made her feel as if he felt this might be the one and only time they would be together and, while this frightened her a little, she responded to the reverence inherent in his caress.

"It's okay," she said, but wasn't sure of the limits of that acknowledgment. At the moment she felt absolutely no boundaries at all.

"It's more than that," he murmured, releasing her hand and bending over her. He pressed his lips to her sensitive inner thigh and pulled back as she shivered in reaction.

"Oh, Pete Jackson..." she murmured.

"Ye-es?" he asked, teasing her, his lips inching upward, his intent all too evident.

"Words are necessary now...but..."

"But?" he asked, reaching his goal and blowing hot air across her.

"But I...can't think...of any."

"Mmm."

"Oh...Pete," she gasped as his hot tongue lightly flicked against her. She reached for him trying to stop him, afraid suddenly and far too vulnerably open to him. She pulled at his shoulders to draw him upward, but he brushed her hands aside.

"Please," he said simply, and the hunger in his voice made her shiver and acquiesce.

She'd been married before, she'd known intimacy. But she'd never known *such* intimacy, such tender regard for her wants. She was both terrified of it and strangely confident, because in some deep hidden recess within her, she knew that Pete would keep her safe while at the same time taking her to places she'd never been before.

His hands cupped her buttocks and lifted her to him, and his tongue drove her insane with a wild, fevered craving.

Her entire body seemed electrified, her veins filled with pure energy. Every part of her ached for him, for that moment when they would join and become one, and still he wouldn't listen to her pleas to come to her.

"Please...please..." she begged, digging at his shoulders, trying to pull him upward. "Pete...*please.*"

He raised his head then and met her gaze. His eyes were glazed and heavy, his breathing ragged and seemingly desperate. There was only one answer to the question on his face and she beckoned him upward with a whispered word.

He gave a low growl and rose above her, his tall, muscular body blotting out the overhead light. He poised between her legs, his eyes never leaving hers, and she felt him press at her opening. He stayed there a moment, not moving, not entering, until she couldn't stand the delay, couldn't wait a second longer. She arched her back sharply and met him, encasing him in a swift, sure capture.

She couldn't withhold her moan of satisfaction, her deep, wholly impassioned response to feeling him inside her, filling her, conjoining him to her. He felt so right; they felt so right together. Nothing had ever felt so right before.

He groaned in reaction and lowered his lips to hers, driving his tongue into her mouth in matching thrusts. He gathered her tightly against him, beneath him, pressing down on her and somehow holding her safe at the same time.

Without searching for it, as naturally as birds flew and grass greened, they found the perfect rhythm. It was slow, deep, and so very, very intense. Every part of her body responded to his touch, every thought in her mind was focused on him. And her heart, moments before uncertain and torn, embraced him and, rather awed, she knew he had penetrated there, as well.

And then all thought, all rationality disappeared completely and, though locked within his arms, tightly held beneath him, he flung her out into the universe, alone

among the shattered stars, fragmenting, shivering, screaming silently, calling his name aloud.

He was there to catch her, to call her name in answer, to bring her back to earth with his shuddering, thunderous roar of completion.

"Carolyn!" he cried out as if in agony, and she clung to him, grasping him to her as tightly as he held her, bringing him back this time, securing him, nurturing him home to her arms, to the real world.

"I never knew," she murmured, not telling him the half of it, not really telling him anything, but trying to say everything in the stroking of his shoulders, the soothing of his still-shuddering body, the wrapping of her legs around him to hold him within her, to keep him there. *Forever.*

Tears filmed her eyes and she felt a couple roll free and down her temples to mingle with her hair. "Oh, I just never knew."

He pressed his lips to the sensitive hollows above her collarbone, still holding her tightly, still pressed deep within her. He raised a shaking hand to her face and, upon stroking it, hesitated, then lifted his head to look down at her.

She didn't open her eyes despite feeling his question, his gaze.

"Are you crying?" he asked, running his hand across her face, dipping his fingers into her hair.

"Mmm. Good tears," she said, and smiled gently, and, scaring her a little, lovingly.

He kissed the corners of her eyes, drying the few tears of release, of realization, with his mouth. His kiss, as he transferred his lips tenderly to hers, tasted of salt and, more, of fulfillment.

He pulled back a little, raising his body to grant her breathing room. She forced herself to loose her grip on his back and opened her eyes then to meet his gaze. The look on his face, compassionate and kind, somewhat awed and

perhaps a bit bemused, made her arch up to kiss him with swift, sure passion before dropping back to the bed.

"Carolyn...?"

The question in his voice made her stiffen slightly, as if the mere sound of her name spoken aloud without the elements of passion was an announcement that the outside world was about to intrude.

Whatever it was he wanted to ask, she wasn't sure she wanted to hear it. She lifted a finger to his lips and pressed gently. "It's okay," she whispered. "It's perfect."

"No," he said against her fingertip. His eyes were sad and his body motionless. The dark bruise beneath his eye was spreading. The cut on his lip stood out in sharp relief against his pale skin.

"Yes," she contradicted. "This is. What we had here. What you did to me. What you do. Tonight. Now. This was perfect."

He didn't argue further, merely gathering her into his arms again, rolling her to the side and slipping away from her in spite of her moan of protest. He drew her closer then and held her against his warm, velvet body.

Pete thought she fit him as if nature had created her body specifically for him. Her skin, satin smooth and silky soft against him, seemed designed for his touch and he knew he could never get enough of the feel of her. And her scent, now mingled with his own, teased at his nostrils like an elusive promise, a forever lingering hint of spring and hope. The scent of laughter and salvation.

He'd wanted her, had ached for her. But in their lovemaking, in the profoundly moving experience of joining with her, he'd discovered something far beyond mere desire. She'd lit the very fires of his soul. He wanted her still, but that want had shifted, after the moment of culmination, to a deep, searing craving.

He didn't want her just for tonight. He wanted her for tomorrow and a thousand tomorrows after that. He wanted her forever. Unconsciously his arms tightened around her

and he shivered a little as she pressed a kiss to his chest and she tightened her own grasp on him.

Now was the time to tell her the truth about himself. Now, with barriers down between them, with her body pressed to his, with the passion imperfectly banked and the shadows pushed to the corners of her bedroom by the glow of her overhead light.

"Carolyn, I want to tell you about the past. About what I am, what I'm—"

"Not now," she murmured against him. "Not tonight. It'll keep. It'll hold."

He stroked her silken hair and lowered his lips to her temple to press lightly, lingeringly. He knew she was wrong; some things didn't keep well. She had the right to know about his past, his uncertain present, and he had the need to tell her.

But a part of him, even in this moment of rare joining, reared its ugly, selfish head and he lay beside her, holding her, reveling in the knowledge that she'd taken him to her bed without assurances, without safety factors. She'd accepted him on nothing more than instinct.

Was it so wrong of him to need that trust? Was it so wrong to allow the night to fade into dawn with the belief that she could trust him, perhaps even learn to love him, on nothing more than pure faith alone?

He, who had trusted no one in ten years, who had believed the milk of human kindness had soured on the streets, who had vowed never to allow himself to believe in anyone again, wanted this lovely, vital woman in his arms now to have faith in him without a single reason for doing so.

That this was patently unfair he knew far better than words could ever express. And yet, it hovered at the crux of his need for her. He wanted to bury his face into the warmth of her neck and stay there for eternity. And longer.

Incredibly, amazingly, she knew about the tattoo on his arm, knew what it meant. And still she'd taken him into

her body, into her passion, and, perhaps, God willing, as deeply as her heart.

She would never know how that realization rocked him to his core. She couldn't know. He scarcely understood it himself. But he held the awareness of the depth of her trust to that opened door in his heart, in his soul, and he felt some broken part him begin to mend.

"Ah, Carolyn," he murmured, needing to kiss her again, needing to go back downstairs and into his wallet to retrieve another measure of protection.

She stirred against him, as in tune with him now as she had been during their union. "Pete...?"

"Yes," he said, in answer and possibly in question.

"Mmm."

"Oh, Carolyn," he said, stroking her face, drowning in her blue eyes. "You were right. This *is* perfect."

Chapter 10

Carolyn woke slowly, as if coming up to the surface through layers of cocooning gossamer filaments. Warm. Cradled. Held safe. Loved.

She opened her eyes and daylight stung them. She tried turning her head and met a broad, warm shoulder blocking her movement.

She didn't have alcohol as an excuse for the night before. She didn't have amnesia or even an unknown second personality to blame. She had no excuses whatsoever. She had gone to bed with a stranger her daughters had found in the desert, a stranger who sported a murderer's tattoo on his forearm.

And she had loved every single second of it.

But...

She sighed, lowering her eyes to the arm protectively encircling her and to the glowing red eyes of his death's-head tattoo. It could be erased, she thought, and immediately chastised herself for the notion. The image might be physically erased, but would she be able to forget it?

Never.

He'd murdered someone and gotten away with it, had apparently exited prison with authorities none the wiser.

But she knew.

And worse, *he* knew.

What kind of a toll would murder take on someone's psyche, on his very soul? The worst kind, she thought. The very, very worst kind.

So much of the tension in Pete Jackson, of the shadows in his eyes, of the bitterness occasionally heard in his voice could be explained by something as dark and damaging as taking the life of a fellow human being.

She'd stopped him from telling her about his past the night before. In the aftermath of their incredible union, in the wake of the shocking truth their joining contained, she hadn't wanted to know about his past. The present was all she had desired, all she craved. She didn't want details, doubts, or baggage from his past to interfere with that rare moment of bliss any more than she would have wanted to talk about Craig, about her days in Dallas, about the sleepless nights that followed his death.

If they had been a normal couple, dating, getting to know each other...no tattoos signifying murder between them...he might have told her what loves he'd had and lost, and she might have opened up about the fears she'd had following Craig's funeral, her eviction from their condo, her desperate struggle to keep her girls safe and happy.

But they weren't, couldn't be, a standard pair of lovers. That notion was as unrealistic as believing a night of perfect harmony could create a future filled with laughter. Even a regular Jane and Joe would encounter struggles with money, moments of losing a dream, times of grief and despair. But a stranger who had *murder* in his past, and a lover who *knew* about it...how could she pretend not to be aware of that dreadful truth? How could she ever hope to pretend that his past didn't exist?

And yet he touched her soul in some inexplicable way.

He moved her with his gentleness toward her daughters. He snared her heart with his lopsided grin. When his gray eyes were lit with humor she couldn't help but smile in response. And the sorrow she sometimes glimpsed in his face, the bitterness that rested so heavily on his shoulders made her sad, hurt and even, upon rare occasion, angry. Not at him, but at whatever had brought such pain to him.

He'd fought for her, been brutally beaten as a message to her, and had thrust his wallet into her hands so that she and her daughters could escape, leaving him behind to fight her battles for her. What kind of a man was he?

A good kind, she thought. The best kind.

As if aware of her thoughts even in sleep, he tightened his arm around her, drawing her closer to his chest. He mumbled something and, amazingly, pressed a kiss to her forehead.

"Are you awake?" she asked.

He didn't answer. He couldn't. He was deeply, soundly asleep. He had kissed her from some level of his unconscious or subconscious mind.

She closed her eyes. Was his past so very important?

Wasn't it more important to consider that she lay, held close, pressed tightly against a man capable of kissing her even while he slept?

Wasn't it equally vital to consider his present actions, to know that he'd held her through the night, had fought for her, had let her into some vulnerable part of him?

Of course the present was important, but so was the past. A person was made up of all the factors in his life, good, bad, even indifferent. She couldn't pretend his past didn't exist. It did exist. He had killed a man in prison. That was a very real part of who Pete Jackson was.

He might kiss her as tenderly as a dawn kissed the horizon or as passionately as stars shone in a winter's sky, but somewhere, perhaps deep inside him, he was flawed, damaged.

Capable of murder.

A slow, sad tear of regret, of pain for him...and for herself...slipped from her eye and dripped onto his arm.

"Mmm, perfect," he mumbled.

Oh, if only that were true, she thought unhappily. If only that were true.

Pete fought waking and even when he did, he kept his eyes closed. He was sure if he opened them, acknowledged the day in any way at all, he would also have to acknowledge the doubts and fears stiffening the woman in his arms. She'd been pliant, warm, and everything a man could ever want through the night. But with morning, she'd grown steadily more tense with each passing second.

He held her fast against him, unwilling to let her go, knowing it was inevitable but wanting to delay the moment as long as possible. He needed to pretend that just for this moment, in the aftermath of a night such as he'd never known before, they were a couple.

He still didn't know about the future, about the part of a man that made him capable of making...and keeping...promises. He didn't trust easily. He couldn't. And he didn't have the kind of faith some men had, faith in a bright tomorrow.

He was used to men like the Wannamachers and their accented friend. That was the world he understood. Women like Carolyn, children like Jenny and Shawna, they were a breed apart. And they simply baffled him. Courage, humor, honesty seemed to bubble up and out of them as naturally as breathing. They deserved every good thing a man could give them...protection, honesty, trust. Love.

They deserved a far better man than he. Knowing this, he still couldn't release Carolyn. He slowly kissed her bare, warm shoulder. And at the sharp gasp and because her spine suddenly became rigid, he let her go.

"Morning," she mumbled, sitting up, turning her back to him.

"Carolyn..."

"We'd better get going. I don't know what time Taylor's bringing the girls out. It's nearly eight, now," she said hurriedly. She all but bolted from the bed and to her closet door for a robe. Still without looking at him, she left the bedroom and seconds later he heard the door to the bathroom close softly. Securely.

He rolled onto his back, groaning a little as the bruises and cuts left by the Wannamachers made their myriad protests known. The incredible and multiple unions with Carolyn had certainly masked any and all pain the night before, but he was fully aware now that they hadn't done anything to help heal the wounds.

He winced as he sat up, and frowned as he swung his legs to the edge of the bed. "Damn," he muttered, catching sight of himself in her vanity's mirror. He looked like a prizefighter who hadn't come close to winning the purse but had managed to go seven rounds before throwing in the towel. He had a black eye, puffy bruises on his cheek, a cut at the edge of his mouth, and a sour expression on his face.

No wonder Carolyn had fled the room.

Whatever her reasons, his battered mug or simply morning confusion after the incredible passion they'd shared the night before, a part of him was glad she'd done so. He had several things he wanted to do before Taylor arrived with the girls. And he needed to be alone to do them.

He pushed off the bed and growled an oath at the stiffness in his body. Not all of it could be laid at the Wannamachers' door, he thought with a rueful grin. Some of the stiffness came from using muscles that hadn't been tested in a very, very long time.

He'd left the clothes she gathered for him in the bathroom, so grabbed a pair of sweat pants from the upper shelf in Carolyn's closet. He winced at the soreness of his arms and at the thought that her husband had once worn these pants.

He decided a man could go crazy thinking that way.

Donning nothing else but the sweatpants and his shoes, mud covered and still damp, he gave a quick look around outside before pelting across the muddy driveway to the bunkhouse.

Staring around the interior, taking in his soaked bed, the wet floor and the streaks of rain down the walls, puddling beside his gear, Pete felt disoriented. The entire world had changed since he packed those bags yesterday. Nothing would ever feel quite the same way again.

Knowing this, he still had to grin. Apparently, except for the beating, he'd been lucky in a variety of ways the night before. And lucky he'd packed his gear before the downpour. He dug into his waterproof bags and found fresh clothing and alternate—dry—boots. Different though the world might be, he still needed the mundane elements that comprised life.

He washed quickly and got dressed and was back in the main house before Carolyn had finished her bath. He started a pot of coffee and, after a quick look up the stairs at the still-closed bathroom door, went to the living room closet and dug into an opened box. He swiftly rifled through papers until he found what he was looking for. A few seconds later he was on the telephone.

The number he dialed was answered by a voice giving another number and he responded with yet a third, this one an extension.

"MacLaine," a deep voice barked.

"Alec…it's Pete."

"Ready for a pickup?"

"Not yet. And I'm not on your place anymore," he said.

"So I was right? You get something?"

"Worked over."

"Bad?"

"I've felt better," he said, but while this was true, some deeper part of himself had not felt as good in years, maybe ever.

Pete heard Carolyn's blow-dryer start up and spoke less

cautiously. "Listen, Alec, you were right, something is going on, but you had the wrong property. The drop is here, on a ranch they call the Leary place. Widow and two little girls are being harassed by a couple of local toughs. But the cowboys have got a friend. Brass-knuckle type. He's giving the orders. Canadian accent. Or non-accent, as the case may be. Just an impression."

"What's the harassment?"

"Midnight spray-paint raids, punk stuff. But their surprise visit last night made it clear they're serious. They want her off the property pretty badly. I was supposed to relay the message that she—or one of her daughters—would be next if she didn't clear out now."

"But you didn't?"

"Yeah, I did, but not all of it."

"Any reason why not?"

"Yeah," but he didn't elaborate. Carolyn had been through enough in the past year without being run off her property to top it off. He was damned if he'd let the Wannamachers take her home.

"If she's got kids..." Alec said.

"I'll make sure they're safe. Carolyn, too. Don't worry, I can take care of them," Pete said, and hoped like hell that was true. Jenny and Shawna's safety was a fairly tremendous commodity to gamble with.

"She just moved in?"

"In the last month. Place was empty for some fifteen years before that."

"Damn, it sure fits," Alec said.

"Yeah, tell me."

"She just buy the place?"

"No, it's been in the family for years, but more or less abandoned. She just got here from Dallas."

"She's a widow, you said?"

"Right."

"Any chance the husband was in the know about how his property was being used?"

"Could be," Pete said coldly, sickened by the notion. This was what he'd withheld from Carolyn, the knowledge that her husband might have accepted money from these men, might be the cause of her current troubles.

The men last night had basically said as much. The papers they'd waved in Carolyn's face early on had been bogus, but their assumption of rights to the property may not have been. The implication that her husband had condoned the situation, had left it to her without explanation disgusted him.

But this, he couldn't tell her anything about. Her husband of some eleven years was dead. Surely she had the right to some illusions.

He told Alec, "The guy left her practically destitute, but I went through some of her papers in her closet and saw that he was receiving a check from a Canadian firm every month like clockwork. Couple of grand a month. And that ties in with what the Canadian fellow said last night."

Alec whistled.

"No kidding," Pete muttered. "And the husband was a prosecuting attorney, wouldn't have much in the way of private practice. Of course, the money could be legit. But my gut tells me I'm right."

"Want me to check out the firm?"

Pete gave him the name he'd seen on the canceled checks from the box in the living room closet.

Pete said, "It's my guess the drop'll take place in the next couple of days. That's how long they gave her to clear out. And, there's a full moon in a couple of days."

"This widow know about you?"

"Some of it. Not all. Carolyn used to be a social psychologist. Of all damned things, she recognized the tattoo."

"Whew! Think of the odds against that. Does she know the rest?"

"No."

"You going to tell her?"

"I don't know."

"Pete—"

"Let me do this my way, okay?"

"You're the boss."

Pete chuckled. "Actually, I'm the hired hand."

Alec MacLaine snorted. "That, I'd like to see."

"Hey, pal, I'll have you know I can saddle a horse with the best of them now."

"What do you want on this end?"

"Just be ready to rally at my signal."

"You got it. I'll get things set up with Lubbock."

"Good deal," Pete said. The blow-dryer stopped. "And Alec? Kiss Cait for me, will you?"

"Not for you, I won't."

Pete chuckled and hung up without a farewell. Between longtime associates, such amenities weren't a necessity.

He had their coffee poured and was sitting at the table when Carolyn came down the stairs.

"Did I hear you talking to someone?" she asked, sliding into her chair and carefully, purposefully not meeting his eyes.

"Phone call," he said.

"Oh," she said, and her nervousness at confronting him by light of day apparently overrode any curiosity.

"Carolyn..."

"Mmm?" She took a sip of coffee.

"I want to talk about last night," he said.

Carolyn's eyes flew to his then. In the harsh morning light his wounds appeared far worse than they had in the shadowy night. The Wannamachers had done this to him because of her, because she'd brought him to her place.

"We should have put something on your eye," she said. "Does it hurt much?"

He shook his head and shrugged. Of course it did. He had to be aching from every pore in his body.

"Looks like hell, though," he said, and grinned crookedly, more crookedly than ever because of the cut on his lip. And she never thought she'd seen anyone more hand-

some, more uniquely beautiful. Those cuts and bruises were a badge of courage and dedication because he'd taken them for her.

"Speaking of wrecked," Pete said, "the bunkhouse leaked like a sieve last night. It looks worse than I do."

She smiled. "That's hard to imagine."

"Thanks a lot."

Her smile broadened. "You're welcome."

She didn't know how he'd done it, but in his offhand manner, in his simple banter, he'd managed to strip the tension and embarrassment from the morning. And he'd managed to make her think about him not as a lover, not as a murderer, but as a man. Just Pete. Who had come to the ranch for her and her daughters, who had believed the kids were conning him about kneeing Bratwurst, who had fixed screen doors, mailboxes, fences and barns, and fed a hungry mother cat to boot.

"Last night was remarkable," he said.

And because he was looking at her so directly and because he'd diffused the sharp fear in her already, she was able to respond honestly, "Yes," she said simply. Starkly honestly.

"There's a lot you don't know about me, Carolyn," he said.

She held up a hand. "That's all right. You don't have to tell me anything."

He smiled a little. Somewhat wistfully, she thought. "You have a right to know."

She stood up and went for more coffee. She poured them both a round before sitting back down. "Pete, I don't want to lie to you. Not just because of what happened between us last night. Knowing that you killed someone in prison scares the living daylights out of me. Not that I imagine for one minute that you didn't have good cause or that it was in self-defence or something...but because that tattoo announces that killing is something to be honored."

"And...?"

"And I think it hurts you."

"And you?"

She felt the wistful smile on her lips now. "And me. Yes."

"Carolyn—"

She interrupted him. "Wait, Pete, let me finish. I was confused, yes. Maybe I still am. I don't know. Maybe I'm just crazy..."

"What are you saying, Carolyn?" he asked hoarsely, forcing her to meet his gaze.

"I'm trying to tell you I don't want it to matter between us. That I think I can live with this. Maybe even forget about it."

Her heart beat wildly and painfully in her chest and it seemed to her that his might have stopped altogether. He closed his eyes with an expression of intense agony.

Oh, dear God, he thought, more moved and more humbled than he could have thought possible. For a split second he wrestled with tears of such exquisite anguish that he was afraid they would spill free. They burned inside, a raging, scalding liquid that poured through him in wave after wave of purifying fire.

He swallowed heavily. She hadn't said she loved him. But those were only words. She'd shown him. She'd granted him the gift of her trust, her faith in him and her unbelievable certainty that a future could exist for them.

He trembled on the threshold of a promise so sweet and so enticing he could taste the possibility of happiness.

"Don't leave me out here all alone," she said softly.

He opened his eyes then. "Never," he said, and had to clear his throat. "What an amazing woman you are."

She smiled softly and stretched her hand across the table to lightly touch the back of his. "So now what?" she asked.

Pete didn't know if she meant them or the situation surrounding them. If he talked about the former, he would flail about in unfamiliar waters, showing her just how little prepared he was to accept the concept of a happy tomorrow.

He chose to answer the latter. "Now we call your sister-in-law and talk to her about getting you and the girls out of town. I'd feel better if she went, too. There's no reason to let these guys have any access to any member of your family."

"I'll call her now, but I'm not going with them."

"The hell you aren't," he said firmly, turning his hand over to grasp her fingers. "You've got to."

"No. I told you last night…I'm not leaving here, either. The girls will be safe with Taylor. But if you're staying here to fight them, I'm staying with you. You can teach me how to shoot or whatever it takes, but I'm staying." She drew her fingers from his tight clasp. "And there's not a bit of use in arguing with me. This is the way it is."

She exited the kitchen like an actress leaving the stage, her head high, her shoulders squared.

Pete was reminded of the morning he'd tried to give her a twenty for a new hammer and a sack full of nails. A smile snagged his lips. On top of her other attributes, this lady was sassy as all get-out.

She came back in a few moments. "Taylor will be out for the girls' things within the hour. She'll take them to Lubbock for a couple of days and wait for us to contact her. She even offered to take them to Disneyland."

Pete was struck anew by the contrasts eddying around them. Drug dealers usurping Carolyn's ranch, and to keep the kids out of it, let's pack them off to a fun park for a few days.

She poured them both another cup of coffee, pulled his cream from the refrigerator and handed the container to him wordlessly, then waited for him to lighten his coffee before putting it back inside. She didn't sit down.

He looked up at her and was surprised by the sharp look of question on her face. "What?"

She held out her hand with the checks he'd found in the closet box. "What are these?" she asked. Her voice ap-

peared no more than mildly curious but carried a note he couldn't identify.

Damn. He didn't want to tell his theory about the checks, about the land...about her husband's involvement. He'd forgotten to put them away after his phone call to Alec. He must be slipping. Want and need of Carolyn was making him careless.

"I found them in the box in the closet."

"You were going through my things?" she asked softly. Dangerously.

Treading on exceedingly thin ice, Pete forced himself to meet her gaze directly. "I did, yes. I'm sorry. I was looking for extra weapons one day."

"In my boxes of unpacked things."

"Yes."

"And what else did you find?"

"Carolyn—"

"What did you want with these canceled checks? What was that phone call about? Who were you calling?"

"What is this, Carolyn?" he asked. "Five minutes ago you trusted me. You don't now?"

A wave of pain swept across her face. "I don't know what to think," she said steadily enough. "I feel as if everything is topsy-turvy, that just as I get something clear, it wisps away. Like fog." Tears filmed her eyes. "I want to trust you, Pete. I do."

"Then trust me on this, Carolyn. Please. Don't explore this particular path. I don't want to see you hurt."

She looked from him to the checks, turned them over to read the countersignature on the back, then slowly set them down beside him. When she looked back up at him, her eyes were veiled, her emotions held behind a barrier that she'd raised in the past few minutes.

"Okay," she said. "For now, I'll buy it."

He knew both what she was saying and what she wasn't. She'd trust him not to hurt her, would trust that knowing about this would. But she was also telling him that her trust

was on a short lead. It was too new, too fragile to accept any and all things he might do.

And that was the moment, the precise and exact moment in time that Pete knew he loved Carolyn Leary. And would love her forever. And he knew this because he had the terrible feeling that he would blow that trust, sunder those boundaries and lose her.

Chapter 11

Carolyn had the girls' bags packed before Taylor's Jeep Cherokee purred into the driveway. Pete carried them outside and stuffed them into the back storage area.

"What happened to your face, Pete?" Jenny called

"Somebody beat him up," one of the triplets said.

"Did they, Pete?" Shawna asked, obviously horrified.

"Ran into the barn," he said.

"Bet it was the Wannamachers," a triplet offered.

"No, it wasn't," Jenny said hotly. "Pete would have laid them out flat. Like use kung fu fighting or something." She demonstrated and poked one of her cousins in the side.

All five cousins entered the fray and soon a rollicking, giggling group set the Cherokee rocking, apparently forgetting all about the bruises and cuts on Pete's face.

But he caught Taylor eyeing him in a combination of sympathy and hard-set anger. He slammed the rear door closed and joined Taylor and Carolyn at the side of the vehicle. "I wish you'd let me call the state troopers," Tay-

lor said. "They'd be here in seconds. If what you suspect is real, they need to be in on it."

Carolyn had said almost identical words the night before. But neither she nor Taylor had heard the cold note in the unnamed man's voice as he spelled out what would happen to Jenny, Shawna or Carolyn if they did so. He had heard it and it echoed still. That he'd called someone else technically couldn't be considered disobeying that arrogant command. He *hadn't* called in the state troopers and he wasn't going to.

He tried one last time to get Carolyn to go with Taylor. She wasn't having any of it. To his surprise, Taylor didn't make any such attempt. When he appealed to her to try, she gave him a cool look of appraisal.

"I don't think you've been around very many western women," she said almost patronizingly. "We're tough as proverbial nails. And we fight to keep what's ours."

"At the possible expense of her life?" he asked.

"Are you staying?" she asked back.

"Of course," he said.

"Then, of *course,* you'll protect her." She turned to Carolyn then and smiled gently. "But you better take care of yourself. We'll be at the Holiday Inn in Lubbock. We'll check in with you morning and night. And if we don't reach you or you don't call us back, I'm sending in the troops. You got it? Doug's friends will be out here like the cavalry. Clear?"

Carolyn hugged her sister-in-law awkwardly and received a full-fledged family bear hug in response. Tears sprang to her eyes. "I love you, Taylor," she said for the first time. And meant it.

"I love you, too. You're my sister, sweetie."

Carolyn, who had never had a sister of her own, clung to the sincerity of Taylor's words…and to the genuine pressure of the arms around her. Finally she pulled back and smiled shakily, blinking away her tears. "You're the one

with all the trouble. You have five kids in the car with you."

Taylor grinned, flicking away the tears in her own eyes, and gripped Carolyn's arms fiercely before letting her go. Then she turned to Pete. "Take care of her," she said solemnly.

"With my life," he said, equally seriously.

She seemed to study him for a moment, then nodded as if accepting him at his word.

With a wave and farewell from Taylor and a cacophonous tsunami from the five cousins, Carolyn's family departed. She watched the Cherokee disappear down the road until a final curve took it out of sight.

"They'll be all right," Pete said.

"I know," she answered, but lifted a hand to swipe at her face.

Pete didn't know how to comfort her. Or if she even wanted him to try. Some things were better left unsaid. Things like husbands selling out to drug dealers. Things like children in potential danger. Things like falling in love with the one woman he'd never even dared dream about?

He wanted to ask her why loving her had to hurt so much. But he knew the answer lay within himself. *He* was the reason it hurt. His past. His choices. His life. It hurt so much because he'd done things that he couldn't reconcile with the way he felt about Carolyn.

"We have to assume they'll be watching the place," he said. "Possibly from the air, or from some rise where a telescope will let them know we're taking them seriously. I think it would be best if we seem to be playing along."

She gave her face a last surreptitious swipe and turned to face him. "So we make like we're packing out?"

He nodded, disconcerted by her use of the pronoun "we."

"If they are watching, they'll have seen the girls leaving with Taylor, so one problem's out of the way." She faltered on her last couple of words. "Unless they follow them?"

"They won't, Carolyn. Trust me, they're not after the kids." At her look of skepticism, he added, "They've got bigger trouble. They've got a cache of drugs coming in—tomorrow night or the next, I'd guess—and apparently they figured they could drive you out before this. It's my theory that's why the outsider is here. He came in to clean up the mess. And, frankly, he's the one that scares me."

"Me, too," she said dryly. She looked so damned beautiful, standing three inches deep in rapidly drying mud, her blond hair softly blowing in the breeze, her imperfectly masked vulnerability radiating out from her like a beacon.

He had to clear his throat. "At any rate, they need to deal with the drugs, not a bunch of kids and the widow of a state trooper. Though, in all honesty, I'd put that bunch up against an army. Maybe even a team of guerrillas."

He found he'd said that just to hear her watery chuckle.

"But—" she began as her laughter faded.

"I know. They want you gone as well."

"Pete…?"

He stilled himself, waiting for the question about the canceled checks, about her former husband's possible involvement. "Thank you," she said slowly. And oh so needlessly.

He exhaled. Tell her now, he urged himself. Let her off. She deserved to know the truth. She needed to know who…*what* she was giving her undeserving thanks to. Let her decide for herself.

She lightly touched his arm and drew her hand back sharply as if afraid of being burned. Before he could so much as force his lips to form the truth, she rounded and squelched through the mud to the main house back door. She slipped her boots free at the door and looked back at him.

How did she know he'd be standing there, as if rooted to the ground, watching her every move?

"I think you'd better bring the horse trailer around," she called. "We can load stuff into that."

He lifted a hand in agreement. And the corners of his mouth in a smile. Yes, Carolyn was one in a million.

Every muscle in her body seemed to be holding a separate and furious protest of the day's activities. And her house was a chaotic jumble of boxes, disarranged furniture...and booby traps.

Together, she and Pete had positioned chairs with casters beneath the windows in the living room; anyone attempting entry through those portals would slip, slide and crash upon first touch. They'd laughingly hung a string of empty cans over the front door no one ever used.

Carolyn had never dreamed she could be up to her neck in sheer danger and be enjoying every moment.

"I must be sick," she unwittingly said aloud.

Pete looked up from his concentrated attention on a wiring project. He'd tried explaining it to her, but he'd also been absently rubbing his leg while speaking. She wasn't stupid, not even close to uneducated. But she was human.

"We'll keep the guns upstairs," Pete had told her, unaware he was letting her know far more than the arrangement of their weapons.

She'd worked beside him all day, hefting boxes out to the horse trailer. That the boxes were mostly empty made little difference, for between sliding through the slowly drying driveway and going up and down steps, the awkwardly sized boxes felt as heavy as if she were hauling books back and forth. And yet, each time she passed him, he'd had a small smile for her or a look that allowed her to regain her flagging energy.

In the past hour, as dusk fell and the temperature had dropped some forty degrees to a shivering cold subfreezing, she'd abandoned the pretense of moving and, after a quick personal cleanup, had gone to the kitchen to stare stupidly at the contents of her pantry and refrigerator. Nothing appealed, and her brain felt too slow to conjure something out of thin air.

Pete passed through the kitchen several times during her silent contemplation, but didn't say anything to her. When she heard his soft, slightly limping footfalls on the stairs, and his progression into the living room, she turned back to the opened refrigerator and inwardly begged it to suggest something to her.

"Carolyn."

She half started. Hadn't he gone elsewhere in the house? How long had he been standing there watching her?

"Sit down."

When she didn't move, he stepped forward and took her shoulders in his hands and turned her to the table. "Sit."

She did as he commanded.

He crossed to take her place at the icebox door. After a couple of seconds' intent study, he withdrew a container of cottage cheese and two apples. He withdrew a couple of spoons from the silverware drawer and a paring knife. He deposited one apple in front of her and the other at his place. He wrested the lid from the cottage cheese and stuck the spoons into the containers.

"Dinner," he said, grinning at her.

She had to chuckle. "That's horrible."

"Horrible? The first sit-down dinner I ever prepare for you and you cast aspersions on it before even trying it?"

He took the paring knife and sliced into his apple, neatly excising a perfect wedge. He tilted the knife, dropping the wedge neatly onto the slender blade, and held it out to her, lifting his hand in a take-it motion. She did so with a shaking hand. How could such an innocent, nearly banal gesture make her feel giddy and liquid?

She bit into the apple slice and looked at him at the same time. His eyes were on her mouth, his lips slightly parted. Whatever he did to her, she realized she did something equally unnerving to him. And the realization gave her a jolt of adrenaline, a fresh flare of energy.

"Better?" he asked.

She remembered a package of thawed chicken in the

meat drawer of the refrigerator. She remembered she hadn't packed the girls' latest reading material. She remembered the night before, the feel of his battered hands on her skin.

She nodded.

He held out another perfect slice, again letting it rest on the blade of the knife. Here, he seemed to be saying, I cut this just for you. I fought for it, I won it. I prized it out of this complex universe and brought it to you.

She took it with the reverence a treasure and gift deserved, but held it out to his lips instead, giving it back to him, sharing it with him. His eyes flashed with an unreadable acknowledgment, a hot, silver blue hunger that made her fingers tremble and her loins ache with sudden longing.

Without saying a word, he rose to his feet and moved to the back door. He locked it carefully, throwing the dead bolt with a loud, definitive clack. He whirled a chair to a safeguard position beneath the knob. He pulled his own .45 from its temporary resting place on top of the refrigerator and tucked it into his pants. He picked up both apples, the knife, and took the pitcher of sun tea from the countertop. When he'd juggled all these items safely into the crook of his left arm, he held out his free hand to her.

She felt as if she floated up from the chair and had to close her eyes against the shock of his touch. Just the barest brush of his fingertips against hers made her weak with yearning, turned her body into a thrumming want.

She followed him up the stairs, knowing where they were going, needing to be there with him. They didn't hesitate on the threshold this time, they had already crossed it, having passed through the storm the night before.

And yet she felt slightly apprehensive. The night before, even with him battered and bruised, chemistry and electricity had taken over, had swept her over a precipice where rational thought had no meaning and desire reigned wholly supreme.

Tonight, after a day's long, hard work, after sending her daughters away with her sister-in-law, after confessing her

doubts of him and announcing her willing denial of them, chemistry was forced to take a back seat to emotion.

He set the foodstuff on her nightstand and the gun beside them. Apples and guns. She was aware of the strange contrast the items and of a certain appropriateness about the picture, that they created a still life as old as time itself.

"Am I taking things for granted, Carolyn?" he asked finally, when she hadn't moved.

"No," she said honestly, and honestly surprised at his question.

"I want you to," he said.

She lifted her eyes to his, puzzled. He looked terrified.

And she realized that he was more stunned by his utterance than she, as if it had come from deep within, a place he hadn't known existed until the words spilled free.

"I don't understand," she said gently. Encouragingly.

He gave a low rasping sound, as if she were dragging something terrible from within him. "I want you to take me for granted. I want you to know I'm here with you. Really here. I want you to believe in that so strongly, so thoroughly, that you can't imagine questioning it."

His words ran over her body like his caresses had done the night before, and deeper, penetrating her fully. But he didn't lift his hands to touch her.

Oh, and they were such sweet words, important words. And as heady as forty-year-old cognac. How she wanted to believe them. How she ached to do as he asked, to simply, easily take him for granted. That was a level of intimacy like none she'd ever dreamed of. But she couldn't say anything yet. She'd already said so much. It was too soon. Everything about him, about them was tenuous, too new, too uncertain.

"I want to," she said, compromising between uttering a lie and blurting out every vestige of the truth.

He closed his eyes and reached out for her then, drawing her tenderly, gently to his chest. He enfolded her in a reverent embrace, a caress made all the more entrancing be-

cause she knew that some part of him understood that like her, he couldn't speak the words to encompass the depths of what he felt for her.

And perhaps he never would be able to. The notion made her feel slightly sad and yet deeply sympathetic. Words were vitally important, but as she knew all too well, they could mask actions. Like, *"don't worry, honey, I've got it all under control,"* then years later seeing Craig's name on the back of checks she'd never seen before nor heard anything about.

Pete's not wanting her to know about them, in a possible attempt to spare her discomfort or pain, spoke louder than words of how much he could care about her. But his action wasn't masking words, it was masking causing her pain.

"In prison, I had ten years to think about the future," he said softly, letting her know more about him in that single phrase than anything heretofore. "But I didn't think about it. I let days and nights, whole years, go by without any sense of wonder, any feeling that the future could be a viable entity with a reality of its own."

That he was talking about her was obvious, especially when his hands pulled her even closer, pressing her tightly against him. Tears stung at her eyes to realize he saw her as a sense of wonder. A poverty-stricken mother of two, widowed and essentially abandoned...and he saw wonder?

She raised her head, surprised anew at his height, at how right she felt against him. She pressed a kiss to one of the few places on his face that didn't sport a bruise. She felt his response shudder through him. Against her.

"Maybe someday..." she said, not even sure what she was suggesting, not sure exactly what she'd intimated that morning.

"I hope so, Carolyn. You have no idea how much I hope so," he said, before lowering his lips to her in a nearly devout kiss, as if sealing a promise or making a vow.

And yet she had the odd notion that what they were

sealing was the moment at hand, that tomorrow was only a dream and, therefore, impossible to reach.

"I'm scared," she said.

"I'm here," he answered.

And without rationality, without thinking about it, his words were enough, his meaning clear. Carolyn knew that the time would come that she would have to consider the empty spaces after his words, the unmade promises.

But tonight...

They stripped each other of clothing that night, a slow, thoughtful shedding. She relished the heat of his bare skin against her knuckles as he unthreaded each button, and the way his roughened, scarred hands brushed against her own inflamed and sensitive body.

As if by mutual agreement, they folded each article of clothing, setting them carefully, solicitously, on either her vanity dresser or draped across the straight-backed chair in the corner of her room.

Undressing seemed to take forever, a slow, unsmiling ceremony that took on the nuances of a ritual or rite. Like dancers in a graceful, mutual parade, they bared their bodies and therefore their very souls to each other. Touching, yet not, seeing clearly what passion and demand had hidden from them the night before.

And when they were both naked, he didn't turn from her to don the latex cloak of protection. He unwrapped it and she sheathed him in it, kneeling before him like a supplicant, a devotee of his sheer masculine beauty, adoring him for thinking of her safety, aching to beg him to disregard the need.

He drew her up and into his arms, pressing against her, not letting her know how much he wanted her, she thought, but rather, to allow himself the opportunity of savoring her wanting of him.

The passion that flared so effortlessly between them rose again, but neither of them stirred. The image of the dancers swept through her mind a second time, but this time it

comprised those still moments when dancers suddenly restrain all movement on stage, limbs frozen as if caught in an endless moment of time, hands touching, bodies together, passion forever trapped in a frieze of undiluted human emotion.

She ached to tell him that she loved him, but she couldn't say the words, afraid they would startle him, make him pull away from that crevasse that surely could be bridged between them. And by the manner in which he cradled her against his body, she knew he was aching, too. For words, perhaps for futures and certainties. And she empathetically understood neither of them would articulate the nebulous, desperate and complex emotions roiling within them.

For Pete it seemed a lifetime had passed since their kiss beside the corral the day before. And it seemed a second lifetime passed in the moment between coming upstairs and now, feeling her satin body pressed to his.

The night before, he'd been caught in a maelstrom of passion, still reeling from the effects of a bashing, afraid for her, and somewhat, of her. Tonight he didn't feel any fears, any uncertainties, except those which were overt... the future, her safety, his unspoken, highly demanding, unvoiced love of her.

Strangely, though his body reacted to her in the purest of animal responses, the lack of tension between them, though fraught with lack of definition, flayed him raw and made him want to bury his face in the soft hollows of her neck and hold her forever.

He'd heard of psychic healers, faith healers, and he'd scoffed at them from the safety of his ringside television seat. He knew now there was something to those seeming charlatans. With one touch, Carolyn had reached inside him to some deeply hidden, darkly buried part of him and, as if by magic, she'd known exactly where to brush a kiss, where to lay a cool, healing hand.

"Come," she said, leaning back, drawing him down to the bed. "Just come to me."

Aroused though he might have been, her request galvanized him, made him utter her name as a groan, an imprecation. Perhaps a plea. He let her guide him and, as much as he might have wanted to create a perfect, lingering impression on her, some rare moment that would last forever in her memory, on her body, he slid into her as if coming home.

Her warmth encased him and her arms slid around him, drawing him closer. Her legs slipped behind his, pressing tightly, pulling him deeper and then deeper still. He plunged his arms beneath her, holding her up from the bed, against his chest, gripping her shoulders with his hands, holding her there, keeping her against him, murmuring her name, forcing her, pleading with her, to feel every nuance of his driving need of her.

The incredible level of emotional intensity thrust him deeper into her, as if by reaching the core of her he would find the core that held her heart, as well. The depth of her. The *soul* of her. She'd said she'd trust him. She'd said she could live with knowing he'd killed someone in his past.

As he arched into her, dipping into that well of molten heat, he prayed that was true. And then thought if that kind of blind, unconditional trust wasn't love, he didn't know another name for it.

As unfair as he'd been to her, in not telling her the truth, or his secondary reasons for hiding out in the desert, he'd clung to her words from the morning like a burn victim would ache for a soothing balm.

And he was burning now. For her.

Only for her.

As her legs hitched higher and her hands lowered to the small of his back, pulling him against her, again and again, deeper and deeper still, he found he could only think of one thing: Carolyn. Loving Carolyn.

Taking Carolyn…to places…neither of them…had known…before.

Faster and harder he plunged into her. Drowning in her.

Dying for want of her. No storm raged outside. But inside a conflagration ignited. Building. Amassing.

"Carolyn..."

Enduring. Rising to fever pitch.

"Carolyn..."

Inflaming him.

And too soon...oh perfect...but too soon, he thought, pleading for more time...he plummeted into her, shuddering, yelling her name, he thought but wasn't sure, digging his hands into her shoulders, dragging her tightly against him to capture him.

To free him.

"Carolyn!" he called again, and she clutched him even more strongly, swallowing his cry with her mouth, taking his oath into her, taking him in an impassioned kiss.

And then her dewy body arched sharply and her head snapped to the right, releasing him, abandoning him, but her fingers pulled him and pulled again. Her hips arced against him and her body heaved in a series of convulsive, shuddering waves. Her teeth were clenched together as if she were in abject pain and he felt her drawing the last of him within her tight embrace.

He felt a near sob of release ripped from him and shuddered as he watched her react to it, a buckling, moaned acceptance. Her breathing was beyond ragged, it was tangled and lost. Her eyes were mere slits, glazed and caught in some other dimension of time and space.

He pressed his lips to her temple and slowly, slowly eased the grip on her shoulders. He bent his head to kiss what surely would be bruised and felt her instinctively tighten around him.

"Don't leave," she said. And though he knew what she meant, he murmured a negative.

Her body continued to spasm around him, but her breathing began to steady, and her heart beneath his own gained a more even rhythm. As she had the night before, her eyes teared and a few rolled free.

"Why tears?" he asked, kissing them away, telling himself he wasn't worried this time, merely curious. And profoundly moved. One day, he vowed, she would laugh instead of cry.

And then he realized what he was thinking...how far his thinking had come.

She didn't answer, merely lifted her arms to enfold him, flexing her elbows at his, jabbing at his muscles, forcing him to press his full weight down upon her.

"I'll hurt you," he murmured, but reveled in the feel of her beneath him absorbing his weight, in the sheer fact that she seemed to relish it.

"Never," she said, echoing his own phrases to her.

God, let her be right, he prayed.

But he knew she was wrong. She might be granting every gift known to humankind...trust, blind faith, acceptance...but she didn't know what kind of man he really was. She didn't know anything at all about him.

Chapter 12

Thunk.

Carolyn sat up. Pete's arm slid down to her thighs.

Thunk. Thunk. *Thunk.*

She cocked her head as if radar equipment had been se-
cretly installed in her body and would allow her to pinpoint
the source of the strange-yet-familiar sound.

Thunk.

She didn't live in the part of the country where shutters
could come loose and bang against the clapboards. Her
blood pressure dropped in sheer recognition of not knowing
exactly what could make that particular sound. She
shivered.

Thunk.

"Pete?"

Her urgent whispering of his name was instinctive.

It had been over a year since a man shared her bed. It
had been her entire lifetime since she'd felt the luxury of
waking someone to help her.

Though he'd been fast asleep only seconds before, seem-

ingly oblivious to the strange noise, she felt him stiffen into wakefulness.

"What is it?" he asked, suddenly and seemingly wholly aware. His arm across her thighs tightened protectively.

Thunk.

"Damn," he muttered, rolling off the bed in a swift, controlled rise. With a fluid, slightly frightening speed, he yanked on his pants, waiting for him on the corner chair. He'd scarcely finished zipping his jeans before he gripped his .45. He crooked his arm upward, elbow tight against his right side, the muzzle of the gun inches from his face and pointing at the ceiling.

"Stay here," he murmured before rounding the bedroom door as if anticipating surprising someone in the hallway.

Thunk.

For a frozen moment, Carolyn stayed put, naked and stunned, doing exactly as Pete had commanded. But suddenly she thought of him facing whatever waited for him downstairs, pictured him facing that nameless something alone, and she sprang from the bed as if catapulted from it.

She flew down the hallway and the stairs, through the silent living and dining rooms and into the lighted kitchen before she so much as considered that naked and unarmed was highly unlikely to be providing Pete any assistance.

She froze on the doorstep, taking in the sight of Pete hunkered down by the back door, head tilted sideways, .45 lax on his leg, doing nothing more dangerous than feeding Ralphette, the barnyard cat.

He glanced up at her. His hair was disheveled and his torso and feet bare. He smiled that lopsided, endearing smile of his. "I forgot to feed her tonight," he said. "She was pulling at the screen door with her paws."

When she didn't say anything, he looked back down at Ralphette. "Poor thing," he said, and stroked the animal.

Carolyn watched a softening transform Pete's face. He was all tough guy—strong, powerful, wholly and utterly

nale, completely and thoroughly in command of a situation—and yet he seemed childlike while dealing with Ralphette.

"Go on up," he said, gesturing toward the stairs. "I'll be right there."

Carolyn didn't move, she could only stare at him.

"Go on," he said. "I've got everything under control."

This was a phrase Craig had used a thousand times, a line he used when nothing had been in control. With a slightly dazed sensation, she realized this man, this stranger from the desert, was speaking nothing but the absolute truth...he *did* have everything under control. Why? Did years in prison hone the senses? Did they make a man focus on what really mattered in life?

She'd helped parolees adapt to life on the outside. Pete made her feel she was the one who needed to learn how to accept life, to take pleasure in the little things like fixing a door, petting a barn cat.

"The Wannamachers somehow believed they could use his property without repercussions," she said. "Craig let them, didn't he? That's what those canceled checks were all about."

Pete's hand stilled on Ralphette's back. "We don't know that for sure."

"We...meaning you and me or 'we' meaning you and someone else?"

He still didn't look at her, and his hand remained motionless on Ralphette's back. "You...me. And an old friend of mine, Alec MacLaine."

Of the MacLaine place. Sammie Jo would be pleased to discover he'd apparently had that couple's permission to camp out on their property.

"Those checks were for two thousand dollars each," she said. "And there seemed to be a ton of them." She tried imagining what an extra two thousand dollars a month would have meant to them in her old life in Dallas. But she failed, because she'd never so much as guessed that

kind of extra money could have been in their lives. Where had Craig spent it, what had he done with it? How could she have lived with him and not known about two extra thousand dollars monthly? How could he have let her clip coupons, pinch pennies, and let her constantly struggle against a seeming tidal wave of bills that so easily engulfed their monthly income.

And if he'd lied about that, kept such a monumental thing from her...what else had he lied about? What other nightmares waited out there for her to stumble across?

"He was leasing the property to them, wasn't he? That's why they think the land is theirs, isn't it?"

When he still didn't answer, she jumped a track and asked him, in a total non sequitur, "When did you find out Craig was involved? Before you came here or after?"

He looked up at that. "After," he said. "Where are you going with this?"

"I need to know," she said.

Pete stared up at the lovely, naked woman standing in the kitchen light. She looked like an angel, he thought, and felt a sharp twinge of longing in his loins. And how could he answer her? Was this to be the moment of truth, a sharing of his past while petting a cat in the middle of the night on a dying ranch in the heart of West Texas?

She sagged against the doorjamb, relief etching every line of her shoulders, her glorious body. "I don't know what I was thinking," she admitted candidly. "I guess was wondering what *else* Craig didn't tell me."

Ralphette meowed and Pete let her back outside. He stayed well out of range of the opened door, and away from the window on the back of the door. This time he latched the screen door before closing the heavier, windowed back door. He threw the dead bolt on the door for a second time that night and the clack sounded oddly final and somehow reassuring.

"I can see why castles used to have moats," Caroly said sleepily.

So could Pete. They had them to keep their women safe inside. He wished they had a moat right now. With a Wannamacher-eating dragon patrolling the waters. He grinned at his own fancy.

"What?"

"I was populating your moat," he said, reaching for her, drawing her chilled, naked form to his torso. He'd thought he couldn't love her more deeply than he had earlier, but found he was wrong. Every time he held her, every kiss she pressed against his chest made his feelings for her swell even more.

She nuzzled his chest with a soft moan, her hands wrapping around his waist. Then, her odd mood jumping to yet another thought, a different plane, she asked, "Were you ever married, Pete?"

"No."

"That's too bad," she murmured.

He smiled against her cheek. "Why's that?"

"You make a woman feel safe."

His arms tightened around her. "I want to keep you safe," he said. He drew a deep breath. "Carolyn...?"

"Mmm?"

"I was in prison for a reason."

Amazing him, she half chuckled. "I should think that was probably a given."

He smiled. "You're right. But it wasn't for the reason you think." When she didn't speak, he continued, "I'm with the FBI, Carolyn. I was in prison on assignment." There. He'd said it. He'd finally told her the truth.

Carolyn had been so prepared to hear something else that his words didn't sink in for a moment and when they did, they made no sense.

"You're with...the FBI," she repeated. She didn't move away from him, but she felt as if she did. She stood within his arms trying to make sense of the past few days, her fears, her doubts...and his lies...and she felt she stood on

the other side of a great chasm, seeing him from miles away.

"I've been with the bureau for fifteen years."

"I see," she lied, feeling the chasm widening. "And prison…?"

"We needed a man inside to gather all sorts of information. Crimes in progress, drug routes, things of that nature."

"And you were that man."

"Yes."

"Ten years?"

"Yes."

"Are there undercover FBI agents in every prison?"

"No. Of course not. But some pens have a higher number of what we call high-yield criminals. See, the bureau always knew an informant on the inside was a dicey customer at best. The information was sketchy, expensive, and too often led to the exposure and subsequent death of the informant."

She just stared at him, as if he were babbling in another language. He explained, "But a man on the inside, a salaried—with hazardous duty bonuses—agent who acted as a prisoner without hope of parole, that person could be invaluable to the bureau, gaining reliable information."

"And you accepted this assignment for ten years?"

Pete's lips twisted in the bitter smile she'd come to know and had so thoroughly misunderstood. "I was thirty-four years old."

"That's a reason?" she asked, staring up at him as if she'd never seen him before this moment.

Pete felt his breath catch in his throat. The look in her eyes frightened him a little because he couldn't read her. He had the feeling he'd just skated onto very thin ice indeed.

"The reason?" she reminded him.

He offered, "My salary was almost quadrupled." It came out as a question.

"You voluntarily went into prison as an informant...for money?" Her tone implied she'd never heard the word before, but suspected it might be a dirty one.

"It was more than that, though I'm not ashamed of that aspect. It was an experimental program. I volunteered for it, Carolyn. It was new. It was unique. I didn't have family like most of the agents. And something about it suited some need in me to understand how criminals really thought, really operated without cops around, without interviews and two-way mirrors."

"And you found out?" she asked.

"In spades," he answered, letting her know by his clenched jaw how much he'd truly discovered.

"And did you gain a lot of information?"

"Yes," he said, remembering finding would-be wife-killer Bill Winslow's wacko journal detailing exactly what he planned to do to his former wife as soon as he was released from prison. The FBI had rushed to Kelsey Winslow's rescue, saving her again from her murdering husband. He'd managed to avert other crimes, other killings.

He couldn't begin to guess what she was thinking, she was so still. "And after a while, I suppose it became habit. It was my job and a life of sorts."

"Did you ever leave the prison...?"

He sighed. "Yeah. They vacationed me to the Seychelles a couple of times. But it felt odd being outside in all that sunshine and water. You get used to life on the inside."

She nodded and he remembered her former profession. "You know the scenario. Pretty soon, I think I didn't feel all that much difference between me and my fellow inmates. Ten years had gone by and I didn't have anywhere else to go, nowhere else to call home."

Carolyn did pull away then and lifted her eyes to meet his questioning gaze. "And the tattoo?"

He held out his arm. "My only protection inside. One of these automatically makes you somebody to stay clear of. Don't pick a fight with that guy—he'll kill you. It

worked. It was a matter of wear the tattoo or fight every man there at some point.'' He gave the ghost of a chuckle, then he seemed to see that she was anything but amused. ''Carolyn—''

''Did you think it was funny to let me believe you'd killed someone?''

The smile was wholly erased from his lips. He paled a little, but when he spoke, his voice was low and steady. ''I did kill someone, Carolyn.''

''What?'' She seemed to be spinning and spiraling in a universe with no gravity. This was all too much information, too fast. And all on the heels of realizing that her husband had lied to her for years.

''It was in self-defense and the guy had murdered four people before he landed in the pen. But I did kill him with my own bare hands. That was it for me. I had to get out. I couldn't see nay difference between them and me any longer.''

His eyes never wavered from hers. She'd been right when she'd wondered what something as dark as taking the life of a fellow human being would do to a soul. It would scar that person forever. She could see the effects of that scarring in Pete's eyes.

''You could have told me all this before,'' she said calmly, but inside she felt an icy wind blowing through her veins, across her heart. How ridiculous she'd been that morning to pour her heart out to him. How foolish to reach the decision that *she* might be able to deal with his past. She hadn't known a tenth of his past.

''You're right,'' he said in that odd way he had of seeming to answer her very thoughts. ''I'm sorry, Carolyn.''

''Why didn't you? Tell me, I mean.''

He had the grace to look away. ''I'm not really sure,'' he said. ''All those years on the inside, I think I really began to feel more like one of them than one of the guys in the white hats. Things like decency and integrity didn't

even have a frame of reference for me anymore. Then I met you..."

"And...?"

"You were everything prison wasn't. You're clean, fresh. Sane. And so damned honest it takes my breath away."

"So it seemed like a good time to lie to me?"

"You needed my help. Mine. I didn't want to be Mr. FBI for a while. Just an ordinary Joe from nowhere. I wanted you to trust me, to have faith in me without a single reason for it other than you just instinctively felt it."

"Why?"

"I don't know, Carolyn. I honestly don't know. But I craved it."

"What you did was unfair, Pete."

"I know," he said, turning to face her. She could see that he did understand that he'd been unfair to her, but she could also tell that he didn't seem to realize how much it hurt her that he'd allowed her to give herself so thoroughly while he'd been lying to her.

"Did you know about the Wannamachers before I asked you to come here?"

He frowned. "What? No. I was out on Alec's place because I needed some space. And because he'd suspected something might be going on out there. When he and Cait bought the place last year, he heard small planes at night. Too many of them. And he put two and two together and hoped he'd come up with forty-four. But now we know he was right."

And for some unknown reason, not from anything in his words or any message on his face, Carolyn was suddenly and embarrassingly aware of her nudity. And realized it was because in the nanosecond between accepting her dawning love for this man and understanding that he'd lied to her, she no longer felt safe. She didn't feel safe at all. She felt adrift on a sea of nuances, lies, and his terribly unfair treatment of her.

"You wanted my unconditional trust," she said, ignoring his last words. "Is that right?"

"Don't hate me for that, Carolyn."

"Hate?" How could he use such a word? But then how could he have lied to her? She shook her head. "But my unconditional trust was what you wanted?"

"Yes."

"But wanting that, you didn't trust me enough to even tell me what you do for a living, that you were in prison on an assignment."

"Carolyn—"

"That flays me to the very quick," she said slowly, carefully, needing him to understand. Really understand. "I can't believe you would let me say those things this morning, make love to me tonight, and all the while you were lying to me."

"I wasn't lying, Carolyn. I just wasn't telling you everything."

"That's splitting hairs and you know it."

He pulled his lips in against his teeth then released them with a small sigh. "What are you really saying, Carolyn?"

"I think I'm telling you to go straight to hell," she said, turning on her bare heel and leaving the kitchen before the threatening storm inside her broke. This would be no mere leaking of a few sad tears, this would be a torrential flood.

"Carolyn!" he called after her, and wrapped his large hand around her arm.

"Don't...touch...me," she said, not looking at him, hurt beyond thought. And yet she wanted to beg him to draw her into his arms and hold her tightly, lovingly, to turn back the clock and tell her the truth from the beginning. Would that have changed things?

He'd *lied* to her.

"Carolyn...please listen," he said, not obeying her stricken command. Instead he tried pivoting her to face him. She averted her face.

"Please. Let me go," she said. She was holding the hurt

ricane within but only by the merest thread. If he didn't let her go now...she would be lost. "Please."

He turned loose of her arms and she fought against sinking to the floor. She managed to get around him and left the kitchen, needing to be away from him for a moment, needing to be dressed, needing to feel safe again.

She wanted to be in Lubbock with her daughters, crying her heart out on Taylor's shoulder. She had to run, to escape, to be away from the ranch where Craig had betrayed her.

And to be away from Pete who had done the same thing.

Tears started to spill from her eyes as she entered her bedroom and saw the tangle of sheets on the bed, the apple cores on the nightstand. Yes, she'd certainly had a taste of knowledge this night and too much knowledge was a tragic and painful thing.

Pete stood in the dim light at the base of the stairs, aching to go up, to follow her, to try to explain the depths of his feelings for her, the confusion that had roiled within him when he first met her.

His involvement with the FBI only took part of the stain of prison life from his soul. The realities of living with a thousand other men—hardened criminals, murderers, rapists, every possible miscreant known to humankind—had left its searing mark on him. Until he held Carolyn in his arms that first time, he'd believed that mark was permanently, indelibly, etched on his heart, as well as carved into his forearm.

He was less the agent than the murderer she believed him to be.

And then she'd kissed him.

And he'd felt hope again.

And now, just when that hope had blossomed to promise, when she'd essentially outlined a possible future for the two of them, accepted him at raw face value as a man she could trust, he'd stolen the dream from both of them. Stolen

it, not because he told the truth, but because he'd told it too late.

Her phone rang and he heard her pick up the extension upstairs and mumble into the receiver. A few moments later she came to the top of the stairs and looked down at him. She was fully dressed, including shoes. But it wasn't the fact that she'd covered her body, hiding it from him, that cut him so. It was her extreme pallor, the bleak, frightened look in her eyes. The evidence of hastily dried tears on her cheeks.

Most of all, it was the stilled, wounded expression of a creature who is sure she will be hurt again.

"Carolyn—"

"That was Bubba Wannamacher," she said flatly. "He asked if I liked their message."

Pete flinched at the dull note in her voice, the flat sound signifying she was being pushed beyond the limits of her endurance. "What else did he say?" he asked gently.

"He said they want use of their property by tomorrow afternoon. That they want us all out of here before then. He seemed to know the girls were already gone. And he knew we'd been loading the trailer. You were right, they were watching us."

Something crossed her face, something causing her to feel despair or pain.

"Did he threaten you?"

"He just said I'd already had one loss in the family, that I'd be wise not to push for a second." She finished on a small sob.

Pete rushed the stairs and was beside her in three bounds. He reached for her but she pulled back, holding her hand up to stop him.

"Don't. Please. I don't think I can take it. I feel too confused. I'm not sure what to think let alone feel."

"I love you, Carolyn," he said, blurting out the second, more important truth, feeling as if the words were torn from him, wrenched from his heart. And praying *this* truth, a far

more vital truth than what he did to earn a living, wasn't too late, too little.

Her eyes lifted to his in swift negation.

"It's true," he said, and knew nothing had ever been more honest, more right.

She shook her head slowly, her eyes filling with tears. "How can you say that to me, Pete? You hid your entire life from me. You *lied* to me." Her tears spilled free and she made no effort to stem them. "You wanted the sun, moon and stars from me and gave me crumbs in return. Crumbs."

The salty waterfall of tears washed her pale face with luminescence. She closed her eyes and tilted her head back a little. The tiny moan that escaped her broke his heart.

"Oh, I never wanted to hurt you, Carolyn. Never."

She drew a ragged breath. "Don't you see? You made me search the very depths of my soul to know if I could be with you honestly and without recrimination for whatever you might have done. You made me question every precept of human nature that I hold dear...when all of that was unnecessary, because you were lying to me. You hadn't killed someone to land in prison, you hadn't gone astray in some horrible way and paid a terrible price. Slowly, agonizingly paying off a debt to society. You were on an *assignment.*"

"Carolyn—"

"The fact that you knew what I was going through, that you *knew* I would feel safe if you'd told me what you did for a living, and you still put me through that...I've been on a roller coaster ride, not knowing what to think, what to do. How could I justify having a murderer around my daughters, and then I'd see you with them and wonder if I was insane for trusting you more than hard cold facts. Damn you, Pete."

"Carolyn. Oh, God, Carolyn—"

"I'm doing as Bubba and Jimmy want. They can have the place. I don't care anymore. Craig rented them his birth-

right, never telling me about letting them use it, never letting me know that if something happened to him, drug dealers would be after us, after his own wife and children. For all I know, Craig was in with them all the way, was part of their circle. Maybe it wasn't an accident that killed him in Dallas, maybe he was murdered because of what was going on here at the ranch.''

''You can't start questioning that, Carolyn. You'll just tear yourself to pieces.''

''I'm already torn to bits,'' she retorted, lowering her head, opening her eyes. ''I've been betrayed by my husband and—''

''Don't say it, Carolyn. Don't even think it. You weren't betrayed by me,'' he said more hotly than he should have, but unable to withstand the sight of her crying, the knowledge of what she was thinking about him.

He felt a fiery lick of anger strike his chest and he wrestled with the urge to tell her she was making too much of his confession, too much of his lack of total honesty. Hell, he'd told her he loved her. He was there for her now. That had to count for something, didn't it?

''What should I think, then, Pete?'' she asked. ''What do you call making someone go down on their knees, bend every rule held sacred in a life, only to tell that person later, it had just been an exercise to see if you could pull it off?''

Her words doused his anger with icy water. Dear God, he hadn't done that to her, had he? In his selfish need for her faith, her trust, by not telling her the truth about himself, he'd made a mockery of the very thing he'd craved.

He reached out for her then, holding her arms lightly.

''Carolyn…please look at me, Carolyn.'' She stood in his grasp without moving, her face turned away from him, her body limp and utterly distanced.

''I'm sorry,'' he said slowly, deeply. ''I'm more sorry for this than I can ever say. I don't have any excuses. The only thing I can tell you is, I never, ever, thought of it that way. Not one single glimmer of such a thought.''

She looked at him dully, then closed her beautiful eyes. Shutting him out. Slamming a door on the future, on them.

Oh, what had he done? What terrible, terrible thing had he done?

Chapter 13

Pete dressed hurriedly, not watching as Carolyn threw items into a suitcase. He couldn't seem to think, couldn't feel. One moment he'd felt more alive than ever before and the next, numb, cold. Lost.

And it was his own doing.

I'm doing as Bubba and Jimmy want. They can have the place. I don't care anymore.

He ground his teeth at the thought. She didn't care anymore because of him. Because he'd lied to her, because he'd made her grapple with issues for no reason at all other than his own desperate—selfish—need for unconditional trust. Because he'd told her the truth too late for it to be anything but damaging.

He'd been right when he'd pictured her hiding her grief and fear from the rest of the world. She'd done exactly that. And suspecting what she was like...*knowing* it, he hadn't told her that he was with the FBI, capable of helping her like no one else, that he had backup help at his disposal merely by dialing the telephone. He'd let her believe him

to be a cold-blooded killer and waited to see if she would still want him.

Sure, he'd told her to call the FBI. Any field office would have found, after some digging around, instructions to patch her call through to Alec. And with his go-ahead she'd have found out the truth about him, that he was the F. Peter Jackson who had staged the big prison rights riot a few years ago. And she'd have found out that he was an inside man for the FBI.

But she hadn't called. And he'd reveled in her not doing so because he'd wanted her—needed her—to rely on him just for himself, as if he really were that murderer she suspected him of being. How sick was that, he thought. No wonder she'd damned him, told him to go to hell. No wonder she'd been so hurt. And no wonder at all that she couldn't so much as look at him now.

She'd given him every vestige of herself and he'd wanted even more. He'd wanted the impossible. And he'd blown his whole universe to the far winds.

He may have just blown every good thing in his life, but he was damned if he'd be a factor in her leaving her home. He was double damned if he'd let a couple of rough-and-tumble thugs and a drug dealer drive her away. Not while he was alive to stop them. That much, at least, he could do for her. Small reparation, perhaps, but one that came from his profession, his training. And one that came from his heart.

She didn't look at him as he moved to the doorway. He hesitated in the threshold, his hand against the doorjamb. "I really am sorry, Carolyn."

She glanced at him, then went back to her packing. "Years ago, when I was still a kid, my mom told me to stop saying 'I'm sorry' over every little thing I did. I was sorry if the sky was cloudy, sorry if the wind was blowing."

"This isn't a little thing," Pete said, feeling the knife blades of her words. He realized there was so much he

didn't know...and so much he'd instinctively known and cast aside.

"No, it's not a little thing. It's a very, very big thing, Pete. It probably sounds ridiculous that I could accept the fact that you might have killed someone and am caviling at a lie...but that lie makes everything we did together seem a lie, too."

"What can I say, Carolyn? How can I fix this?"

She sat down on the edge of the bed, not contemplatively, but as if every nuance of her energy drained suddenly, totally. "Some things can't be fixed, Pete." She looked at him through pools of tears in her blue eyes. "Now I'm sorry."

He had to close his own eyes against the sharp, agonizing pain that ripped through him at her words. He pushed himself from the doorjamb, fighting the rock-hard need to go to her, drag her into his arms and demand that she take the words back, that she understand he'd blundered but that he loved her. Loved her.

He found himself downstairs in the dimly lit living room, staring at the photographs on her wall. Carolyn...Carolyn, he called silently, anguished by the loss he felt, by the raw need for her, sickened by the intensity of the pain rippling through him. Through her.

He whirled away from the photographs, from the smiling faces, and grabbed up the phone receiver. His hands were shaking as he pressed Alec MacLaine's home phone number. He grinned bitterly as he realized it was shortly after five in the morning in Washington.

"This better be really good," Alec growled into the phone by way of hello.

"It's Pete. You got a scrambler handy?"

"Yeah, hang on."

The phone gave the shrill whine of protest that initiating a scrambling device always made.

"All set," Alec said, coming back on.

''The deal's going down anytime after tomorrow afternoon.''

''We're ready for you. You want us in place first or in for the reception afterward?''

''I want these bastards nailed. Being here first might scare them off,'' Pete said. ''They were fairly graphic in their description of what would happen if we called the state troopers.''

''Going in for mop-up is riskier.''

''I know. But it's important to get them all.''

''The widow and kids off the place?''

''The kids are.''

''The lady wouldn't budge?''

''Sort of,'' Pete said. He could still hear the pain in her voice as she said she was giving in to Bubba and Jimmy's demands.

''Are you having trouble with her?''

That was the understatement of the century, Pete thought, but added another lie to his seemingly endless string. ''Nothing I can't handle.''

''It'd be better if she were gone,'' Alec said, not knowing that she already was, in the only way that really counted.

''Who will I be contacting?'' Pete asked.

''Our guy in Lubbock is Tom Adams. He's a good agent. Tough. Clean. Bit of a wild card. He'll be working with a Texas Ranger. Steve Kessler. Adams says he's one of the best in the business.''

''Good enough. And fliers?''

''Four helicopters from Cannon Air Force Base over in Clovis, New Mexico. They're fueled up and ready to go. They promise they can be on-site in less than thirty minutes from your call to Adams and Kessler. And they'll each be carrying five of our boys. That ought to be enough to round up a few desert rats.''

''Good work, MacLaine.''

''By the way, I checked out your Canadian connection.

The firm exists, all right, Canadian Chemical Concerns. And it's legit. Up to a point.''

"Up to the point of what's going on in the basement chem labs?"

"You got it. If this deal really does go down, and we manage to nab them at your end, your discovery of those canceled checks is going to put the capper on the case. We'll be able to nail down the lid on Canadian Chemical.''

"Any word on who my Canadian friend might be?"

"We've got him narrowed down to two possibilities: Eric Thorteneaux or a runner by the name of Chet Dubois. Both of them hang out in Santa Fe during the winter months. Play the jet-set, trust-fund-baby routine. Thorteneaux usually runs the western distribution and Dubois makes the eastern connections. They've been tagged for a long time, but we wanted the drop location.''

"I think you've got it.''

"And the source, if we're lucky. Ditto on the good work, Jackson.''

Yeah, he'd done some really good work around the Leary place, he thought. He'd managed to break Carolyn's heart and his own in the process. He should get a medal or two for that.

And yet, he recognized that making arrangements for a raid on the men who had been hassling her made him feel as if some of the numbness could be alleviated from his body. The need for action, for resolution, steadied him somewhat.

"What are you going to do about the widow?" Alec asked. Pete found he didn't care for the tag. Carolyn epitomized beauty, grace...love.

"I'm going to keep her with me," he said. An hour ago he'd hoped that might be forever.

"Can she shoot?"

"The broad side of the barn," Pete said, remembering the hole in the barn, the first time he'd wrapped his arm around her. Only a few days ago, he thought, recalling how

nervous he'd been to touch her, how skittish she'd been when he had.

Alec chuckled. "Well, just make sure she doesn't shoot you."

"Oh, she wants to right about now."

"Those years in prison make you rusty in the charm department?"

"Hell, I was never any good at charm. I always manage to stick my foot in it," Pete said, unaware he had an audience.

Carolyn leaned against the stairwell and listened unabashedly. This was her property, after all. Her crisis. Her trouble. Even if he'd come into it at her request, gotten beaten as a rough message to her, even if he'd made her feel she'd gone to heaven and back. Even if he'd lied to her.

Since she could only hear Pete's side of the conversation, she had to imagine the other caller's phrases. But she was able to make some fairly good guesses as to the content of the other side of the conversation.

Pete chuckled, ruefully, Carolyn thought. "Can you do me another favor, Alec? We sent Carolyn's daughters with her sister-in-law and her kids to Lubbock for a few days. They're staying at the Holiday Inn there...no, I don't know if there's more than one...yeah. Right. Around-the-clock, okay?... Thanks, I owe you...yeah. Little, eight and ten. Just buttons...no, she's a widow, too. State trooper in the line of duty...yeah, she's okay...let me know, all right?"

Carolyn closed her eyes. Knowing that Pete was apparently arranging for around-the-clock protection for her daughters and the rest of her family took some of the chill from her heart. And he was obviously setting up some scheme whereby they could catch Bubba, Jimmy and the mysterious Canadian fellow in the proverbial act of distributing drugs.

She'd told him she didn't care anymore. Hearing him

rallying his army on her behalf made her feel as if she'd said the words only to hurt him. And perhaps that was true. She'd been so hurt herself that staying on the ranch was a matter of supreme indifference. At that moment.

At this moment, hearing him making arrangements with another agent—*FBI*, she thought incredulously—she wondered how she could even have considered departing, walking away from her home, her ranch. And for the first time since she'd moved in, she felt it *was* hers. Not Craig's, not Craig's daddy's. It was hers. The Leary place, a small farm-ranch peopled with the next generation of Learys.

And, only this morning, she'd considered, with Pete.

"Okay then. Cross your fingers...oh, and kiss Cait for me, will you?" Pete fell silent, listening for a while, then chuckled aloud. Carolyn felt an irrational stab of jealousy. Who was Cait?

"You think so? I'd say that's about as remote a possibility as finding little green men on Mars." He chuckled again. And the laugh wasn't rueful this time, it was rough and bitter. "I'll let you know if it ever happens."

Pete hung up the phone without saying goodbye and turned. Carolyn hadn't meant him to find her eavesdropping, but he'd rung off so abruptly, she'd been caught at the impolite observance.

The smile faded from his lips. "Are you all right?" he asked.

She knew the question went far deeper than the words implied. She tried telling herself that he wasn't a stranger, that the truth he'd withheld hadn't turned him into another man, that he was same man who had held her in his arms, had loved her with such incredible passion, that he was still Pete Jackson. The man who worried about her, her feelings, her emotions, her needs.

He was also the man who had deliberately let her believe he was a cold-blooded killer. A man who had lied to her.

"Fine," she lied back. "I'm just fine."

"Did you hear everything?"

"No," she said, meaning she couldn't possibly have heard it all.

"I was checking in with Alec," he said. His voice was low, more clipped than usual, as if he were desperately holding a tight rein on his words. "We've set up a raid for tomorrow night. Let's just hope it's scheduled for then and not four days from now. I'll be the one signaling them in."

"What kind of a signal?" Carolyn asked, picturing lights flashing across a vast distance. "Two if by air, one if by desert?"

He gave her a surmising, appraising look, as if trying to guess if she was being sarcastic or merely attempting to lighten the tension between them. Maybe she *was* trying to diffuse the situation, set her pain aside until the bad guys were caught and the crisis was over. He made that possibility seem real.

"Good idea...but I was thinking more in the lines of using your cellular telephone," the FBI agent said prosaically and then grinned crookedly at her. Apology and regret were inherent in every line of his face, in the steady regard of his eyes.

She shook her head, fighting the wave of sympathy that threatened her. She forced herself to say lightly, "How disappointing."

"But we'll get to sit up on the roof of the barn," he said, as if offering a rare treat. *Laugh with me,* he seemed to be saying. *Tell me it's okay.*

She couldn't. She felt too raw, too hurt by his lie. "Not my barn, we won't," she said. "We'd fall through."

"That bad?"

"Wasn't the floor wet today?"

"Soaked."

"You have to be up high so you can see all around?"

"Yes."

"There's the top of the roof...or the rise out where the girls first found you."

He flinched, as though she'd said something hurtful. Be-

cause that was the time to have told her the truth...that first night, that first meeting?

He shrugged, and the cut at the side of his mouth made him look as though he were grinning. "The roof of the house would be perfect."

She remembered how they'd exchanged the word "perfect" in the aftermath of passion and was stung by the gulf that stretched between them now. Then, he'd had his arms wrapped around her, mumbling in half sleep, pressing a kiss to her temple. Now he stood clear across the room, a solid, strong presence miles and miles away from her.

Dawn was still three hours in the future and she knew both of them should be nearly falling asleep where they stood, but they were wide-awake, fully clothed, and any kind of intimacy seemed utterly impossible, from simple conversation to sharing a cup of coffee together. How on earth was she to get through the next twenty-four hours in his company?

As if aware of her confusion, Pete stuck to talking about his plans for them. "I think it would be best if we make a grand show of leaving the place tomorrow afternoon. This afternoon I mean. I'll call our guy in Lubbock when it's light. Maybe he can show up here as if he's buying or just hauling Bratwurst for you."

"How do we get back here ourselves?" she asked.

He made a scissored walking motion with his fingers.

"Won't they see us?"

"My hope is that they'll watch us pull out, dust their hands and figure they're home free."

"That's a pretty big gamble," she said. She remembered saying exactly those words to Craig on multiple occasions.

"It's the only one we have at the moment," he said, unknowingly echoing Craig's standard response.

Taylor had said Pete reminded her of Craig. The kids had said the same thing. Was Pete more like Craig than she'd allowed herself to believe?

No. Some things, maybe. Height. General build. Sammie

Jo's cute buns. *And the lies.* But Craig had lied to her about their life together, *her* life, their future. Pete had lied to her about *his* life.

His *past.* His present. Wasn't that different?

Who was splitting hairs now? she asked herself.

Everything went as planned once daylight arrived. Getting to the dawn, in the strained, tense silences between them now, had seemed pure agony. And surviving the tension in the clear, cool light of the first March day seemed impossible.

Pete was on the phone a great deal during the early morning hours, making sure the arrangements they'd planned in the night were likely to come off. Carolyn paced the floor, wishing he'd let her have a crack at the phone; she was worried about Jenny and Shawna, and knew that Taylor couldn't have gotten through this morning as they'd contrived because the phone had been tied up the entire time and on the rural telephone system, such conveniences as call waiting didn't exist.

But if anything were wrong with the girls, Pete would already have known about it through his contacts.

Incredibly, she managed to doze off sometime between Pete's carefully phrased phone call with Tom Adams and his cautious shaking of her shoulder two hours later.

"Mmm?" She rolled over, her arm brushing against his thigh. "What is it?" she asked then, startled into wakefulness.

He gave her a gentle, reassuring smile that quickly faded from his bruised features. "Everything's all right," he said. "I think we'd better be seen doing some last-minute loading."

At something he must have seen on her face, some lingering hurt, a lot of confused longing, he asked, "Are you going to forgive me, Carolyn?"

"Yes," she said.

"Forgiven but not forgotten?"

She had to lower her eyes. How could she forget? And yet, just the feel of his hand on her shoulder caused a flash fire through her body.

They made a terrific show of hauling a few last boxes to the horse trailer. Pete led Bratwurst out of the barn and tethered him to one of the corral fence posts, as if the horse were waiting to be carted away.

Carolyn fed Ralphette, but made it appear she'd gone to the barn for a few last items to load into the trailer. She and Pete passed each other in the still-muddy driveway and she felt the hurt tension flaring between them.

A single phrase was all it would take to douse the painful raging fires, she thought, but she couldn't utter it. That it caused her as much pain as it was obviously causing him didn't make it any easier to pass by him without reaching out, touching him, forgiving him, accepting whatever motivations prompted him to lie to her.

She wasn't so inflexible as to believe that a lie could never be condoned, forgiven and therefore, eventually forgotten. But he'd known from the beginning what trouble she faced…how much simpler it would have been to have just told her he was with the FBI. Simpler and kinder.

And it was the kindness issue that kept her from stretching her hand across that seemingly endless chasm. That and his amazing selfishness. Unconditional trust, my foot, she thought. Except maybe mother love, nothing was unconditional.

But she felt the lack of his encouraging smiles, his uplifting crooked grins. Yesterday the hard work had flown by in an almost lighthearted camaraderie. Today, the minutes dragged by, the tension increasing with each glance in his direction.

Shortly after four o'clock, a white half-ton pickup and horse trailer pulled into the driveway. The driver honked the horn twice, making Carolyn's heart jolt.

She went with Pete to greet the "horse traders." Standing so close to him, matching his stride as they walke

across the driveway, she ached to slip her hand in his and hurt all the more because she couldn't bring herself to do so.

"Tom Adams," the driver said, holding out his hand after hopping down from the cab. "And this here's Steve Kessler."

Carolyn didn't know what an FBI agent—aside from Pete—should look like, but she didn't think Tom Adams was it. He was only slightly taller than she, roughly five-eleven, maybe six feet in height, and so broad shouldered he looked like an inverted pyramid. His hair was jet black and his eyes a warm brown. He was dressed like any normal cowboy from the Almost area, dusty boots, brightly colored but slightly worn shirt, stained felt cowboy hat.

Steve Kessler, the Texas Ranger, looked more the part, except for the broad, open grin. He was also dressed cowboy fashion, but sported a baseball cap and tennis shoes instead of hat and boots. He was nearly Pete's height.

"Been thinking about your plan, Pete," Adams said. "Mind if we make a couple of changes?"

The changes entailed loading Bratwurst in their trailer, taking him down the road quite a ways and turning him loose. "He'll come on back to the barn—"

Pete looked a question at Carolyn and she nodded, smiling.

Adams grinned. "Meantime, you all will drive on out of here, making a good display of it. You'll drive on down the road a piece, till you catch up with us. You'll pull up alongside of us, like as if to ask us what the problem is. You all will hop in our horse trailer, and Steve'll get in your rig and drive it on out, in case anyone's watching down the road. I think we can make it look right enough. Any rate, I'll mosey on back here and swear and curse and load up your horse while you two nip on in the house. Work for you, pardner?" Adams said.

Pete grinned. "Like a charm."

Adams tipped his hat at Carolyn and he and Kessler loaded a much protesting Bratwurst into the trailer.

Adams turned to shake Carolyn's hand before departing. "Your horse played his part right well. If we're watched, won't be no one surprised if that horse is kicking up a ruckus fit to beat the band. Now if you two can do the same, I think we'll have us a little party going on."

He and Kessler jumped up into the cab of the half-ton and moments later were gone from sight.

"Show time," Pete said quietly.

Carolyn's heart was already pounding faster. But part of the reason was that he was looking at her as if he meant something else altogether. His eyes were lit with a sorrow-filled tenderness.

"You already put whatever you wanted upstairs, didn't you? Anything else you think of, go ahead and leave in the girls' bedroom. That's the best access to the roof. Be sure to throw in some food. I'm already starving. And, whatever you do, don't forget the cell phone and a flashlight."

"Roger," she said, turning for the house.

"Carolyn," he called, stopping her. "I feel it," he said.

"What?" she croaked.

"That we're going to get them tonight. That you won't have to worry about those guys anymore."

Strangely, the Wannamachers were the least of her real worries.

Less than fifteen minutes later, Carolyn carried an empty suitcase—her packed ones still lay on her bed—and loaded it into the Ranger. Pete hauled a couple of things out from the bunkhouse, making the illusion complete.

They got into the car with Carolyn at the wheel. She gave her house a long, lingering look before putting the car in gear.

"We're not even positive they're watching," Pete said. "And if they are, I don't think they can see clearly enough to catch the expression on your face."

"I wasn't acting," Carolyn said, driving forward. "It's

funny, but I didn't even know I liked the place until I was getting ready to leave it. Acting out or not, it still bothers me.''

Pete let the silence gather between them again, though he wanted to talk to her, longed to do so. Carolyn Leary was a remarkable woman, he thought. Courageous, strong. Determined. As filled with integrity and grit as an artesian well.

He'd told himself he loved her, had even blurted out the words to her. But he'd played the fool. He should have met her with half the honesty and decency that she'd shown him. From the first moment she met him, she'd been nothing less than utterly direct, incredibly straightforward.

Was his excuse that he'd lived a lie for ten years and didn't even remember how to go about telling the truth? No. He had no excuse. He'd simply and horribly ignored one of the things he loved about Carolyn the most: her innate character. She'd been right to be angry with him, doubly right to be hurt by his lie. That's the way people should feel when lied to, he thought. That's the way people should feel when hurt by the lie.

He might not be able to have Carolyn and the bright promise that had dangled so briefly before his eyes, but he could help secure her future, save her ranch for her. That suddenly seemed such a very small thing.

Adams and Kessler had already released Bratwurst by the time Carolyn pulled alongside their pickup and trailer. Adams came to Carolyn's door. "Now I'm going to keep on standing here, leaning on your window, chatting like I'm doing now." He turned and pointed across the field toward her place. She followed his gesture and realized it was only for show.

He turned back around. "And you're going to slide on out the other side and you and that big fellow with you are going to slip in the side door of the horse trailer. You with me?"

"With you," Carolyn said, almost foiling the entire plan by pocketing the keys. She gave a nervous laugh and poked them back into the ignition.

"You're doing fine, now, little lady. You just scoot on across now. Pete, we're going stay real close now, so you don't hesitate a second to send up the balloon. We've got binoculars and a pair of night visions, so we'll be watching, too. You remember the cell number, don't you? Just don't let your guard down. It's a cinch they're going to make an appearance at her house sometime tonight, otherwise they wouldn't have gone to such trouble to clear you all out of there."

While he was talking, Pete was guiding her across the seat and out the passenger door. She could still hear Adams's voice clearly as they crossed the narrow separation between the vehicles and climbed into the horse trailer, taking care to stay well below the roof of the Ranger.

"It's not too late to just keep going," Adams said. "We can take it from here."

"No," Carolyn said firmly. "I want to be there. It's my home. My life."

Once the side door was closed, she leaned her forehead against the side of the trailer. "Think we did okay?" she asked.

"You were perfect," Pete said, dropping his hand to her shoulder.

She couldn't help it, she stiffened. He pulled his hand back as if she'd slapped him. But he was wrong; she hadn't tensed out of any sense of rejection of him. She had straightened because at that moment, she'd had to fight the urge not to melt into him, had to war with the need to feel his strong arms around her, his warm breath playing against her temple as he assured her that everything would be all right.

Through the slatted window, she saw her own vehicle drive away and proceed down the road that would eventually take Kessler through Almost. She felt disconcerted

watching her only means of transportation in the world—except for Bratwurst—disappearing down the road.

Tom Adams pitched a split fit outside the horse trailer, swearing, kicking the side of the trailer and shaking his fist first in the direction of her departing Ranger, then in the direction of her ranch.

Pete chuckled. "This guy missed his calling. He should be on the stage."

"You FBI types seem to have a variety of interesting talents," she said. The second she said it she knew he'd misunderstood her. Hurt flashed in his eyes and changed them from gray to a searing blue.

That was the trouble with the first lie, she thought. It had a domino effect of creating misunderstandings, hurts and stings. "I didn't mean anything hurtful by that crack," she said steadily, meeting his gaze directly.

The rig lurched forward then, pitching her into his arms. "What did you mean?" Pete asked, catching her easily, holding her tightly against him. She tried pulling away, but he wouldn't let her go. And it felt so good to be there.

"Mending fences, fixing screen doors...doing Shawna's math homework for her. That's what I meant."

He actually blushed and she had to look away to keep from kissing him. But she couldn't resist just resting her head against his broad shoulder for a brief moment. It simply felt too right to deny herself this one small boon.

All too soon they were back at the ranch. Adams pulled the trailer as close as he could to the house, so that the trailer itself would serve as a wall to whoever might be watching.

Pete held her a second longer, then let her go. He opened the side door cautiously and slipped through it. He held back a hand for Carolyn. For a split second, she only stared at the broad palm. The expanse between the horse trailer and the back door of her house seemed endless and fraught with danger.

But the distance between her hand and his seemed immeasurable and the dangers too great to fathom.

Then she slipped her fingers against his warm skin and sighed as he enfolded her hand.

"Come," he said.

She shivered and stepped down from the trailer into his waiting arms.

"I'm here with you," he said softly.

Still holding her hand, he wrapped his other arm around her shoulders and pulled her against him as he led her to the house.

"Just stay beside me," he said.

Didn't he understand that was all she'd ever really wanted to do?

Chapter 14

Climbing out Jenny and Shawna's window and onto her roof wasn't as easy as Pete had made it sound earlier. The overhang was narrow at that point and probably rotted underneath. And the roof itself, some six feet beyond the overhang, pitched at a thirty-five-degree angle perpendicular to the window.

"The plan was that I come out on the roof, not you," Pete said from his position on the overhang.

"I distinctly heard the word 'we' when you posed the plan," she said tartly, and found she'd said it just to see that grin of his.

The cut on the side of his lip, healing swiftly, made his grin look permanently gamin, as if he were on the verge of cracking a joke. For all his silences, for his moods, even for his lies, she'd come to expect a measure of earthy humor in Pete. Smiling came more naturally to him than frowning. That, like so many other of his attributes, was a good thing, she thought suddenly.

"What are you thinking?" he asked, his grin fading a little, his eyes silver gray in the waning light.

"I don't know," she said, but she was lying now. She was thinking that his bruises, fading to that sickly yellow purple, stood out like badges of honor on his face. She'd seen Tom Adams taking in the evidence of Pete's beating and had also witnessed the exchange of glances between Adams and Kessler. There seemed to be an unwritten code among the three men not to speak of the battering Pete had taken on her account.

Somehow she didn't want him going out on that roof without knowing that internal bruising, a hurt to the heart could heal as well. The one he'd dealt her, the devastating one she'd aimed at him.

But she didn't know how to form the words to bridge the gap between them. How did she go about applying a curative to blows to the heart? Was such a thing even possible?

He reached through the window, cupping her face in his large hand. "It's all right," he said softly. "You stay here."

"No," she said, shaking free of his hand and stepping over the windowsill. She felt a pang of embarrassment at seeing their handprints in the thick layer of West Texas dust.

"I really do clean once in a while," she said.

Pete glanced down at the handprints. "Is this some of that soil that Taylor said is on its way to Arkansas?"

Carolyn nodded. "Good thing they think we're gone," she said. "If they saw those handprints, they'd know exactly where we are."

"I don't think there's much worry about that."

Pete led the way down the overhang to the point it disappeared beneath the sharply pitched roof. Grunting, he hitched his body up and over onto the old wood shingles before holding down his hands to help her up. Then they wriggled up the shingles on the upward slant of the back

ide of her house. From that position they could lie against
he sun-warmed and worn shingles and peek over the sag-
ing center point of her roof.

Carolyn's heart was racing, not so much from fear of a
rug deal going down soon, but of the old roof and the
heer, dizzying height. It was a long, long way down to the
tterly ungiving ground.

"I don't think we'll miss much from up here," he said,
ooking through a large pair of binoculars Adams had given
im earlier.

Carolyn wanted to tell him she was missing too much
lready.

He touched her arm and a frisson of reaction coursed
rough her. His merest touch could transport her, she
ought, creating a chain reaction within her. Like the dom-
o effect of hurts causing more hurts, his single touch
arked a series of fires inside her.

Despite their amazing position on the roof of her house,
e ancient wood shingles digging into her, Carolyn closed
er eyes and absorbed the strange peace. She could hear
ete's slow, steady breathing, the whisper of the tall grasses
oving to the rhythm of the late afternoon breeze, a horned
rk calling a warning to his mate. In the sharp quiet, she
uld even hear Ralphette's kittens mewling way off in the
arn.

The horned lark called again, then was quiet. Ralphette's
ttens fell silent as their mother apparently rejoined them.
ete's breathing hitched.

"Damn," he said.

"What?" she asked, feeling her heart jolt at the sudden
nsion in his voice. Her eyes flew open. "What's wrong?"

"Somebody's coming."

"Who?"

Pete didn't answer for several seconds. "Red-and-white
alf-ton pickup."

"Wannamachers," she breathed, ducking down and roll-
g to her side, nearer to Pete, her heart pounding so loudly

she was sure he could hear it, that *they* would hear it whe
they arrived.

"Don't move at all," he whispered, inching down besid
her. "They're getting out of the truck."

"Why would they come here?"

"The drop site must be closer to your house than w
guessed. Or else they're coming to make sure you reall
got out."

"They'll see everything in the house is still there."

"They'll see a chaotic mess. And the doors are locked."

"What if Craig gave them the keys?"

"Sh-h-h," he said, pressing a finger against her lips.
was warm and callused and, for some odd reason, feelin
it made tears spring to her eyes.

"We're safe here," he said, and brushed his finger alon
her cheek. "Perfectly safe."

She smiled tremulously. That's what she'd been missin
since the night before, that sense of safety, that securit
she'd felt around him before.

The cellular phone gave a bleat and Pete nearly threw
from the rooftop as he grabbed it up. He listened for a fe
seconds. "We know," he whispered. "We're literally rigl
on top of them."

He depressed the switch and set the phone to "ring
off." "Damn," he said. "I about had a heart attack."

Carolyn rolled from her side to her back, hysteria wellin
up in her. She pressed her hands over her mouth to kee
from giggling aloud. There was nothing funny at all abo
the situation but the expression on his face and the wa
he'd juggled the phone tickled her in too many ways.

A loud bang from down on the ground drove all hum¢
from her. She was glad she'd already covered her mout
for at the thunderous crash, she would have cried out. Sl
looked a question at Pete. He shrugged slightly, frownin

Then she recognized the sound. Someone below ha
thrown open the cellar door. It rested at a slant to tl
ground, stairs leading down into a dirt-floored root cell

r tornado safety zone. And the fold-out door had a tin
aceplate that sounded like Thor striking the sky whenever
was pitched over onto its cement rests.

"Cellar," she breathed. "They're in the cellar."

"Can they get into the house from there?"

"Yes. But I think the door's locked."

"Must stash something there. Maybe their own private
ache."

Sure enough, a few minutes later, the pickup started
gain and they could both see the packages jouncing in the
ack as Bubba or Jimmy drove the half-ton out of the drive-
ay and onto the road leading toward town.

Pete switched on the telephone and called Adams.
Coming your way with something in the back of the
ckup. They took it from the cellar...no, can't see the en-
ance from here...we're fine. We'll just sit tight."

In his unusual fashion, Pete depressed the Off button
ithout a farewell. Was that an Eastern thing? Carolyn
ondered. A prison thing...an FBI trait? She didn't know,
at she did know it seemed suddenly very important to find
t. There were a whole host of things she had a burning
sire to know about him. His favorite foods, drink, all the
tle habits that made up a person.

She closed her eyes again, feeling a wave of serenity
veeping through her. When this was all over, when they
ere off the roof and the Wannamachers and their Cana-
an friend safely locked up, she would tell him how she
lt about him. Let him know that she past the place
hurt. She'd been able to stomach the idea of his being
killer but had flown into total despair when she discov-
ed he was respectable? What possible sense did that
ake?

What had hurt her so deeply was that he'd withheld the
ath from her. Lied to her. Made her feel foolish and
trayed.

She'd only been hurt...not completely destroyed. To
alk away from Pete would do that to her.

She listened to the renewed calling of the horned lark and heard the countermelody of a nighthawk. And the tele phone ringing inside her house. She stiffened, knowing in stinctively who was calling.

"Oh, my God, it's Taylor," she said.

"What?"

"Taylor. Remember? She said she'd try us morning an night and if we didn't answer either time, she was sendin out the troopers. She'll do it, too. She couldn't get throug this morning. And now...tonight the phone's just ringing She'll keep calling until I answer—or she'll call Doug' friends.

It'll ruin everything."

"Damn," Pete said, inching down the shingles. H would have to roll over her to get there.

"No, I'll go," she said. "You stay here and b watchdog."

He looked as if he would argue, but apparently saw th logic in her argument, and since she was closer to the win dow and because she was already halfway there, he nodde and lifted the binoculars to his eyes. "Just tell her we'r fine and get back up here ASAP."

She felt like giggling again as she crossed the windo ledge and ran for the stairs. Her realization that she didn want to live without Pete, that a hurt could be mended b simply accepting it and letting it go, that her troubles wer all likely to be over that night, forever, filled her veins wit effervescence, made her step light and easy. She grabbe up the phone.

"Taylor?"

There was a pause, then, "Wrong," a male voic drawled. "Guess again, Miz Leary."

Numb as she felt at that second, a different voice speak ing directly behind her made her jump and pitch the pho ne's receiver to the floor.

"You! How'd you get back here? We watched yo leave. Damn. Dubois's gonna pitch a hissy."

"Bubba," Carolyn breathed.

"You should have listened to us," he said, shaking his head and drawing a .45 from his belt. "You just can't tell some folks nothing."

He strolled toward her, leveling the gun at her chest.

Pete counted the seconds Carolyn had been gone. When he'd reached a full minute and a half's worth, he laid the binoculars aside and wrestled with the need to go check on her.

She could have felt the call of nature, he told himself. Taylor might have told her that something had happened to one of the girls—his stomach knotted at the thought— or she might have tripped going down the stairs.

Or, he thought, suddenly realizing that there had only been a single crash of the cellar door. The Wannamachers hadn't closed it. Maybe one of them had stayed behind.

Carolyn might be taking so long because there might have been someone waiting for her in the house. Just because the Wannamachers employed poor grammar and spoke in West Texas drawls didn't mean they were at all stupid.

He was already inching toward Jenny and Shawna's window when he heard the voice.

"Now where could he be?"

Bubba Wannamacher, Pete thought, somehow knowing which brother was inside Carolyn's house. Funny, he couldn't tell Jenny or Shawna's voices apart, but he could a Wannamacher.

Bubba called loudly, in a singsong voice, "Come out, come out wherever you are...or the little lady gets it."

He heard Carolyn give a bitten cry and his jaw clenched. He'd let her walk right into them.

"He's not here!" Carolyn said. Her voice was loud and strong. And Pete knew they were in Jenny and Shawna's bedroom.

And he remembered the clearly defined handprints on the windowsill. His and hers matching prints.

"He left!" Carolyn said. Her voice was so clear, she sounded as if she were right beside the window. There was no way Pete could scramble off the roof without making noise and no way that noise wouldn't alert Bubba.

He knew Carolyn was trying to buy time, talking loudly so that Pete would be alerted to Bubba's presence.

His fists clenched as he heard Bubba threaten Carolyn again. "I really will do something to the little lady. And you know I can do it, too," Bubba called out.

Because the window stood open and the house was so poorly insulated, Pete could hear Bubba dragging Carolyn across the hall to her bedroom. He slithered down the shingles, tensing himself, preparing to swing down to the overhang.

He paused as he heard Bubba's voice, louder now, apparently still in the hallway, not all the way into Carolyn's bedroom.

"Well, well, what have we here? Two apple cores. Two suitcases. Why, Miz Leary, sleeping with the hired hand? When you coulda had fun with me all along."

It was all Pete could do not to swing down from the roof when he heard Carolyn's disgusted protest.

"Now where is he?" Bubba asked, his voice getting louder again as he moved back into Jenny and Shawna's bedroom.

"He left!" Carolyn called. "He...he was afraid."

"You know something, Miz Leary...or since we're getting to be such good friends, can I call you Carolyn?... don't think that hired hand of yourn is all that skittish. Fact is, if we hadn't held a gun on him the other night, I think he'd a took us all three on."

"I tell you, Bubba, he left. He took the Ranger. You don't see it anywhere, do you?" she demanded.

Nearly overriding his fear for her—and his anger at whichever Wannamacher was holding her—was admiration

for Carolyn. She must be terrified and yet she was still trying to cover for him, give him time to help or get it there.

"Now, why do you suppose that window's open?" Wannamacher asked.

"Airing out the room from your smell!" Carolyn snapped, then gave a sharp cry.

Pete inched down the roofline, trying not to make a sound. He wouldn't be able to help her if Wannamacher met him at the windowsill with a gun. And he sure couldn't help her if he fell off the damned roof by moving too fast.

But when Bubba said, "You know what? Let's just see what you look like under all these clothes," Pete felt Carolyn's cry to his soul. He couldn't hold back a second longer. He didn't inch down onto the overhang, he flung himself down, catching the rotting trim in one hand and grabbing for the window ledge with the other.

The trim gave way with a sick groan and the screech of pulled nails.

For a moment he hung in midair some thirty feet above the ground, swinging in front of the window, seeing Bubba Wannamacher digging at Carolyn's clothing, bending her back against Shawna's desk.

The stark horror of what he saw saved him, spurring him into a swinging kick that jettisoned him through the window with an avenging force and an appalling clatter of broken glass and shattered wood. He was on Bubba before the man had even turned to see what the noise was.

"What the—?" Bubba cried out as he went down.

"Pete!" Carolyn called as she was also flung to the floor. She skidded wildly for a moment and came up against Jenny's bed.

Pete took all this in with one part of his mind while the other focused on making certain Bubba Wannamacher would never touch Carolyn again. Over and over again his splinter-laden hand pummeled Bubba's face.

"Pete," he heard Carolyn calling as if from miles away.

"Pete, stop! Pete, it's okay, Pete." But she was too far away and he was too violently snared by the tremendous anger that held sway in him.

"Don't, Pete...we don't need this between us." He felt her digging at his shoulders. Trying to hold him back. "Pete!"

His fist slowed and his hand at Bubba's throat loosened its grip a notch, then another.

"Pete, I was wrong to shut you out like that. I was hurt, I was angry. But that didn't change my feelings for you. Nothing could change that."

"What—?" he panted, afraid to look at her, afraid he was delirious, dreaming this somehow. He stared into Bubba Wannamacher's bloodied face, took in the fact that the man was nearly unconscious. He dropped his own bleeding hand to his thigh.

"I love you, Pete," she said. Softly. Steadily.

And then he felt her hand gentle on his shoulder, stroking him now, soothing him. No longer afraid for him, possibly of him.

"I love you, Pete."

He closed his eyes, surprised to be feeling pain instead of joy at her words. Then he realized it was the pain of intense, staggeringly profound relief.

"I thought..." he murmured. "Oh, God, I thought I'd blown it all." He was still gasping for air. "Everything that mattered to me...I thought I killed it because I lied...to you."

Her hand squeezed his shoulder and he felt her kneel behind him. "For a minute, I thought so, too," she admitted, laying her head against his back. "We're too new. We don't have the stuff between us yet that could glue us back together."

"Do we now?" he asked, feeling like a little kid alone in the dark, seeing a flashlight coming his way: scared to death and hopeful at the same time. "Do we, Carolyn?"

"Yes," she said simply. "Because we want to love each

other. We want each other. Yes. I really think we'll be okay.''

Pete blinked his eyes against the tears that threatened to fall free. He looked at Bubba Wannamacher's battered face and up at Jenny and Shawna's poster-studded ceiling.

''Let's call in the troops,'' he said. ''I'm about ready to call it a day.''

''Yeah,'' she agreed, not moving. ''And we better hurry. I think Jimmy's on his way back. It was him on the phone, not Taylor.''

''And I'd rather be holding you than Bubba,'' he said, and felt his first true grin in almost twenty-four hours as she chuckled against him.

''That makes two of us,'' she said.

She rose first, holding out a hand to help him up. He unstraddled the heavyset and thoroughly subdued thug and stiffly pushed to his feet, one of his hands wrapped around hers, the other grasping Bubba's .45 automatic. He swayed for a moment as he stood and found he was more than half-afraid to meet her eyes, afraid of seeing she hadn't really meant her words.

He thought of her courage, her strength, the way she'd been pawed by Bubba, and shifted his gaze to find her waiting for him. And the love she felt for him blazed in her blue eyes, a luminescent, liquid fire, quenching a thirst that had raged in him all his life.

He dragged her to his chest and held her close against him, breathing in the scent of her hair, the feel of her supple body pressed to his.

''I love you, Carolyn. God only knows how much.'' He struggled against a new wave of raw emotion. He closed his eyes, fighting it, glorying in it. He didn't feel the tear snaking down his face, only her soft, trembling hand wiping it away.

''I love you, too, Pete.''

He kissed her fingers and tasted mingled salt, blood and the sweet love of Carolyn.

"But we'd better make a couple of phone calls," she said.

"Right," he answered, drawing her upward for a long, deep kiss.

"I think I broke the phone downstairs," she said, finally, gently cradling his bruised face with both her hands.

He kept his arm around her waist, his hand at the small of her back, holding her to him. "And I left the cell phone on the roof."

"Well…I've wanted to sit in the moonlight with you for a long time now," she said, pressing a soft, delicate kiss to his lips.

"Mmm," he moaned, a soft, strangely satisfied growl. "Let's go."

They made their phone call to Adams then lay together on the roof, watching planes arriving from the east and west, watching the moon, pointing out the helicopters flying in from the north, and the flash of the state troopers' warning lights approaching from the south. And they watched Jimmy Wannamacher's abortive attempt to escape and his subsequent arrest in the middle of what had once, in predrought days, been a wheat field. And clasped hands as a battered and handcuffed Bubba was led from the house and eased into the back of a state trooper's black-and-white car.

Carolyn's driveway seemed a sea of Smokey Bear hats and gray uniforms, FBI agents dressed in black jumpsuits with gold-lettered identification on the front and back, and a couple of cowboy-dressed undercover operators—Adams and Kessler—who left Pete and Carolyn alone.

The stars twinkled dimly in the full moonlight and the fields flanking her house looked frost covered and silver.

"Are you cold?" Pete asked.

"Not anymore," Carolyn answered, snuggling against him.

"We'll have to go in sometime," he said.

"Mmm. But not yet."

"Are you sure about this?" he asked.

She knew he wasn't referring to staying on the roof. She chuckled a little. "Very," she said. "Very, very sure."

"What else do you want to know about me?" he asked.

"Everything."

"That'll take awhile to tell," he said, gently stroking her hair.

"I hope it takes a lifetime," she murmured.

Epilogue

Carolyn bit her lips together as she smeared a painkilling unguent onto Pete's naked and upraised inner thighs. She wasn't afraid of hurting him, she was trying desperately not to laugh.

"You're shaking the whole bed," he said. "Why don't you go ahead and let it out?"

She chuckled.

"Oh, sure," he said. "Laugh at your poor husband's pain and agony."

She dropped a kiss in a place designed to take his mind from his current woes.

"That's more like it," he said, reaching for her.

"It's your own fault," she said sternly, but continued to take the pain away with her kisses.

"I said I was going to learn to ride that damned horse if it killed me."

"Yes, but I didn't think you meant it literally!"

"It would have been fine, but he bounces when he runs," Pete complained, still trying to draw her up.

''That was a trot,'' she said, wiping her already numb fingers on a cloth. ''If he'd run, you'd be lying in the driveway.''

''You're awfully sassy today,'' he said.

''According to you, I'm always sassy.''

''Mmm. And I love it.''

''And I love you.''

He made the grunting sound that seemed to mean anything from ''me, too'' to ''good dinner.'' It was a low, rumbling growl of repletion and every time she heard it, she felt a slow frisson of delight work down her spine.

The rumble was like his grin, crooked and low, enigmatic and slow.

She crawled up the bed and lay down beside him, settling naturally into the crook of his arm. He gave that low rumble again and drew her a bit closer.

''This is nice,'' she said.

''Sure, you don't have a broken tailbone.''

''Neither do you,'' she chuffed. ''Just saddle sores.''

''Great. Something new for you to tell Alec and Cait next time they call.''

''Did I tell you they're planning on coming out here during the Christmas holidays?''

''No! Are they really?''

She poked him in the ribs and then shifted her hand to a slow caress.

''I suppose they're planning to round up the usual suspects,'' he said, followed by a hum of pleasure.

''Adams, Kessler, you, somebody named Chandler, also in the Lubbock office. And his wife.''

''Kelsey Winslow,'' Pete said, and she knew from his tone that he was remembering something from his days in prison. Assignment or not, those ten years were permanently marked on her husband's soul.

However, daily loving, daily living was making its mark too, slowly smoothing some of the harsher scars, erasing some others altogether.

"A regular FBI enclave," Pete said. "Good thing we added on to the house."

Carolyn pressed a kiss to his chest, thinking about all the changes that had taken place in her life the past six months. Seven, if she counted from the night she'd found her daughters in the desert with a perfect stranger.

Pete had taken an early retirement from the bureau. He'd resigned the morning after the big raid back in March. "It's just not for me anymore," he'd said. "I need to be as far away from that kind of life as is humanly possible."

She'd asked him to stay on the ranch with her. In fact, she'd asked him to marry her at that moment.

"Are you sure?" he'd asked her then, as he'd asked her when they'd been up on the roof.

"Who's ever sure?" she'd asked him back. "But I know—as Shawna would say 'like in my soul or something'—that we're supposed to be together."

It had been scary to take such a step, but there hadn't been a single moment of regret. Not one.

He'd taken some of his incredible pile of savings and sunk the money into fixing up the ranch. But he'd done most of the work himself, not because they couldn't afford help now, but because he enjoyed it. He said he liked the work, the being outdoors, and the transformation he could create with his own two hands.

And he volunteered his time at the Almost Public School, teaching about hunting for arrowheads and taking the kids on field trips onto the MacLaine place and coming back dirty, dusty, and thoroughly happy.

All Carolyn knew was that the Leary place—technically Jackson now—changed from a ramshackle, falling-to-bits ranch a couple of miles outside Almost, Texas, to a lovely, working home and family. His magical touch could be seen everywhere, from the barn to the house, to well-behaved, happy newly adopted, on Pete's part—daughters, to the most contented woman this side of the Pecos.

"We've come a long way," she said.

"Nah. Just got started."

She smiled. "Sometimes it seems hard to imagine we haven't known each other forever."

He pulled her tighter to him and lowered his hand to her breast. His warm fingers slid beneath her to cup her fullness, to mold it to his almost absent caress. But he knew her so very well. He knew exactly where to touch, where to press, how to make her shiver with desire and shudder with pleasure.

"I learn something new about you every day," he said.

"Like what?" she asked. "I never do anything different."

"Oh, yeah?" he asked, shifting to lightly tug at her already hard nipple.

She gasped and arched upward, but said, "That's nothing new."

"Oh, yeah?" He scooted down the bed and captured her nipple in his mouth, lightly grazing her with his teeth.

She shivered and gripped his arms in response. "N-neither is...that," she managed to say between clenched teeth.

"What about that chess game last night?"

"What chess game?" she asked, her entire focus on the warmth of his mouth, the raw-silk feel of his tongue on her aching nipple.

He lifted his head from her breast as he slid a finger into her honeyed core. "The chess game you trounced me at."

Her legs fell open to him and he slowly, deeply stroked her inside. "You'd just...never...asked if I could play."

"Play? That wasn't playing...you're cutthroat." He added another finger and lowered his mouth to her breast again, laving her with his tongue, sucking sharply, then gentling her while his fingers worked a wicked magic. "One minute you're my beautiful sweet little wife and the next, *whoa*, berserker mode. I tell you, Carolyn, it was scary to watch."

She chuckled throatily. "Berserker mode...like the

night...you Errol Flynned in the window at Bubb
Wannamacher.''

He held her nipple gently in his teeth and talked aroun
it. ''That *was* rather impressive, wasn't it?'' He suckled he
then pushed her slightly sideways to find her other breas
He said, en route, ''Especially considering the trim pulle
away in my hand smack-dab in midflight.''

She gasped again as he found his prize. And all the whil
his fingers were slowly, sensuously claiming her, makin
her molten with renewed desire.

She tried getting out her words, though her ragge
breathing and her inchoate thoughts didn't help. ''The big
gest drug bust in West Texas history...and the Guine
World Record for the mo-oh-st amount...of splinters in
human hand.''

She decided she'd found a new sensual delight, that
his chortling while he suckled her.

Then Carolyn couldn't think about the past, about t
aftermath of that terrible moment, the arrests of the Wa
namacher brothers, the getaway of the unknown Canadia
the capture of millions of dollars' worth of uncut cocain

She could only feel the warmth of his hands, the fi
unleashed by his hot, hot tongue. She shuddered benea
his touch and begged him to join her. ''Please...'' s
called.

And he came to her with a groan, his go-around w
Bratwurst holding him back, his desire for her pushing h
forward. And she knew the old desert horse was forgott
as he uttered that wonderful rumble of satisfaction befc
capturing her lips with his own.

Later, sated, lying beneath the covers now, not becau
it was at all chilly, but because Jenny and Shawna w
due home from swimming lessons any moment, Pete lit
invariable cigarette and blew a cloud of smoke into the
circulated by the ceiling fan.

''There's really just one thing I want to know,'' he sa

''Mmm?''

"That first morning in your kitchen...why did you get so mad when I said you didn't have to cook for me? Was that some East-West thing or what?"

Carolyn opened her eyes, a blush working up her cheeks.

"Carolyn?" he asked, shifting to see her face.

"No," she said in a little voice.

"Then what was it?"

"Oh, you might as well know. I'd dreamed about you that night, and when the girls brought you inside, I was rattled. I mean, there you were and you looked good enough...oh, never mind."

Pete chuckled. "If you'd told me that then...we'd have been here a lot sooner."

"You'd have run away."

"Right up these stairs."

"I love you, Pete."

He pulled her tightly against his chest, where she felt safe, loved. Trusted.

But all he said was, "Mmm."

* * * * *

Don't miss Marilyn Tracy's next book in the ALMOST, TEXAS series, coming soon from Silhouette Intimate Moments.

TRACI ON THE SPOT   BY TRACI

1

Morgan Brigham slowly set down his coffee cup on the kitchen table and stared at the comic strip in the center of s paper. It was nestled in among approximately twenty hers that were spread out across two pages. But this was e only one he made a point of reading faithfully each orning at breakfast.

This was the only one that mirrored *her* life.

He read each panel twice, as if he couldn't trust his own es. But he could. It was there, in black and white.

Morgan folded the paper slowly, thoughtfully, his mind t on his task. So Traci was getting engaged.

The realization gnawed at the lining of his stomach. He dn't a clue as to why.

He had even less of a clue why he did what he did next. Abandoning his coffee, now cool, and the newspaper, ignoring the fact that this was going to make him late the office, Morgan went to get a sheet of stationery from den.

He didn't have much time.

Traci Richardson stared at the last frame she had just wn. Debating, she glanced at the creature sprawled out the kitchen floor.

"What do you think, Jeremiah? Too blunt?"

The dog, part bloodhound, part mutt, idly looked up fro[m] his rawhide bone at the sound of his name. Jeremiah ga[ve] her a look she felt free to interpret as ambivalent.

"Fine help you are. What if Daniel actually reads th[is] and puts two and two together?"

Not that there was all that much chance that the ma[n] who had proposed to her, the very prosperous and busy D[r.] Daniel Thane, would actually see the comic strip she dre[w] for a living. Not unless the strip was taped to a bicusp[id] he was examining. Lately Daniel had gotten so busy he['d] stopped reading anything but the morning headlines of [the] *Times.*

Still, you never knew. "I don't want to hurt his fe[el]ings," Traci continued, using Jeremiah as a soundi[ng] board. "It's just that Traci is overwhelmed by Dona[ld's] proposal and, see, she thinks the ring is going to swall[ow] her up." To prove her point, Traci held up the drawing [of] the dog to view.

This time, he didn't even bother to lift his head.

Traci stared moodily at the small velvet box on [the] kitchen counter. It had sat there since Daniel had asked [her] to marry him last Sunday. Even if Daniel never read [the] comic strip, he was going to suspect something eventua[lly.] The very fact that she hadn't grabbed the ring from [his] hand and slid it onto her finger should have told him [that] she had doubts about their union.

Traci sighed. Daniel was a catch by any definition. [So] what was her problem? She kept waiting to be struck [by] that sunny ray of happiness. Daniel said he wanted to [take] care of her, to fulfill her every wish. And he was e[ven] willing to let her think about it before she gave him [an] answer.

Guilt nibbled at her. She should be dancing up and do[wn,] not wavering like a weather vane in a gale.

Pronouncing the strip completed, she scribbled her signature in the corner of the last frame and then sighed. Another week's work put to bed. She glanced at the pile of mail on the counter. She'd been bringing it in steadily from the mailbox since Monday, but the stack had gotten no farther than her kitchen. Sorting letters seemed the least heinous of all the annoying chores that faced her.

Traci paused as she noted a long envelope. Morgan Brigham. Why would Morgan be writing to her?

Curious, she tore open the envelope and quickly scanned the short note inside.

Dear Traci,

I'm putting the summerhouse up for sale. Thought you might want to come up and see it one more time before it goes up on the block. Or make a bid for it yourself. If memory serves, you once said you wanted to buy it. Either way, let me know. My number's on the card.

Take care,
Morgan

P.S. Got a kick out of *Traci on the Spot* this week.

Traci folded the letter. He read her strip. She hadn't known that. A feeling of pride silently coaxed a smile to her lips. After a beat, though, the rest of his note seeped into her consciousness. He was selling the house.

The summerhouse. A faded white building with brick rim. Suddenly, memories flooded her mind. Long, lazy afternoons that felt as if they would never end.

Morgan.

She looked at the far wall in the family room. There was large framed photograph of her and Morgan standing before the summerhouse. Traci and Morgan. Morgan and

Traci. Back then, it seemed their lives had been permanently intertwined. A bittersweet feeling of loss passed over her.

Traci quickly pulled the telephone over to her on the counter and tapped out the number on the keypad.

* * * * *

*Look for TRACI ON THE SPOT
by Marie Ferrarella, coming to
Silhouette YOURS TRULY
in March 1997.*

At last the wait is over...
In March
New York Times bestselling author

NORA ROBERTS

will bring us the latest from the Stanislaskis as
Natasha's now very grown-up stepdaughter,
Freddie, and Rachel's very sexy brother-in-law
Nick discover that love is worth waiting for in

WAITING FOR NICK
Silhouette Special Edition #1088

and in April
visit Natasha and Rachel again—or meet them
for the first time—in

The Stanislaski Sisters

containing TAMING NATASHA
and FALLING FOR RACHEL

Available wherever Silhouette books are sold.

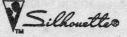

From the bestselling author of *Scandalous*

Cam Monroe vowed revenge when
Angela Stanhope's family accused him
of a crime he didn't commit.

Fifteen years later he returns from exile, wealthy
and powerful, to demand Angela's hand in marriage.
It is then that the strange "accidents" begin. Are the
Stanhopes trying to remove him from their lives
one last time, or is there a more insidious,
mysterious explanation?

Available this March at your favorite retail outlet.

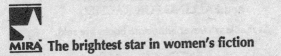

Harlequin and Silhouette celebrate
Black History Month with seven terrific titles,
featuring the all-new *Fever Rising*
by Maggie Ferguson
(Harlequin Intrigue #408) and
A Family Wedding by Angela Benson
(Silhouette Special Edition #1085)!

Also available are:
Looks Are Deceiving by Maggie Ferguson
Crime of Passion by Maggie Ferguson
Adam and Eva by Sandra Kitt
Unforgivable by Joyce McGill
Blood Sympathy by Reginald Hill

On sale in January at your favorite
Harlequin and Silhouette retail outlet.

FORTUNE'S Children™

Bestselling Author

MAGGIE SHAYNE

Continues the twelve-book series—FORTUNE'S CHILDREN—
in **January 1997** with Book Seven

A HUSBAND IN TIME

Jane Fortune was wary of the stranger with amnesia who
came to her—seemingly out of nowhere. She couldn't deny
the passion between them, but there was something
mysterious—almost dangerous—about this compelling
man…and Jane knew she'd better watch her step….

MEET THE FORTUNES—a family whose legacy is greater than
riches. Because where there's a will…there's a *wedding!*

Look us up on-line at: http://www.romance.net

COMING NEXT MONTH

Silhouette® INTIMATE MOMENTS®

invites you to meet the folks of

ALMOST, TEXAS

a brand new mini-series
by
Marilyn Tracy

ALMOST, TEXAS, a small town where suspense runs
high and passions run deep, and a hazard-free
happily-ever-after is *almost* always guaranteed!

It all begins with
ALMOST PERFECT
(February 1997)

A drifter has hired on at widow Carolyn Leary's ranch.
Pete Jackson may be handsome as sin and know his
way around horses, but the loner is just a might too
handy with a gun. What's his secret? And does
Carolyn even want to find out?

Be sure to look for other stories set in this unforgettable
town, coming later in the year—only from
Silhouette Intimate Moments.

Dear Reader,

Once again, you've come to the right place if you're looking for that seductive mix of romance and excitement that is quintessentially Intimate Moments. Start the month with *The Lady in Red*—by reader favorite Linda Turner. Your heart will be in your throat as rival homicide reporters Blake Nickels and Sabrina Jones see their relationship change from professional to personal— with a killer on their trail all the while. And don't miss the conclusion of the HOLIDAY HONEYMOONS miniseries, Merline Lovelace's *The 14th...and Forever.* You'll wish for a holiday—and a HOLIDAY HONEYMOON—every month of the year.

The rest of the month is fabulous, too, with new books from Rebecca Daniels: *Mind Over Marriage;* Marilyn Tracy: *Almost Perfect*, the launch book in her ALMOST, TEXAS miniseries; and Allie Harrison: *Crime of the Heart.* And welcome new author Charlotte Walker, as she debuts with *Yesterday's Bride.* Every one of these books is full of passion, and sometimes peril—don't miss a single one.

And be sure to come back next month, when the romance and excitement continue, right here in Silhouette Intimate Moments.

Enjoy!

Leslie J. Wainger

Leslie J. Wainger
Senior Editor and Editorial Coordinator

Please address questions and book requests to:
Silhouette Reader Service
U.S.: 3010 Walden Ave., P.O. Box 1325, Buffalo, NY 14269
Canadian: P.O. Box 609, Fort Erie, Ont. L2A 5X3

"Your past isn't any of my business," Carolyn told him.

"Of course it is," Pete said. "I'm living in your bunkhouse, eating my meals with you and your daughters. I'm taking my baths in your house, for God's sake. Who's business is it, if not yours? You should want to know what kind of man you brought in here."

Halfway throug his and widened while he'd been mentioned kissing enticing her beyon might as well have shouted it, for it hung between them like a palpable presence waiting to be acknowledged.

"Run a check on me, Carolyn. If you want the truth, go to the source," he said with a slow, bitter twist to his lips. "Call the FBI."